— DRIVEN —

— DRIVEN —

A Novel

IRWIN L. HINDS

Order this book online at www.trafford.com
or email orders@trafford.com

Most Trafford titles are also available at major online book retailers.

This is a work of fiction. All of the characters, names, incidents, organizations, and dialogue in this novel are either the products of the author's imagination or are used fictitiously.

Printed in the United States of America.

ISBN: 978-1-4269-6884-6 (sc)
ISBN: 978-1-4269-6885-3 (e)

Trafford rev. 11/15/2011

www.trafford.com

North America & international
toll-free: 1 888 232 4444 (USA & Canada)
phone: 250 383 6864 • fax: 812 355 4082

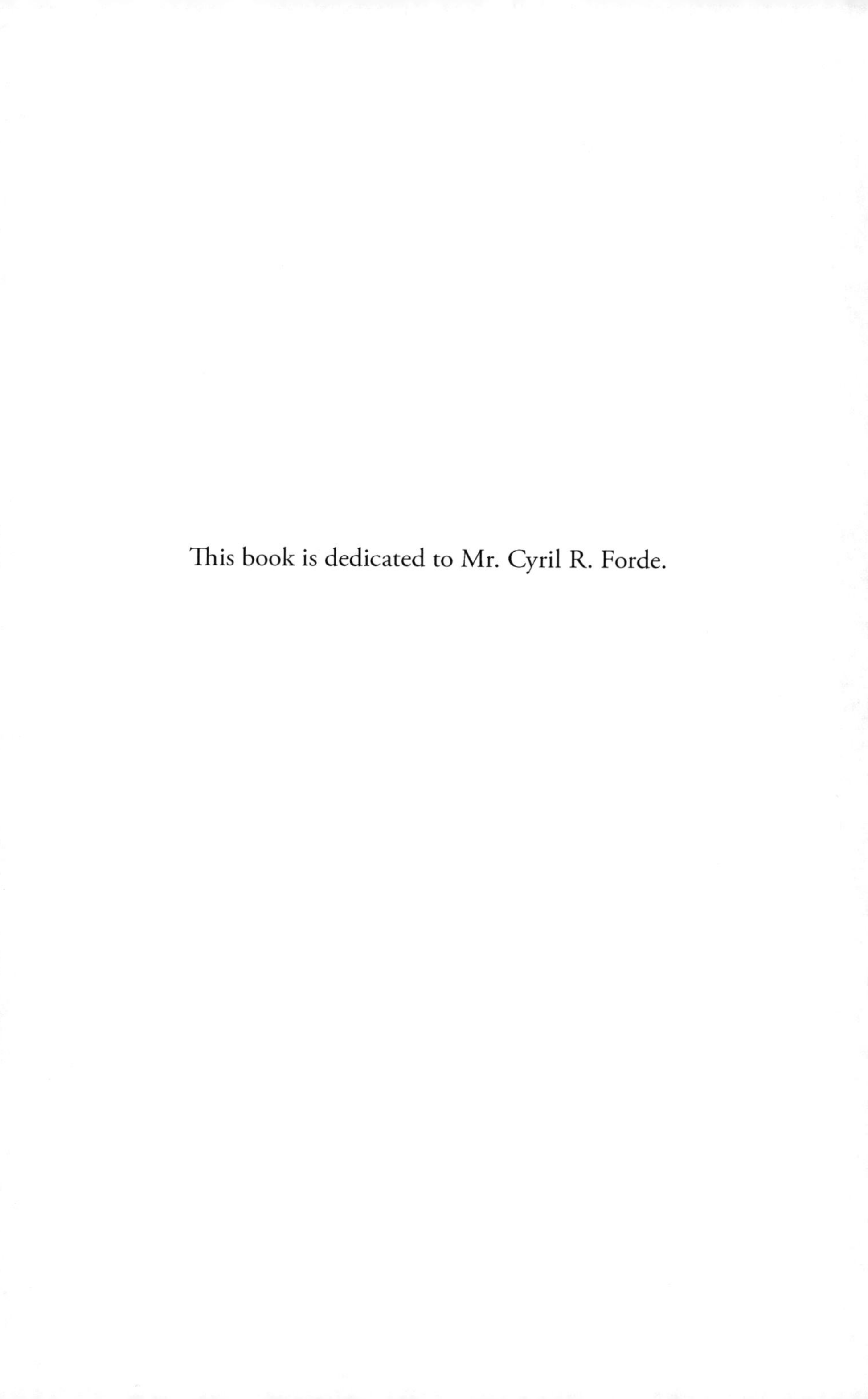

This book is dedicated to Mr. Cyril R. Forde.

ONE

He left her just when she needed him most. Tyrone Khadevis was nowhere to be found when Carmelita Orr returned home from the hospital with their newborn baby. It was 6:55 p. m. on Thursday, February 15, and one of the coldest wintry evenings of 1968 when she gave birth to a healthy six pounds/five ounces baby boy at the maternity ward of the Unitarian Hospital on Eastern Parkway, Brooklyn, New York. At precisely the same time in Trinidad, the larger of the twin-island nation of Trinidad and Tobago, Jane Hackett was in labor with her first child, a girl, who was born two hours later at the home she shared with her mother, Emelda Hackett, in the remote fishing, agricultural, and petroleum producing village of Mayaro.

It was from that same sleepy little enclave nestled along the bank of the Ortoire River that Carmelita migrated to the USA less than a year earlier. Although she was a product of the same archaic system of maternal care Jane was receiving, she was glad to have received the kind of advanced modern medical care made available to her and her baby.

Jane's baby was delivered by a mid-wife known as Madam Greenwich whose only qualification hinged on the fact that she had eleven children of her own and had delivered or assisted in the delivery of twenty-eight others. That undoubtedly placed Jane and her child at greater risks than Carmelita and her baby could have experienced at the Unitarian Hospital with its staff of highly trained doctors and midwifery nurses. Yet, there was never any concern.

After three days in the hospital, during which time Tyrone, aka TK, never visited Carmelita and or their baby, she was, nevertheless, glad to be discharged. She returned to the one room efficiency she shared with him on Herkimer Street, Brooklyn, New York, only to discover that he was not there. *He abandoned the place*, she thought. The next day she contacted several of his friends in the neighborhood but no one knew of his whereabouts. Two days later, Mark Benefield, a young drifter who came to New York from Virginia together with TK, informed her that he left the city. Not only did he abandon their home, he had abandoned her and their baby knowing quite well that there was no one else she could have turned to for help.

For months Tyrone had been complaining about the way he was treated in New York City. He contended that he came to New York to escape the harsh realities of Jim Crow laws in the South but found that life here, though different, was no better. He was constantly being stopped and questioned by the police. Sometimes he was asked to assume the position; hands up over his head, legs apart, and body forward against his car. Then he was frisked. To him there was no justification for that because he had always been a law abiding citizen. He felt constantly violated.

When he wasn't harassed by the police, TK felt unduly persecuted by his peers. Often the very guys who always borrowed money from him and whom he frequently assisted in their times of constant need, were the ones who criticized his efforts to get an education. They were the very ones who berated him for the jobs he accepted and worked at as a means to attaining his goals, even when they had no jobs themselves or pretended to be interested in jobs for which they were not qualified. In fact, they much preferred to beg him or even a stranger for money to sustain their many bad habits.

In spite of his efforts, they continued to tease him. Some called him professor sear cropper. Some called him pachyderm because of his size. He was six feet seven inches tall and weighed an even three hundred pounds. There were those who called him Cotton because he liked to wear white cotton shirts. For a while he persevered but the bantering seemed endless. When he met Carmelita it eased a bit. That perhaps, was because he started spending more time with her than with his so-called buddies.

Carmelita was a concerned, caring, affectionate, and giving individual. Those who knew her well interacted with her at two extremes. There were those who loved her dearly and felt happy for her and TK as a couple. At the other extreme were the envy, jealousy, anger, and hatred. On one occasion someone she trusted as a friend remarked, "Girl, I don't know why you are here. You should go back to Jamaica on the banana boat."

Carmelita was shocked and deeply hurt by the hateful, derogatory statement but elected not to respond. The irony of it was that her perceived friend, Lillian Paul, knew that Carmelita was from Trinidad. But she somehow believed that Trinidad was in Jamaica. Either she never finished high school, was poorly schooled, forgot her geography, or she simply disliked women of color, her own color, if they were born outside of the USA.

When Carmelita became pregnant, TK vowed to be there for her and their baby. He never suggested that they got married although she hinted several times that they should. "It is the right thing to do," she said often. Nevertheless, her pregnancy weighed heavily on his mind. He didn't think that he was ready or prepared for the responsibilities of fatherhood and a family. As a result, he never considered marrying Carmelita. His father abandoned his family when TK was only eight years old. One would think that should have strengthened his resolve to do better for his offspring, considering the fact that Carmelita wanted him to. On the contrary, it scared the Dickens out of him.

For several days Carmelita pondered over her situation. Then on the eighth day after realizing the impact of TK's departure which left her alone with a new-born baby, no job, no money, and no immediate family to turn to, she decided to call her mother,

Mrs.Tracy Jackman. One major problem existed. Well, to her at least, it was major. Her mother and step-father lived in Beaumont, Mayaro, Trinidad, and did not have a telephone. While their neighbor next door would not have objected to them receiving a telephone call from her, the question of privacy weighed heavily on her mind.

Her mother's neighbors, Fred and Mary Landcomb, were known to be effusive and unable or unwilling to keep anything to themselves. Carmelita was concerned that very soon all of Mayaro would know of her predicament. Nevertheless, out of desperation she made the call. Mr. Landcomb answered the telephone and did not hesitate to get her mother on the line.

When Mrs. Jackman got to the house and took the telephone from Mr. Landcomb who by then had spoken with Carmelita, her hands were shaking. The urgency with which he called out to her to say that she had a telephone call from the USA, instilled a measure of fear in her. *Is Carmelita in some kind of trouble*? She wondered just before he handed her the telephone. "Hello! She said and waited.

"Is that you, Mama?"

"Yes," she said, but she was tentative.

"This is Carmelita." There was a long pause and Mrs. Jackman could hear her daughter sobbing. Then Carmelita said, "I am home with the baby, Mama. Tyrone has left us. I don't know what to do, Mama. I have no money, no job, nothing!" She was sobbing louder and the words she spoke became muffled.

"Why would he leave you with a young baby?" asked her mother. "He seemed to be such a nice young man. I was always impressed whenever I spoke with him on the telephone."

"I don't know, Mama. However, he is gone and I don't know what to do."

"Don't you worry, child. Ah just get meh sue-sue (a cooperative saving among private individuals) and it is the last hand (payment). Me eh ha nothing more to pay so ah go send you ah ticket (airline ticket) to come home."

"That is not what I want to do at this time, Mama."

"Well, ah doh know what else to say. Maybe ah could buy a ticket for meh-self and come up to stay with the baby while you look for ah job."

"Would you do that, Mama?"

"Yes, of course."

"Oh! Mama! That would be so nice," said Carmelita. "How soon can you get here?"

"Perhaps in one week from today. After ah go in town to the embassy (US Embassy) and apply for ah visa ah go let you know exactly."

"Thanks, Mama. That is great news. I am looking forward to seeing you already."

"I am too, child. I cannot wait to see you and little Elvin, my grandson. Imagine that!"

"I hope to see you soon, Mama."

"Ah hope so, child," said Mrs. Jackman. She then whispered, "We have to get off the people's telephone now."

"I understand, Mama. Thanks. Bye."

"Good bye, meh dear," Mrs. Jackman said and hung up.

There were tears in her eyes but she tried to compose herself before saying anything to Fred and Mary Landcomb. While she appreciated the use of their telephone which was the only one in a private home in the entire Mayaro district, she was concerned about their propensity for gossip. She felt she could have had more privacy at the Telephone Exchange but that was beyond her control.

Carmelita gave some thought to the tendency of the Landcombs to gossip but she had no other choice. She was grateful that they received the call and contacted her mother right away. That brought some immediate, though temporary relief from the stress she was experiencing. Immediately, she started thinking of what she can possibly do to improve her lot and ensure a secure future for her son. *I do not know how long Mama can stay with us but I would like to go back to school,* she thought.

Suddenly, there was a knock at the door. She responded hesitantly, opened the door and saw David Cassel standing there smiling. He was a young foreign (international) student who lived in one of the kitchenettes on the upper floor. He handed her a single red rose he had in his hand and said, "Mrs. Mendoza told me what happened so I came to say how sorry I am."

Your sorrow wouldn't help me right now, she thought but said, "Thank you, David. Wouldn't you come in?"

He looked at his watch and said, "I do have a few minutes to spare." Carmelita stepped aside and he entered. She then closed the door behind them.

"Please sit down." She pointed to the sofa-bed in the room. David hesitated but eventually he complied.

"What exactly did Mrs. Mendoza tell you, David?"

"She said that TK never visited you in the hospital and that he seemed to have disappeared before you were discharged. Carmelita looked amazed and confused, so David continued. "I don't think she meant any malice or disrespect by it. She seemed genuinely concerned."

"She is probably concerned as to how I will pay the rent at the end of the month. I am too. I really don't know how I will manage but my faith is strong."

"Don't worry too much."

"That's easy for you to say, David. I, however, have this little boy to think about. He has to be fed and he needs a warm and comfortable place to live."

"I understand," said David. "I have to run off to work now and I have classes until ten o'clock tonight, so I will get home very late. However, I shall speak with you again tomorrow morning."

"Okay. That will be nice. Thanks."

"Bye."

David left and Carmelita closed the door. Baby Elvin was sound asleep in a bassinet she and TK had purchased in anticipation of his arrival. She sat on the couch, mused about her predicament while admiring her new born as he lay peacefully in the bassinet. *God is good*, she thought. *We will survive.*

For some reason, which he didn't quite understand himself, David was thinking of ways in which he might be able to help her. Neither could claim that they were close friends although they always conversed amicably, perhaps more so than any of the other boarders and lodgers that the Mendoza's had at their four story dwelling. One mitigating factor, he thought, was that they were all from Trinidad, including Mr. and Mrs. Mendoza. Yet, he questioned himself as to why he, more than any of the others, was so inclined to be sympathetic toward Carmelita.

TWO

The door bell rang early Wednesday morning, February 21, 1968, almost one week after Carmelita came home from the hospital with little Elvin. She moved toward the door timorously and opened it hoping that it might be TK. It was not. Her level of anxiety lessened as she smiled and said, "Good morning, Mrs. Mendoza."

"Good morning, Carmelita. How are you today?"

"I am okay."

"That's not good but it's not bad either," said Mrs. Mendoza. "May I come in?" she asked as she handed Carmelita a package.

"Thank you," said Carmelita. "Of course you can come in." She stepped aside and held the door open for Mrs. Mendoza to enter.

"Have a seat, Mrs. Mendoza."

"How are you getting along?" Mrs. Mendoza asked as she sat down.

"We are doing fine, for now at least. In fact, our resources would take us to the end of the month. However, my mother is expected to be here next week. As soon as she gets here I will go out and find a job."

"I am pleased to hear that," Mrs. Mendoza said as she got up to leave.

"Are you leaving already?"

"I wish I could stay longer but I have quite a number of things to do before lunch today."

What a ruse! You just wanted to know whether I can afford the rent now that TK is no longer here, Carmelita thought but she said, "Thanks for the package. That's very thoughtful of you."

"You are welcome," Mrs. Mendoza said as she walked through the door and pulled it shut behind her. Carmelita then locked it, sat in the couch, leaned back and closed her eyes. As Mrs. Mendoza climbed the stairs to her third floor apartment, she heard water flowing heavily. She stopped, listened, and smiled. *That could only be David. He is the only one who is there this late,* she thought. She hurried inside and changed into a sheer, yellow nightgown. It was early enough she thought that anyone who saw her would think that she just woke up. Only Carmelita knew otherwise. Mrs. Mendoza stepped out into the hallway but did not close the door behind her. By then the sound of running water from the shower upstairs had stopped. David had gotten out of the shower, wrapped a towel around him and walked across the hall to his room where he proceeded to towel-dry himself. He did not lock the door behind him. It was rare that anyone locked their doors in that building. Mrs. Mendoza came up the stairs and entered David's room smiling.

"You shouldn't run the shower so forcefully, David," she said. "It wakes up everyone."

He was startled and scrambled to wrap the towel around himself again. She stepped forward, rested her right hand on his left shoulder and wiggled her index and middle fingers down to his chest. "I used to be a nurse. There is nothing I haven't seen," she said.

She was not wearing a bra and her nipples could be seen through her yellow, sheered nightgown. She looked down at her chest and asked, "Do you like them, David?" He did not answer. He smiled but it was not genuine. It was a smile of chagrin.

"I am running late for work, Mrs. Mendoza."

"Call me Carmen," she said.

"I do not want to be late again today."

"Carmen. It is okay for you to call me Carmen. I was not responsible for you being late yesterday," said Mrs. Mendoza. "You didn't say that to Carmelita, did you?"

"What?"

"You heard me," she said.

"Please, Mrs. Mendoza," David pleaded.

"Are you asking me to leave?" David did not answer. He stood there amazed as she reached out, grabbed the towel that was wrapped around him, and walked out the door laughing. "I will see you in the morning," she said, and before going down the stairs she hung the wet towel on the banister. She was still smiling when she reached the door to her apartment. *He is very well endowed*, she thought.

David got dressed but the last words Mrs. Mendoza spoke kept playing on his mind. *Does that mean she will not leave me dinner tonight*? He wondered. *I cannot imagine what she meant, but I will certainly get something to eat before coming in tonight*, he thought.

Mrs. Mendoza had always prepared dinner for David and the three other young men from Trinidad and Tobago, each of whom received boarding and lodging from her for a fee. She was disappointed that David did not succumb to what she had hoped to be a morning of sexual escapades, something different from the run of the mill chores she performed every day. However, she wasn't going to withhold food as punishment, not for the moment at least. She felt confident that he was tempted, and that it was only a matter of time before he succumbed. *At fifty-one I am not over the hill*, she thought. She gave no consideration to the fact that David was half her age and that her daughter, Dallas, was a classmate of his at the Municipal College of Arts and Sciences.

David was perplexed. He sulked and mused all day at work as he recalled conversations he had several weeks earlier with Mrs. Mendoza's husband, Victor. They spoke about many things, including politics, religion, education, interpersonal relationships and the family, but what bothered David the most were the frequent threats Victor Mendoza made about the lengths to which he would go to protect his family, particularly his daughter, from people he viewed as sexual predators. *Was he aware of his wife's predatory inclinations*? David wondered. *Her actions this morning were pretty much like that of a cougar*, he thought.

Victor Mendoza worked hard for long hours on any given day. He owned and operated a dry-cleaning plant where he had only one employee. He, therefore, had to have taken a hands-on approach to making the business a successful venture. He didn't do much for recreation. His six days per week schedule did not allow it. On most Sundays, instead of resting at home, he involved himself in activities of the church. He was a devout Roman Catholic. He was also an avid gun collector and had on several occasions threatened to blow the head off anyone whom he perceived was taking advantage of his daughter. *What will he do to someone his wife is taking advantage of, or someone he perceives is taking advantage of her?* David wondered.

As the end of the work day approached, he was thinking less of Mrs. Crystal Mendoza and her husband, Victor, and more about Carmelita. He decided that he should get some take-out food and wondered whether she might want some herself. The idea of food for two played heavily on his mind. He thought it was a good idea but he didn't want to appear too presumptuous, aggressive, patronizing, or overly sympathetic and in the process hurt Carmelita's pride. Being a Trinidadian, he was well aware of the fragile nature of his compatriot's sense of self-worth. After considerable deliberation, he decided he would call her. As soon as his work schedule ended that evening he used a pay-phone and dialed her number.

"Hello!" She answered softly.

"Carmelita, this is David."

She hesitated for a moment before she asked, "How are you, David?"

"What's the matter, girl. Don't you recognize my voice?"

"You surprised me."

Long before TK left Carmelita had given David her telephone number but he had never called her. Although they had spoken often before TK's departure and several times since, the conversations were always in person. She just was not accustomed to hearing his voice on the telephone.

"I am sorry. I should have mentioned to you this morning that I intended to buy take-out food for dinner, and ask whether I can get you some also."

"What's the matter? Is it that Mrs. Mendoza is not cooking this evening?"

"She never cooks every day. You know that."

"That doesn't answer my question, David."

"I don't know whether or not she is cooking. Now, would you like me to bring you some food?"

"If you intend to have dinner with me, yes"

"Okay. What would you like to have?"

"I would have anything other than fried rice."

"Would you like some home-styled Caribbean cooking tonight?"

"Where will you get that?"

"Leave it up to me, girl. I know this town."

"Okay."

"I will see you at six o'clock."

"Aren't you going to class this evening?"

"No," he answered. He didn't say why he wasn't going to attend classes and Carmelita didn't ask.

"I will see you then," she said.

David called the restaurant, *Caribbean Cuisine*, and immediately placed his order. Carmelita did not specify what she wanted, so he ordered the items on the menu that he liked with the hope that she too would enjoy them. When he arrived at the Mendoza's on Herkimer Street, Crystal Mendoza was at the mail box in the foyer.

"Good evening, Mrs. Mendoza," he said politely.

She immediately handed him two air mail envelopes she had in her possession although she had not yet opened the mail box. The letters she handed him originated from Trinidad and Tobago. He knew that from the date and country of origin stamped on them.

"Those are for you," she said acknowledging his presence with a smile, but she did not respond directly to his greeting.

"Thank you," he said as he took the letters from her.

Mrs. Mendoza retrieved the day's mail and walked up the stairs to her third floor apartment. David followed on his way to his room on the fourth floor. Crystal Mendoza was careful enough to lift her long skirt to avoid stepping on it and tripping as she climbed the stairs. David viewed that as a seductive act. *Her skirt isn't all that long*, he thought as he lowered his gaze to the carpeted stairway. When she entered her apartment, he breathed a sigh of relief and continued on to his room. The door was open and his telephone was ringing. He rushed in, put down the food, and picked up the telephone. By then it was too late. The caller had already hung up. He had no way of knowing who called so he dialed Carmelita's telephone number.

"Hello!" She answered.

"Carmelita, this is David. Did you call me?"

"No."

"Anyway, I am home. I have your dinner, so I am coming down right away." He glanced at the letters Mrs. Mendoza had given him. *They seemed to have been tampered with*, he thought, but he left without opening either of them.

Carmelita wondered why he didn't knock at her door as soon as he came in but she quickly dismissed the thought. Minutes later he was there. "I have to go and see what Mrs. Mendoza has prepared for dinner," he said hurriedly.

"Why?"

"She always leaves us dinner. It would be rude of me if I didn't put away the food."

"Where will you put it?"

"I can take it up to my room. She doesn't have to know that I did not eat it."

"Okay."

"I will be right back," he said and left.

He knocked at the Mendoza's door but no one answered. He entered and went directly to the kitchen as was customary. His dinner, as well as dinners for three other young men who lodged and boarded there were on the kitchen table. The dinners were labeled with each individual's initials. He took his without uncovering it and headed to his room. Once there, he tasted the meal only to realize that it was not palatable. *Could the dinner of the others be the same*? He wondered. *How on earth does one get freshly cooked white rice to taste sour*? Perhaps it wasn't freshly cooked, he reasoned. *Even if this food had been cooked a week ago and refrigerated bacterial putrefaction should not have occurred*, he thought. He left the dish on a small table which he used primarily as a desk in his room, and hurried down to dinner with Carmelita.

THREE

They sat next to each other on the couch and ate from the compartmentalized Styrofoam containers in which the restaurant served the take-out dinners. Baby Elvin was sleeping soundly and Carmelita was careful not to wake him up, so while they conversed, the level of expression was forcibly subdued. She outlined her plan to find employment that will allow her to meet her daily expenses, including the rent, while at the same time continuing her educational pursuits.

"That is an ambitious plan but it will not be easy."

"I am aware of that. Nothing has ever been easy for me but what else can I do?"

"You can wait until the baby is at least one year old before going out to work."

"What! Who will support us in the meantime?"

"I see how that can be a problem."

"That is the problem, David," said Carmelita. "If or when my mother gets here that should be resolved, partially at least."

"How long can she stay?"

"I don't know. That will depend partly on my stepfather and partly on the type of visa she gets from the US Embassy in Trinidad."

David wondered what assistance he might be able to render but asked instead, "Where would you seek employment?"

"I would prefer to work someplace that is centrally located."

"Centrally located in relation to what?"

"Central to where we live here and where I would like to attend college."

"Where would you like to go to school?"

"I plan on applying to the Municipal College downtown."

"I assume you mean downtown Brooklyn?"

"Yes, of course."

"Then you should apply to several schools instead of one."

"Why?"

"That will increase your chances of getting accepted to at least one of them."

"There are fees associated with the applications and I cannot afford them."

I can help, David thought but he said, "I understand."

"I am confident that I will be accepted to whichever institution I apply to."

"I am too. I know that you are very well qualified for college admission, so why limit yourself to the Municipal College?"

"As a New York City resident, if I am accepted there the tuition would be affordable."

"What is the cost of tuition for residents anyway?"

"It is free."

"What?"

"Why are you so surprised? Do you mean to tell me that you have been in attendance there and you didn't know that?"

"I honestly didn't know."

"Well, now you do."

"Why then aren't more residents like us taking advantage of that opportunity?"

"If you are asking why aren't more black folks taking advantage of the opportunity? I cannot answer that, David. You are taking full advantage of it I see."

"I am not a resident. I am a foreign (international) student and I pay my tuition, girl."

"I wasn't aware of that. I assumed that like me, you were here permanently."

"Your assumption was wrong but now you know the facts."

"That must be very difficult for you, I imagine."

"Actually, it is not. I work and pay the tuition. I am willing to work and jobs are available."

"That must have been quite an adjustment for you to leave your family and a respectable position with the Ministry of Health at home to work and go to school here. Wasn't it?"

"It was, just as I imagine it had been for you to leave home."

"That is reason enough why we must stay focused and not lose sight of our goals. I have made a few mistakes but hopefully, I can redeem myself."

"You have the perfect mindset and the right plan. Persevere and you will succeed. Remember also that I will be here to render any assistance I can." David finally said to Carmelita what he had been longing to say since Mrs. Mendoza informed him about her predicament.

"Thanks, David," she said with a broad smile.

"Seriously, I will pick up an application form for you next week. If you apply now you can enter during the first summer session."

"That would be nice."

That conversation with David was very encouraging. It seemed to be just what Carmelita needed. Suddenly, the future did not look all that gloomy for her and her little boy.

"David, you have lifted my spirit today."

"Tonight," he corrected her. "It is already nine o'clock."

"Wow! Is it that late already?"

"It certainly is. I guess I will leave you now," he said and stood up. Carmelita also got up. She walked with him toward the door and he said, "Good night."

"Good night, David. Thanks for the dinner, the company, and the words of encouragement."

"You are welcome. I will see you some time during the day tomorrow. Bye."

"Good night," Carmelita said again with a smile as David walked away.

When he got upstairs he sat at the table he normally used as a desk. He sighed, picked up the letters Mrs. Mendoza had given him, scrutinized them, and concluded that they had indeed been tampered with. Nevertheless, he proceeded to open them. They were from his mother and were written and mailed two weeks apart. The later dated of the two was mailed three weeks prior. "Why am I receiving them now?" he questioned himself softly. He had long suspected the Mendoza family of tampering with his mail, a concern he heard the other three young men who boarded there expressed from time to time.

What do they have to gain by opening our mail? He wondered. *I am apolitical and none of us is involved in anything shady as far as I know. We are all here as students trying to achieve some measure of higher education. What possible interest or motive do they have in knowing what our families write to us about? We do not pose a threat to them nor to the nation*, he thought.

David could not find answers to his questions or explanations for his thoughts. He was puzzled as he thought about Mrs. Mendoza's actions that morning. He tried desperately to link her behavior with the mail tampering but nothing was revealing. The more he thought about it, the more questions there were than answers. *If they are trying to find out more about our personal lives it would be just as easy for them to ask us. I have nothing to hide, and I doubt whether any of the other young men do.* His thoughts were interrupted when his telephone started ringing. He answered it.

"Good evening, David. This is Mildred," the caller said.

"Hello, Mildred. How are you?"

"I am fine. I was wondering if it would be convenient any time tomorrow for me to get that book from you."

"Oh, yes. The textbook I promised to lend you. Which one was it again?"

"*The British Approach to Politics*."

"What time would you like to come and get it?"

"Well, I am going to the library in the morning and I should be there until noon. I can come any time after that."

"Would three o'clock be okay?"

"I think so. If you know the author's name, however, I might be able to find the book at the library and save myself the trip."

"The book was written by Michael Stewart, MP. The latest edition was printed this year."

"That's great. I shall let you know if I am able to find it there so you wouldn't waste your time waiting around for me."

"I would never consider waiting to see you a waste of time. On the contrary, I was looking forward to that."

Mildred was flattered but she said, "You are such a tease, David. You and I know that you are just being kind by lending me the book so I can complete my thesis."

"I wasn't even aware that you were writing a thesis. I thought you needed something to supplement you assigned text."

"That's very nice of you, David. I will see you at three o'clock tomorrow." Mildred seemed to have abandoned any hope of finding the book at the Public Library on Saturday. She was captivated by what David said and wanted to see him immediately but was content on waiting another eighteen hours. She was a scholar by all accounts. She was ten years younger than Mrs. Mendoza but fifteen years older than David.

"I will be here when you arrive," he said.

"See you then, bye."

He hung up the telephone, put his letters away and went to bed. He lay there with racing thoughts for a while. He was thinking mostly of Carmelita and of ways in which he might be able to help her. He thought briefly of Mrs. Mendoza and her husband, Victor before he fell asleep.

FOUR

David slept later than usual that Saturday morning. Eventually, the ringing of his telephone woke him up but he missed the call anyway. Since he was awake he decided to get out of bed and head to the shower. He did so timorously. He adjusted the hot and cold water so that the flow from the showerhead was tepid but gentle. That wasn't the way he preferred it but it was how he thought Mrs. Mendoza wanted it. *I hope that will be enough to stem the tide of her curiosity*, he thought before stepping into the bathtub and under the flowing water from the shower head.

After about seven minutes in the shower, he wrapped a large towel around himself, pushed the sliding door open, and stepped out of the tub. Mrs. Mendoza was standing at the bathroom door smiling. Their eyes met. "What the…." David started to say something but she placed her right index finger at the center of the tip of her nose and across both lips, indicating that he should not speak. He complied because he realized that although Victor Mendoza would have left for work at his dry cleaning plant, the Mendoza's adult children were still at home that Saturday morning.

"Are you feeling any better this morning?" Crystal Mendoza asked.

"I am fine. Nothing was ever wrong with me."

"Well, I am glad to hear that, David. Yesterday you seemed to be very upset."

"Upset? No! I was surprised, rather shocked I should say."

"Why were you surprised or shocked as you say?"

"That was not the sort of thing I expected from someone……"

"Yes! I know." Mrs. Mendoza interrupted him. "You think that I am too old for you, don't you?"

You are as old as my mother. Furthermore, you have a husband who threatens to be vicious with anyone who pursues his daughter. What will he do to someone his wife pursues? David wondered but he said, "I do not know how old you are, Mrs. Mendoza."

"Crystal. You can call me Crystal in our private conversations."

What private conversations? He wondered, but before he could say anything further, Crystal Mendoza asked, "How old do you think I am, David?"

"Thirty-five, perhaps," he said.

She smiled, stepped forward, hugged him and whispered, "You are so very sweet."

Fifty-one is more like it, he thought as he struggled with his feelings. He did not hug her although he felt an urge to reciprocate. Instead, he simply said, "Thank you." She eased her embrace and he stepped back clutching the towel that was still wrapped around him. Crystal smiled and sat on the single-bed in the room. She could have sat on the chair at the table which he used as a desk but chose not to do so. She was hoping that David would sit next to her but he did not.

"Aren't you going to get dressed?" she asked.

"I will when you leave."

"I have no place to go."

"You can't stay here all day."

"Why can't I? Perhaps you are forgetting something."

"What's that?"

"I own the place."

"I know that," David said. He was still clutching the towel and that did not escape Crystal Mendoza.

"That's funny. Yesterday you seemed so bothered that I saw you undressed but today you are more relaxed in the nude in my presence."

"I am not naked," he said as he looked down at the very large towel that was wrapped around him. Crystal laughed.

"What is so funny?" he asked.

"You are," said Crystal as she got up to leave. "I will see you later, David. Enjoy the rest of your day."

He waited until she descended the stairway before closing the door to his room. He then dressed hurriedly while thinking of what he should have for breakfast. Eventually, he decided on pancakes and coffee and left the building to eat at a restaurant two blocks away. He could have fixed his own breakfast in the kitchen to the apartment where he lived on the fourth floor. He and the other young men had done that many times before. However, on that Saturday morning he wanted to get as far away from Crystal Mendoza as possible. When he arrived at the restaurant, the place was crowded. He had to wait to be seated but he did not mind. *Anything is better than having to deal with her again this morning*, he thought. *She is relentless and somewhat alluring at the same time.*

Crystal Mendoza realized the kind of effect she was having on young David Cassel and she was very pleased. *After all, he is a man and a very nice young one at that*, she though, *I should have asked him to come with me to do the grocery shopping. I certainly could use some help this morning.* She gave no consideration to the fact that her twenty-three year old son was the person she should have considered asking to accompany her to the supermarket. She was only thinking of opportunities to exert her influence over David. *He will succumb sooner than later*, she thought.

David sat at the table in his room and reached for the telephone to call Carmelita. Just then it started ringing. He answered. "David, this is Carmelita," the caller said excitedly.

"What's up with you, girl?"

"I am so happy. I just had to share this with you."

"What is it?"

"Mama got her visa, David. She got it!"

"When did she get it? I thought the US Embassy was closed on Saturdays in T & T."

"She got it yesterday but she arrived home too late to call me."

"How late is too late? You never go to bed before midnight."

"While that is true, remember that she had to ask the neighbors to allow her to use their telephone."

"I wasn't aware of that."

"Yes. Not many households in Mayaro have telephones. You know that, don't you?"

"No. Where we lived in Belmont, everyone I knew had a telephone."

"That was very unlike Mayaro, my friend. Nevertheless, Mama got the visa and she already bought her airline ticket."

"So when is she coming?"

"Next Wednesday."

"That will be February 28th, isn't it?."

"Yes," Carmelita said after she glanced at a large calendar that was hanging on the wall over the couch.

"That is reason for a celebration. Would you like to go out to lunch?"

"I would love that but I am reluctant to take Elvin out in weather like this."

"Oh yes! You are so right. Why don't I call up and have some food delivered instead?"

"That would be nice but please, no fried rice."

"What do you have against fried rice, girl? I love that stuff."

"Then I will refrain from telling you why I object to having it."

"Okay, I will get some home-styled Caribbean food instead."

"Good. I shall see you later."

"Okay. Bye."

"Bye, David."

As soon as he hung up the telephone, it rang again. He answered, "Hello!"

"David, this is Mildred."

"Oh! Hi, Mildred"

"Can I come a little earlier than three o'clock today?"

"How much earlier would you like to get here, Mildred?'

"Just after mid-day, maybe."

"I may not be back here by then."

"I am sorry. I didn't know that you were going out."

"I am not going out as such. I am meeting a friend for lunch."

"What might be a convenient time for you then?"

"Since you want to be earlier, would 2:00 p.m. be okay?"

"Yes."

"Then I shall see you at two."

"Thanks, David. I will see you then."

"Okay then, bye." They both hung up the telephones.

David sat on his bed and wondered what he might be able to do for Carmelita besides picking up the application for admission form at the Municipal College of Arts and Sciences that coming Monday. After considerable deliberation, he decided that the work-load (number of credits) he was carrying every semester was not necessary to maintain his status as an international student as set forth by the Department of Immigration and Naturalization Services. *Right now I am taking sixteen credits each semester when only twelve are required to be considered a full-time student*, he thought. *If I reduce my work-load to twelve in the Fall Semester when I enter graduate school, I can then help Carmelita to pay for her books since her tuition will be free. That's one way for her to get started if her pride would allow her to accept help.*

He looked at his watch and saw that it was 10:55 a.m., so he dialed the telephone number for *Caribbean Cuisine* and placed an order for lunch. He was told that it could be picked up in half an hour. At 11:30, therefore, he left home and walked over to the restaurant. His order was ready. He paid the cashier, received the food, and left. As he approached the building where he lived, Mrs.

Mendoza and her daughter, Dallas, were entering the lobby. He assumed that they had not seen him so he waited until they were out of sight before entering himself. He walked up to the second floor and rang Carmelita's door bell. Baby Elvin was crying. She picked him up before opening the door.

"Hi, dear," David said.

"Hi, I thought it might be you."

"It's me alright. Hello cutie," he said while smiling at the baby. He then placed the index finger of his right hand in the baby's left palm and repeated the phrase, "Hello, Cutie." The baby stopped crying and smiled at him. "You are so cute," he said as he turned his glance to Carmelita.

"He likes you," said Carmelita as she took the food from David and passed the baby over to him. "Hold him," she said and David did just that.

"You are a pro at it I see."

"Well, being the first of five children, what can I tell you?"

"You will probably say that you had to take care of your siblings."

"I did."

"Did you take care of them all?"

"No. I had to care only for the third, fourth, and fifth."

"Why? What happened to the second child?"

"Nothing happened to him. We were just too close in age."

"I understand."

Carmelita transferred the food from the Styrofoam containers to dinner plates. Little Elvin was sleeping by then. She took him from David and lay him down in the bassinet. Then she sat on the couch.

"He is sleeping just so peacefully," David said.

"He is a good baby. Come on, let's eat," said Carmelita. "You can wash your hands in there." She pointed to a door that led to the bathroom. "The towels are clean. I just changed them in case you are wondering."

David came out of the bathroom and joined her on the couch. "Excuse me for a minute," she said as she got up, took one of the plates of food and handed it to him together with a fork wrapped in a napkin.

"Thank you," he said. She then took the other plate of food with a fork and napkin for herself and rejoined him on the couch. They sat close together as they ate and conversed.

FIVE

Mildred arrived just when David was returning to his room after having lunch with Carmelita. He heard the door bell ringing and ran downstairs to answer it, hoping he could have accomplished that before Mrs. Mendoza became interested in knowing who was there. There was a certain curiosity about her which in many ways was justifiable. She always wanted to know who was entering or leaving the premises. It was her way she claimed, of keeping the undesirables out. *If they know that somebody is watching them, they wouldn't come*, she often said.

David opened the door and greeted Mildred who seemed hesitant to enter. "Aren't you going to come in?" he asked.

"I don't know, David. Should I?"

"Somehow I thought that was why you came."

"I am here to get the book you promised me. You know that."

"Well, if you prefer to wait on the stoop, I can run up and get it for you, or you can come up and get it if you wish." Mildred hesitated for a moment then stepped inside. David closed the door and said, "Come on up. I am on the fourth floor." She followed closely behind him. As they approached the second floor landing he stopped, looked up, and saw Mrs. Mendoza standing at the door to her apartment.

"Hello, David," she said condescendingly.

"Good afternoon, Mrs. Mendoza."

"I wanted to ask a favor of you but I see you are going to be busy all afternoon."

"Oh! This is Mildred. She is in a class with Dallas and me."

"She is a classmate, eh? It is nice to meet you, Mildred."

"The pleasure is mine, madam."

That I can tell, Crystal Mendoza thought but she said, "Enjoy your evening."

"Thank you," Mildred said as Mrs. Mendoza turned and walked away.

As they reached the fourth floor, David stepped back and ushered her in. They entered his room and he turned the chair away from the desk and said, "Have a seat, Mildred."

She sat down and immediately asked, "Was that your landlady downstairs?"

"Yes."

"Is she Dallas Mendoza's mother?

"Yes."

"Is she always that nosey?"

"Yes," said David. "Does that make you nervous?"

"It does make me a little uncomfortable but not nervous."

"Please don't be bothered by it. She does that all the time. As soon as the door bell rings, she positions herself where she can see who is entering the building."

"Either she has a lot of time to spare or very few people ever come here."

"You are correct on both counts. Most of us here are working and going to school. We have little time for anything else," said David as he looked around his room for the book. "Here it is," he said. He found it among a pile of used textbooks on the floor at the foot of his bed and handed it to her.

"Thank you," she said as she took the book, looked at the index, and quickly browsed through the text.

"You are welcome."

"This would be very helpful."

"I thought so."

"Thanks again for inviting me to get it."

"You are welcome anytime," said David. "Now, can I get you something to drink?"

"Yes, if you can offer me something hot."

David laughed, and Mildred asked, "What is so funny?"

"I don't think it is fanny."

"Then why are you laughing at me?" Mildred was laughing too although she didn't know why. "The things I can offer you that's hot are either coffee, tea, Old Oak or Mount Gay Eclipse."

"What are the last two?"

"Oh, those are liquors from Trinidad and Barbados respectively."

"Hold the rum. There is no need to get me drunk."

"It wasn't my intention to get you intoxicated. It's just something to warm you up."

"Some coffee will do just fine, thank you."

"I'll be right back." He left the room, went to the kitchen and got the coffee percolator started. He returned and asked Mildred, "How do you like your coffee?"

"I'll take it with cream and sugar."

"Come with me because I wouldn't know how much cream or sugar you need."

She followed him to the kitchen and they sat at the table where he had everything that was needed to serve the coffee.

"You have a well equipped kitchen here I see."

"Yes. There are three other students living here."

"Do you prepare all of your meals here?"

"No. Mrs. Mendoza serves us dinner Monday through Friday."

"I see. You are boarders."

"We are boarders and lodgers."

"No wonder she is so nosy. She wants to protect her own interest."

"You can look at it anyway you want to, although I do not see the connection."

Mildred did not attempt to clarify her statement. Instead, she allowed David to lead their discussion, and he wittingly took it in another direction; education. That was something dear to him and she too was conscious of its virtues. Both were school teachers at one time or another in their respective countries, Jamaica and Trinidad and Tobago, although neither was yet qualified to teach in the USA.

They enjoyed their coffee while they discussed a variety of issues including, but not limited to sports, politics, race, ethnicity and gender. Foremost among the topics they discussed was the absence of black men on college campuses and their presence downtown at Fulton and Nevins Streets where they were either soliciting something or hawking something.

"What can we do to encourage the brothers to register for classes at *The Municipal College of Arts and Sciences*?" David asked at one point in their conversation.

"By we, do you mean you and I as individuals?"

"Yes, off course."

"Not much I suppose."

"There is an observational study of street corner men that was published last year. In it the author chronicles the behaviors of groups of brothers who hang out constantly at street corners in urban centers. In the article the author tries to explain the reason for their behaviors."

"What was her conclusion?"

"His conclusion, the researcher was male."

"I should have known. Nevertheless, what was it?"

"There was no single conclusion."

"Come on, David. If the research is published there must be a conclusion."

"There really wasn't any. I can tell you some of his findings in a disjointed sort of way as I remember them."

"Okay."

"He found that the men were obsessed with skin color, shades of black that is. He also found that he was at a disadvantage because he couldn't speak their language fluently......"

Before allowing David to continue, Mildred asked, "What language did they speak, weren't they all Americans?"

"Yes, they were Americans."

"So what language did they speak other than English?"

"You know."

"I do not know, David. Fill me in."

"In a sense they spoke very much like Trinidadians, Jamaicans, or the manner in which other people from the Caribbean do."

"They did not."

"You know what I mean. It is as if several of us got together and spoke just the way we did at home, it might be difficult for other people to understand."

"What difference would there be? The way I speak now is just the way I spoke then."

"You may be different from other Caribbean folks I know. Very often in conversations with them I have to ask for further explanations from time to time."

"I suppose some people speak like that. They stick with the vernacular whether it is Ebonics or patois. I do not. I never did."

"Neither do I but I do understand the language. Don't you?"

"When my compatriots speak I understand but I have difficulty understanding yours."

"That's what I am talking about."

"It is not the same thing. We are from different countries. The researcher, Elliot Liebow, and the street corner men were all Americans."

"This discussion could go on and on. However, I am just going to tell you the findings as I remember them."

"Okay."

"*In Tally's Corner*, he described the street corner men as cynical, self-serving, and constantly exploiting one another and the women in their lives as useful objects or income generators. The men prided themselves as exploiters of women. Their assessment of a woman as nice and desirable was based on the balance in her bank account or the amount she earned weekly, fortnightly, or monthly."

"Is that all?'

"No."

"What else did he determine?"

"He found that for the most part, the men were anti-marriage. Most were single. Those who were married believed that they were forced into it against their will. Many had children they did not support."

"What else did he conclude?"

"I don't think any of these were conclusions per se. However, he did mention that the men ranged in age from twenty to forty. Most were unemployed. Those who did work had unskilled or menial jobs which they hated."

"Why as American citizens couldn't they find better jobs?"

"They lacked proper qualifications, I suppose."

"Why was that, when so much is available here to choose from?"

"If you look back twenty years when the forty-year olds should have been in college you would realize how many obstacles there were, especially for some of those men who came up North from the South."

"I understand your point of view but they are here now."

"While they are here now and the opportunities abound, they lack the fundamentals and, therefore, do not have the desire or the will to acquire the necessary skills."

"What will happen to them? How will they inspire their children to persevere and achieve?"

"I do not know, Mildred. I am concerned that these things will remain the same for them and their descendents for many years to come and that the population of street corner men will increase over time. Ten, twenty, thirty, or even forty years from now if we are still here, we might witness the same pattern."

"There has to be a way out of this cycle of dead end jobs and self-imposed destitution."

"I am not sure that it is self-imposed destitution. There are several factors that impede the progress of the street corner men."

"What are some of those factors?"

"The chief factor is discrimination which in its variety of forms has accounted for the fact that these men were never able to acquire the fundamentals I mentioned earlier."

"You never said what those fundamentals were."

"Perhaps I took it for granted that you knew."

"Well, I do not."

"Those men obviously lacked the education necessary to attain better jobs. They were also never given the opportunity to experience apprenticeships that eventually would have led to skilled trades."

"So they are stuck where they are for life."

"They are for the most part, yes."

"Come on now, David. There has to be a way out of that quagmire."

"The best way out is through education. It determines one's quality of life for the rest of one's life."

SIX

Mildred thanked David for the book again and for the wonderful afternoon she had with him, although he did not think that he provided much to make the afternoon as wonderful as she said it was. However, she thought that their discussions were inspiring and uplifting. She was glad that she made no effort to find the book at the Public Library. If she did, she would have missed the opportunity for a quiet afternoon of straight talk with David. Apart from her activities at work and with school, one might say that her lifestyle was sedentary. Occasions like the afternoon she spent with David were rare and she was somewhat saddened when she had to say goodbye.

"I wish I could stay a while longer, David, but there is so much I need to get done, it is necessary that I leave you now."

"I understand. It was nice of you to come."

"It was nice of you to have me. Let's face it, you could have brought me this book on Monday."

"You needed the book and the time to work on your thesis this weekend, didn't you?"

"I am so glad that you understand. Thanks again."

"I am not so sure that I would have understood had I not been a student myself, but you are most welcome."

As Mildred was ready to leave she took the textbook and her purse, and David got up to walk with her to the train station. Before stepping out of the door, they hugged each other. Then they walked down the stairs, through the front door, and onto Herkimer Street.

"I think I will take a taxi," she said.

"Are you sure?"

"Yes. The train takes too long on the weekends and there is a lot that I would like to accomplish this evening."

"Are you certain about this?" David asked again as he thought of his own financial situation which would have precluded any thought of him taking a cab that evening.

"Yes," said Mildred. "I almost forget to give you this." She took a ticket from her pocketbook and handed it to him. It was an invitation to a dance. "Let me know if you would like to attend," she said.

"Okay."

As soon as he said that, a gypsy cab stopped in front of them, Mildred climbed into the back seat and waved to him as the taxi drove off. He then turned to walk back into the building. At the same time Mrs. Mendoza and her daughter Dallas were coming out.

"How are you, David?" Dallas asked.

Before he could answer her mother said, "He is fine. His girlfriend, the older one, was with him all afternoon."

She is no older than you are, David thought but he said, "I am doing just fine, Dallas. By the way, that lady is just a friend." For some reason he felt the need to explain that.

"There is no need for you to explain, David. You are grown so pay no attention to the things my mother says." Without further comment, Dallas and her mother left and David entered the building and closed the door behind him. His first thought was that he should check on Carmelita on his way up, but he quickly dismissed that thought and went directly to his room. He tossed himself across his bed. He felt somewhat doleful by what Mrs. Mendoza said. As he lay there looking at the ceiling, his thoughts were drifting. He thought of his aging mother in Belmont, Port of Spain, Trinidad. He thought of his job, Mildred's invitation, Carmelita's predicament, and Mrs. Mendoza's forwardness.

David didn't have a television in his room. He viewed the device as a distraction from his studies. He wished he had a radio though and vowed to purchase one the next time he got paid. After about an hour or so of lying there despondent and thinking, he decided to get out of the bed and get something for dinner. He knew that in order to get dinner he had to go out and he wondered whether he should get something for Carmelita also. However, having had lunch with her earlier he didn't want to pester her by asking about dinner so he decided against it. As soon as he was ready to leave his room the telephone rang. He answered and the caller said, "David, this is Crystal. What are you doing right now?"

He was taken aback by the question but quickly gathered his thoughts and said, "I am about to go out to dinner."

"Are you going alone?"

That's none of your damn business, he thought of saying but he said, "Yes"

"Would you be out long?"

"I don't know," said David. "Why are you asking me all these questions, Mrs. Mendoza?"

"Crystal! There is no one else here so you can call me Crystal."

"Okay."

"You still can't say Crystal, can you?"

"Say what?"

"Crystal."

"Okay, Crystal. Why are you questioning me?"

"Well, if you weren't going out I would have asked whether I could come up and speak with you or if you prefer, you can come down here."

"You never needed anyone's permission to come upstairs before. You own the place! Have you forgotten?"

"Aren't you getting a little beside yourself now, David?"

"Maybe I am, and it is probably because I am tired of your shit."

"Huh! That's mannish. I like that of you."

"You are a very sick woman," David said. Mrs. Mendoza offered no objection. Instead, she was laughing hysterically, so David hung up the telephone and left.

Although he didn't venture out of the neighborhood, it was 9:00 p.m. when he returned home, exactly two and a half hours after he went out to dinner. Before he could take off his coat, the telephone started ringing. He hesitated to answer fearing that it might be Mrs. Mendoza. He felt that he had been rude to her and he was concerned about the repercussions. He suspected her to be vindictive. He had never disrespected her before but was convinced that it was the only way he could have gotten her to cease her aggressive, repugnant sexual advances toward him. Shortly thereafter the caller hung up. David took off his coat, sat down, took a deep breath and exhaled loudly. Just then the telephone rang again and he answered. It was Carmelita. "What's up, girl?" he asked.

"That's what I want to know. I have not heard from you all afternoon. Are you okay?"

"I am fine," he said but wondered why she was expecting him to call her again.

"There is something I want to ask you, David."

"Okay, I am listening."

"I cannot ask you that on the phone. Actually, I can but I would prefer not to."

"Can you come up or would you prefer that I come down?"

"Would you, please?"

"Certainly, I can do that."

"When can I expect you?"

"I will be there in half an hour."

"Great!"

Two minutes later Carmelita's door bell rang. "That was quick," she whispered to herself as she moved toward the door and opened it. She was surprised and it showed.

"Sorry if I startled you," said Mrs. Mendoza. "Can I come in?"

"Yes." *What else can I say*, Carmelita thought as she stepped aside so Crystal Mendoza could enter.

"How is the baby?" she asked.

"He is doing very well, thank God. He sleeps a lot though."

"That's good," said Mrs. Mendoza. "I wouldn't take up too much of your time but I wanted to know whether your heard anything further from your mother."

"Oh yes. Didn't I tell you?"

"No."

"I am so sorry, Mrs. Mendoza. There is just so much going on in my head."

"I can imagine," said Crystal Mendoza while thinking, *with older and more financially stable women showing so much interest in David you must be going nuts*, but she asked again, "Did you hear from her?"

"Yes! Mama got her visa. She will be here next Wednesday."

"Is that February twenty-eighth?"

"I think it is the twenty-first."

"You think?"

Carmelita looked at the calendar that hung over the couch and said, "Sorry! It is the twenty-eighth"

"So when were you planning to tell me?"

"Once again, Mrs. Mendoza, I am very sorry. I sincerely apologize." There was no response from Crystal. She got up and walked out the door without saying another word. As she walked up the stairs she whispered to herself, "That poor girl, she has to endure so much." David was coming down at the same time and their eyes met. "Hey! Handsome," she shouted.

"Good evening, Mrs. Mendoza."

"It is Crystal, baby, and that's only for you," she said. David smiled but said nothing more. Instead, he bowed his head and his right foot slipped. He grabbed the railing to regain his balance and continued on his way.

"You need to pay attention to where you are going, son. I wouldn't want you to fall down the stairs and hurt yourself."

"Thank you," he said.

As he reached where she was standing close to her doorway, Crystal Mendoza reached out, held his hand, looked directly in his eyes, smiled, and asked, "Are you okay?"

"Yes."

"Take care of yourself, hon." She released her grip and he eased his hand out of hers. They both smiled and walked away.

David rang Carmelita's door bell and she quickly opened the door. "What took you so long?" She asked with a tremor in her voice.

"Someone called just when I was about to leave the room but in any case, it hasn't been half an hour since I spoke with you."

"That might have been a good thing."

"Why? Why are you crying?" David asked the two questions in quick succession as he noticed tears in her eyes.

"Mrs. Mendoza was here and she was quite upset because I didn't tell her when Mama was coming."

"Why didn't you tell her?"

"I intended to but I forgot."

"Well, don't fret about it."

"I don't want to worry but I am concerned."

"I know. She can be very intimidating," David said as he held Carmelita's hand and guided her toward the couch. They sat down and she leaned her head on his shoulder.

"What was it you wanted to talk about?" he asked.

"As soon as Mama arrives here next week I want to christen the baby."

"That's a good idea."

"That's not all."

"What else is there?"

"I would like you be his godfather." David did not respond right away so Carmelita asked again, "Would you do that for me, David?"

"Yes, of course." Carmelita smiled for the first time that evening and David asked, "Who will be the godmother?"

"At first I thought of asking Lillian but she was really mean to me before TK left."

"Is she Lillian Paul?"

"Yes. Do you know her?"

"Yes."

"What do you think I should do?"

"I do not know her well enough to give you an opinion."

"The only other person I was considering was Mrs. Mendoza but she too was very nasty to me."

"When was that?"

"When she came here earlier today, a little while ago really"

"Don't pay her any mind. She could probably be his grand-godmother if there had ever been such a thing."

"That's not very nice, David."

"She is not very nice."

David viewed Mrs. Mendoza as a wicked sex-starved individual who chose to do a few good deeds as a swathe for all the evil she perpetrated on people with whom she came into contact daily. He had lost all respect for her and was adamant about not giving in to what he considered her attempts at reeling him in.

SEVEN

After careful and considerable deliberation, Carmelita decided that David and her mother would be Baby Elvin's godparents. She concluded that it was just a formality. In today's world, she reasoned, no one expects a child's godparents to assume parenting responsibilities for him or her in the event something awful or untimely should happen to the natural parents. *On the contrary, in this part of the world, she thought, the state will make that decision if the parent or parents neglected to do so in a will.*

Carmelita was much more relaxed once the matter of Elvin's christening was settled. She confided in David that she did not want to place any undue burden on her mother who had sacrificed so much already to ensure that she received a private secondary school education. That was commendable for a woman, herself a single mother who was poorly educated. As the first member of her family to attain a General Certificate of Education (GCE), everyone was proud of Carmelita's accomplishments but she felt that she could have done even more. That was the reason she left her position with the Ministry of Education and migrated to the USA.

She arrived in Brooklyn in May,1967 with every intention of starting college the following September. That was until she met Tyrone Khadevis at a party she attended with Lillian Paul. She was impressed by his keen acumen and witty sense of humor. Soon they were going out together regularly and before she could land a decent job or register for classes, she became pregnant. Suddenly she was no longer welcomed where she resided with a friend and former classmate. The situation became less and less tolerable every day. Then TK suggested that she moved in with him. She did and their relationship floundered from then until his departure a few months later after Elvin's birth.

David was always sympathetic toward Carmelita but he didn't know why. As far as he was concerned nothing should ever get in the way of one's education. He never did understand why she hung out with TK who, although he had a job and went to school sporadically, he spent more time with his pot smoking buddies than he ever did studying or looking after her interest. Nevertheless, David had vowed to do whatever he could to help her. He never told her that, so he had the option to change his mind without reneging on a promise. *That,* he thought, *would not be necessary if she stayed the course she was on.*

It was approaching 11:30 when he said good night and left Carmelita's place to return to his room. He took his shoes off to climb the stairs carefully, and he threaded lightly so that his movements could not be heard, especially by Mrs. Mendoza whom he knew stayed up late, particularly on weekends for no apparent reason. Carmelita wondered about the barefoot act but did not question it. She just smiled and closed the door as he left. He managed to reach his fourth floor room relieved that Crystal Mendoza was nowhere in sight. Well, he didn't see her although he couldn't be sure that she didn't see him.

There was complete silence on the floor. His compatriots were either out for the evening or they were all asleep. He had no way of knowing with certainty and didn't care very much about that anyway. He got himself ready for bed and as he lay there thinking about Carmelita he quickly fell asleep. He slept soundly through the rest of the night and well into Sunday morning. It was 10:15 a.m. when the ringing of a telephone next door woke him up. Very soon thereafter his phone started ringing. "Hello!" He answered.

"David. This is Mildred."

"Good morning. How are you?"

"I am fine, and you?"

"I am okay."

"You sound as if I woke you up."

"Not really. I was already awake when the telephone rang."

"I want to let you know how helpful that book is to me."

"I thought it would be. I found it to be well written when I used it for GCE (General Certificate of Education)."

"Was it an assigned text?"

"Yes."

"What subject was it for?"

"It was the assigned text for *British Constitution*."

"Well, I am so glad you brought it with you."

"I am glad that it is helpful."

"It is. Thanks again."

"You are welcome."

"Listen! Did you think about that other thing?"

"What was it again?"

"The ticket I gave you to the dance, David."

"Oh! I am so sorry. I really didn't give it much thought. However, I will get back to you on that this evening."

"Please do."

"I certainly will."

"Okay, thanks."

"I will call you later, bye."

"Bye, David." Mildred said with a pleasant Jamaican lilt. David smiled and tossed himself across the bed again. He thought about the mundane things he usually did on Sundays and wondered whether that Sunday would have been any different since he had gotten closer to Carmelita. She too was hoping he would spend the rest of the day with her and her son but she was reluctant to ask for fear that he may have thought of her as becoming too demanding. She contemplated calling him and picked up the telephone, then decided against it.

Victor Mendoza and his adult children, Dallas and Daniel left for church. Crystal did not accompany them. In fact, she never did. Generally on Sundays when they were gone she would spend time preparing lunch for the family and meals to be frozen, reheated, and served to the boarders until mid-week. That Sunday was no different. As she went about her chores it occurred to her that she needed some canned foodstuff from the uppermost shelf of the kitchen cabinet. Previously, she used a stepladder to retrieve them. On that occasion, she called David.

"Good morning," she said when he answered the phone.

"Good morning, Mrs. Mendoza."

"Crystal," she said and asked, "Are you busy?"

"Not really."

"Could you come down here for a minute?"

"Must I do that right now?"

"Preferably, yes."

"I would need a few minutes in the shower." As soon as he said that he regretted it.

"Remember not to open the tap too forcefully."

"I will remember that," he said with relief as he went into the bathroom, brushed his teeth and showered quickly. He came out, got dressed and headed down to the Mendoza's. He entered the kitchen and saw Crystal making a feeble attempt at climbing a stepladder.

"Be careful," he said.

"Oh. You are here. I got tired of waiting and decided to get the things I need myself."

"I am sorry. I didn't think I took that long but maybe I did."

"Okay! If you can hold the ladder steady I will get what I need."

"Why don't you let me get it?"

"Alright," Crystal said as she started to climb down the ladder. Upon reaching the last rung her left foot slipped to the floor, or so it seemed. As she stumbled, David held her. She regained her balance and held on to him. Although by then he had relaxed his grip, she held him close, and looked directly into his eyes with her lips pursed.

"What is it?" he asked.

"What do you think?"

"I think I should get you what you want and get out of here."

"Why? Am I that repulsive?"

"I never thought of you as being repulsive."

"So what is it?"

"Would you just tell me what it is you need out of that cabinet."

"What I really need is for you to..." Crystal paused then she said, "Two cans of golden corn kernel and two cans of sweet green peas."

He raced up the ladder, fetched the items and handed them to her. He climbed back down, folded the step ladder and asked, "Where do you want this?"

"Just lean it against the refrigerator. Victor will put it away."

David did as he was told and asked, "Is there anything else you need before I leave?"

"No."

"Then enjoy the rest of your day."

"Do you really think I can?"

"I know of no reason why you can't."

"That is right. You do not know. Why don't you sit for a while and let me fill you in on a few things."

David sat at the kitchen table reluctantly and waited to hear what Crystal Mendoza had to say. She didn't seem to be in any hurry to speak at first. Then she sighed and said, "Things are not always as they appear to be, David." He looked at her puzzled and she continued. "I know that you think of us as the ideal family; husband and wife and two dynamic children but we are not all that. My husband is a hard working man, a good provider. My children are the best any parent could desire under the circumstances. That is, growing up in this crime ridden, drug infused neighborhood."

Where is she going with this? David wondered but he asked, "What then is the problem?

"Don't you see it? I am miserable. Victor works twelve to sixteen hours a day for six days a week and he spends the seventh day either at the church or with other parishioners. My kids are busy with what they as young people do." Crystal paused and waited for a response from David but there was none so she continued. "What am I supposed to do? I am sick and tired of the domestic chores."

"Then join your husband at Sunday mass."

"I can't do that."

"Why can't you?"

"I am not Catholic."

"That shouldn't matter if you believe in God."

"It matters because I am not even Christian and we started off badly because my parents vigorously opposed our marriage."

"But you got married anyway and it seemed to have worked out quite well so far."

"Things are never quite what they seem, David." Once again Crystal waited for David to comment but he did not, so she continued. "I must say that everything was fine with us up until about five years ago."

"I take it that us refers to the family as a whole."

"By us I mean Victor and I."

"What happened five years ago?"

"His interest in me began to wane."

"How could you say that? Whenever I speak with Mr. Mendoza he expounds the virtues of his family."

"Yes, I know. He has a textbook view of the ideal family but the warmth and affection are lacking."

"Well, maybe you can do something about that."

"Believe me, I have tried everything."

"You probably have tried everything you know or could think of but there are lots of other things you may not have thought of."

"Like what, David?"

"Well, let me ask you this: Have you been away on vacation together as a couple since the kids have grown up?"

"No."

"Have you gone hiking, on a picnic, or just for a stroll in the park or on the beach in the summer time lately?"

"No.

"When last have the two of you gone out to dinner?"

"It has been a while."

"It has been a while! Does that mean you had dinner out together six weeks ago, or six months ago?"

"More like six years ago."

"Oh, my world!"

"Now, are you beginning to get my drift?"

"I think so."

"At times I feel so isolated even though the children are still here. I dread the thought of what will happen to me when they leave."

"They are not likely to leave home anytime soon."

"You are wrong, David. Just last week Victor went with Dallas to look at an apartment and Daniel has been talking about moving out himself. Over here things are different from back home in T & T."

"Yes. I have heard it said on campus that young adults do not live with their parents for very long."

"You heard right. I am surprised that Dallas and Daniel are still here. Don't get me wrong, I am happy that they are, but surprised nevertheless." Crystal Mendoza said with a cracking voice. David noticed that she was crying.

Gee! I didn't think you could be that emotional. You always acted so tough, he thought but said, "Please don't cry, Crystal."

EIGHT

Crystal was determined to use the occasion to gain sympathy from David but he had other things in mind. He was sympathetic alright but was determined not to become involved the manner he thought she wanted him to. Just then he heard a telephone ringing on the upper floor and assumed, or rather, pretended it was his, excused himself, and left the Mendoza's apartment. By the time he reached his fourth floor room the caller had already hung up. He still wasn't sure whether it was his phone that rang or one of his compatriots' but he was glad to get away from Crystal.

As he lay across his bed thinking, he recalled that although Dallas was attending college Daniel was not. He was not in a vocational school or an apprenticeship either. He could have assisted his father and learn the dry cleaning business but he did not. At age twenty-three, he preferred to hang out with friends at street corners. David remembered a conversation he had with Victor Mendoza in which he justified his son's actions and lifestyle as youthful exuberance.

The fact that the young man smoked reefers did not bother his father. "I had my share of indiscretions," he often said. "And look at me today, I am beyond that. He will rise above his. Right now he manages to stay out of trouble. He goes to church with me regularly and is very respectful. What more can I ask for?"

Not only can you ask for more, you can demand more, David thought. Just then his telephone rang. He answered. It was Mildred calling.

"I called you earlier but your telephone just rang and rang," she said.

"So it was my telephone that was ringing and you were the one calling. I ran up the stairs a while ago hoping it would be mine but thinking it could be someone else's."

"I am sorry about that. Anyway, have you given any thought to the invitation?"

"What invitation?"

"David? The invitation I gave you to the dance."

"Oh, I am so sorry." said David. "As a matter of fact I think I will attend."

"You think, David? I need to know whether or not you plan to attend."

"Yes. I will attend."

"Good. That's nice to hear."

"What's the price of the ticket?"

"Don't worry about that. It has already been paid for."

"Thanks," he said.

He wasn't very happy about that because he did not want to be looked upon as a sponger. However, he couldn't dwell on it because Mildred quickly said, "Good bye, David."

"Bye, Mildred."

As soon as he hung up the telephone it rang again. When he answered a very excited Carmelita asked, "What are your plans for lunch today?"

"I have no specific plan."

"Good! Then keep the scheduled period open."

"Now that statement leads me to ask you two questions. First, what exactly is the scheduled Sunday lunch period? Secondly, why should I keep it open?"

"That is not exactly fair, David."

"Why isn't it fair?"

"You asked me two questions in rapid succession leaving me no time to think."

"What is there to think about? I haven't asked you about the quantum theory."

"Don't get smart with me when you know exactly what I am telling you."

"I am not being smart or facetious. I am simply telling it like it is."

"How is it, David?"

"Come on, Carmelita. Just answer the questions." Carmelita started laughing which caused David to laugh also, although he didn't know why he was laughing. When the laughter subsided she said, "Listen, lunch can be served anytime between two and three o'clock today or on any given Sunday. In answer to your second question, I am asking you to keep the period open because I am preparing lunch for you." David did not respond so she asked, "David, are you there?"

"Yes! Yes, I just don't know what to say."

"Say okay, but only if you mean it."

"Okay! I must say that I am flattered."

"Are you flattered or flustered?"

"Perhaps it is a little of both."

"There is no reason for you to be anxious. I can assure you that you will be thrilled to taste some good Mayaro, country cooking."

"Is your cooking better than that of *Caribbean Cuisine's*?"

"I will let you be the judge of that. I can assure you though, if it is not the very best out of Mayaro, it is right up there with the best of them."

"I like your confidence."

"You will love my cooking even more."

"So what time should I come down?"

"Lunch will be ready by one o'clock but you can come now if you wish."

David looked at his watch. It was 11:45 a.m. so he said, "I will see you at half past one."

"1:30 it is. I am looking forward to seeing you then."

"Okay."

They both hung up and David wondered what he might be able to take along to show his appreciation. Then it occurred to him that he could take the train downtown, go over to Junior's Restaurant and purchase one of their nationally renowned, delectable cheese cakes for dessert. He looked at his watch, decided there was enough time, and rushed out of the building.

After purchasing the cake, he crossed the street and bought a bouquet of yellow roses from a florist at the corner of Flatbush Avenue and Fulton Street before re-entering the subway. He arrived back at his Herkimer Street dwelling a little before 1:30 p.m. and went directly to Carmelita's. He knocked at the door rather than ring the bell but she opened it without hesitation.

"These are for you," he said as he handed her the roses. "Oh! David, they are beautiful. Thank you."

Has there ever been a time when a woman said roses were ugly? David wondered but said, "You are welcome. Take this also."

"Let me guess. It is a cheesecake, a Juniors Restaurant cheesecake!"

"That is for your sweet tooth."

"Thanks again," Carmelita said as she kissed him on the cheek.

"I have to ask you this," said David. "Don't you check to see who is at the door before you open it?"

"Most times I do."

"So why didn't you when I knocked?"

"I knew it had to be you."

"You couldn't be sure about that."

"I was certain."

"How could you have been certain?"

"It was by intuition perhaps."

"You shouldn't take such chances in this part of town, girl. It is not safe."

"Doesn't Mrs. Mendoza monitor who enters and leaves the building?"

"She tries but she is successful only if someone rings the bell downstairs before entering."

"I understand."

"Good."

Suddenly little Elvin cried out. That was something he seldom did. "Perhaps he is hungry," said Carmelita. "I should have fed him an hour ago."

"Why didn't you?"

"He was sleeping and I was trying to have lunch ready before he woke up."

"Well, he is awake now and lunch is ready I suppose."

"That is true."

"Then feed him."

"Perhaps I should," Carmelita said as she walked to the bassinet and picked up the baby. As she sat in the couch next to David he wondered, *where is the bottle with the infant formula*? Carmelita sensed his concern and said, "I breast feed him. It is better for him and more economical than formula."

"I understand. I will be back when you are through."

"No. You do not have to leave."

"Please give me a call after you have fed the baby."

"Really, David, you do not have to leave," Carmelita pleaded but David insisted and she eventually walked with him to the door and closed it as he left.

He is such a gentleman. I hope this is it so that no other woman gets to take advantage of him, she thought as she nursed the child. Ten minutes later Elvin was sleeping again. Carmelita got up, held him to her shoulder until he burped. She then put him back into the bassinet, washed and dried her hands, dished out the food and placed it on a small table that seated two. Then she called David. His telephone was busy so she waited for five minutes and called again. That time he answered, "Hello."

"David, I am ready."

"I'll be right there," he said and as soon as she hung up the telephone there was a knock at her door.

He couldn't get down here already, she thought as she moved toward the door. She was right. When she opened it, Crystal Mendoza was standing there with a dish in her hand. It was covered with a white kitchen towel. She handed it to Carmelita and said, "I hope you would like this."

"Thank you," Carmelita said with a smile but she did not ask what it was or why Mrs. Mendoza felt the need to bring her something that Sunday afternoon. She also did not invite Crystal in although it seemed as if she was waiting for an invitation. Since none was forthcoming, she said, "Enjoy the dish."

Before she turned to leave, David who was on his way down spotted her and rushed back up the stairs to his room. Carmelita saw that and struggled not to laugh out loudly but she managed to exude a child-like giggle at the same time she said, "Thank you, Mrs. Mendoza."

"I like that. You are in a good mood today."

"Thanks."

"Enjoy your day and keep smiling, girl. Bye."

"Bye," Carmelita said as Crystal turned and walked away.

David picked up his telephone and dialed Carmelita's number. When she answered he asked, "Is she gone?"

"Yes," she said while laughing.

"That was close."

"Are you afraid of her or simply avoiding her?"

"It is perhaps a little of both."

"Why?"

"Believe me! You do not want to know."

"Already you are wrong. I asked because something heightened my interest."

"You may be curious but certainly not interested."

"Okay, David. Whatever it is, keep it to yourself but you can come down now. The door is open."

He walked down the stairs quietly and into Carmelita's second floor efficiency. The table in the room was set for dining. The yellow roses were in a vase at the middle, and the food she prepared and dished out was at each place setting. The dish Mrs. Mendoza brought was to her left, that was after David was seated. She expected him to bring up the issue of Crystal Mendoza's visit earlier but he did not.

"Let's say a prayer," Carmelita said. She clasped her hands and bowed her head, and David did the same. Nothing either of them said was audible to the other except *amen*.

"Everything looks and smells so good," he said.

"I hope you find the taste to be as good as the look and smell."

David did not respond to what Carmelita said, instead he asked, "What is covered there?"

"Oh, that is something Mrs. Mendoza brought me. I haven't even looked at it"

"Don't you think you should?"

"Yes, of course." She uncovered the dish and saw that there were actually two dishes with prepared food. A smaller dish containing curried chicken was inside of a larger one that contained two roti (a type of flat bread) *skins*.

David looked at the food Mrs. Mendoza prepared and said, "Huh."

"What's that about?"

"It's nothing really."

"Come on, David. Is that all you can say?"

"That is all I am saying." He was thinking of the dinner Crystal Mendoza left him on Friday evening. It was putrid and he wondered again what she might have done to effect that taste and why. *Is it possible that she had done the same thing to the preparation she brought to Carmelita?* His thoughts were racing even before either of them tasted Mrs. Mendoza's roti and curried chicken.

Although David never told Carmelita of his experience with the dinner he took upstairs on Friday, she found his reaction to having food from Crystal Mendoza, a person whom she knew served him dinner every evening from Monday to Friday, to be strange. She decided, therefore, to taste the food she received from Crystal first. When she did David looked at her and asked, "Is it fetid?"

"No, it is very harsh of you to ask that!" said Carmelita. "The food is delicious."

"Good for you!"

"Aren't you going to have some?"

"No, thank you."

"Why wouldn't you even taste it, David?"

"I taste her cooking five days per week already. That is enough."

"That sounds as if you do not like the way she cooks," Carmelita said as she wondered, *what will he think of my cooking today*? Her self-confidence was a bit shaken.

"I didn't say that."

"You didn't have to." By then David tasted the food Carmelita prepared and he said, "Yours is truly delectable."

"Well, I am glad you didn't find it to be fusty."

David laughed. Then he asked, "Why are you trying to start a quarrel?" The question reminded Carmelita why she had invited him to dine with her in the first place. *It certainly wasn't to haggle about Crystal Mendoza's cooking*, she thought.

She reached over, held his hand and said, "I am sorry. We really shouldn't quibble about such things."

"We shouldn't ever quibble about anything."

"Let's just stop it now, David, please!" Carmelita pleaded. He smiled as if he agreed and they continued eating. When they were finished, he washed the dishes while she attended to the baby. The rest of the evening they conversed amicably about many things but the emphasis was on what lay ahead for Carmelita and Elvin since David was expecting to graduate with a Bachelor of Science degree in May of that year. Cognizant of the fact that the future was not assured, they agreed on a plan of action that emphasized, but was not limited to Carmelita's pursuit of higher education. "It is a way out of this quagmire," David suggested and Carmelita agreed.

NINE

It was 11:35 p.m. when David returned to his room from Carmelita's. Before he left her place, he had asked her to give him a wake-up call sometime between 5:30 and 6:00 a.m. Monday morning. He was concerned that he might oversleep and be late for work. However, instead of going directly to bed he decided to look for the invitation Mildred gave him to the dance. He found it in a pocket of the parka he wore that Sunday afternoon when he walked with her to get transportation home.

When he examined the ticket carefully he realized that the dance was scheduled for Saturday, March 2, 1968, the same day that Carmelita had asked him to be at little Elvin's christening to stand in as his Godfather. Although the christening was scheduled for 11:30 a.m. at the church Mr. Mendoza attended, he was uncertain as to the number of people Carmelita had invited to witness the ceremony and eventually gather at the house for a reception. The dance was scheduled to start at 10:00 p.m. and he hoped that any reception to celebrate Elvin's christening would have come to a close by then.

In spite of his concerns, he placed the ticket on the table in his room and went to bed. The night was quiet except for the occasional emergency vehicle siren, so soon after lying down he fell asleep. He slept soundly until his telephone started ringing at precisely 5:30 a.m. Monday morning. He rolled over and reached for it thinking it had to be Carmelita, but the caller hung up before he could answer. Ten minutes later the phone rang again.

That time he was in no hurry to answer but the caller stayed on the line until he did. It was Carmelita. She was giving him a wake-up call as he had asked her to. He inquired about the earlier call and she assured him that it was not from her. *Who could it have been*? He wondered, but quickly dismissed it.

By 7:20 that morning he was dressed and left the building. He managed to do that without any interruption by or intrusion from Crystal Mendoza. His major concern was whether he would have been able to stay awake during his late night class which ended at 10:10 p.m. Somehow, he managed, went home, picked up his dinner from the Mendoza's kitchen and took it to his room rather than eating at the kitchen table as was customary. On the contrary, he did not eat at all that night. He went directly to bed. He did not visit Carmelita or telephoned her. Crystal was not at the mailbox when he arrived there. She wasn't leaning over the banister as he went up the stairs, nor did she venture up to his room, or called him on the telephone.

All should be well in dreamland, he thought. After all it was a good day. As he lay on his back thinking of Carmelita and Elvin, his thoughts drifted momentarily to Crystal Mendoza before he fell asleep. He slept all through the night. As soon as he woke up he called Carmelita to ask what time her mother's flight was coming in the next day. She informed him that the flight was due to arrive at 8:35 a.m. and that by the time she clears custom and immigration it could be 10:00 a.m.

"Do you plan on meeting her at the airport?" he inquired.

"I most certainly do, although I do not know how I can manage that with Elvin."

"Huh!" David paused while thinking of how he can possibly help.

In the meantime Carmelita continued, "If I had a stroller it would be much easier," she said.

"What would you do then?"

"I would take the train to the airport and back."

"If you take the train you would still have to get off at some point and take a bus."

"I am aware of that."

"It would not be any easier, would it?"

"I didn't say it would, but what choice do I have?"

"I will think of something and call you back." Twenty minutes later he did just that from his job. "I will call in sick tomorrow," he said. Carmelita did not respond so he asked, Carmelita, are you there?"

"Yes! Yes," she said and he repeated his earlier statement, "I will call in sick tomorrow so I can go with you to the airport."

"Isn't that risky?"

"I do not think so," said David. "Whenever I have exams I call in sick two days prior in order to review."

"Do you do that with every exam that is scheduled?"

"No. I do it only when I think I need the time."

"Doesn't that cause a problem with work scheduling for your employer?"

"To be honest, I have never thought of it. My education is my number one priority. The job is only a means to achieving that end."

"That is not a very nice approach to work, David."

"Listen, Carmelita, it is a menial job. I do what I think is necessary so that I wouldn't be stuck in this or a similar position for life."

"You cannot be stuck in positions like that for life. You are there only because you are a foreign student. You have a good educational background. You couldn't be in college without it, and if your circumstances were different, you and I know that you wouldn't be working there, at least not in your current position."

"That is my point exactly."

"I cannot keep up with you, David. You have lost me."

"Why? What I am saying is simple. My education is my priority. Very few other things are as important."

"What are the few other things you consider as important?"

"What I plan to do tomorrow."

"Do it your way, David. It has worked very well for you so far," Carmelita said in resignation.

"There you go! Thanks."

That conversation with David left her exhausted. She was becoming impatient and no closer to solving the problem she was facing. *How could she have gotten to Kennedy Airport to welcome her mother with a newly born infant in freezing cold weather, and with no money for a taxi?* What she didn't know was that David had the solution. He could have told her up front but he preferred to surprise her.

That Tuesday evening, February 27, 1968 David Cassel left work and went to a small department store on Fulton Street. There he purchased a stroller and a soft, light, woolen baby's blanket and headed home. The items were in their original cartoons and he hoped that neither Crystal nor any of her family members would be hanging out at the front when he arrived. He was lucky, perhaps only because it was a very cold day, there was no one in sight. He opened the front door gently, climbed the stairs to Carmelita's second floor efficiency and knocked at the door.

That could only be David, she thought as she approached the door and opened it. He smiled, handed her the packages and said, "These are for you. They are for Elvin really."

"Oh, my God! Thank you! Thank you, David."

"You are welcome," he said. By then Carmelita had put down the packages, reached out and hugged him tightly. She wanted to say something more than thank you but hesitated because there was nothing in David's demeanor to indicate that he felt the same way, or that he would respond favorably to what she so longed to express.

They stood motionless in each other's arms for more than a moment before they moved to the couch and sat down. "I will be forever grateful, David," she said.

"Please don't mention it again."

"I shall try but that will be difficult."

"Why?"

"No one has ever done anything as wonderful for me before."

"Oh really?"

"Really, you are truly an amazing man, David."

"Well, it's nice to know that someone thinks of me that way. Anyhow, I would like to go with you to the airport tomorrow."

"Is that the reason you said you were going to call in sick tomorrow?"

That is exactly why."

Carmelita rested her head on David's shoulder and tears began flowing from her eyes. She wasn't sobbing so he didn't realize that she was crying until he felt his shirt sleeve wet.

"Why are you crying?" he asked.

"I don't know, David. I am just a little overwhelmed."

"Why? Do you think I am smothering you?"

"No. You are such a kind, giving, loving person, I consider myself lucky to have met you."

"Well, thanks," said David. "Anyway, you didn't say whether or not I can go with you to the airport."

"Of course you can go with me. I want you to. I was just too shy to ask."

"What time shall we leave?"

"We want to be there for 8:35 a.m. but I have no idea how long it takes to get there by public transportation."

"I will inquire about that tonight."

"Whom will you ask?"

"Victor will know."

"Please don't ask Mr. Mendoza about that."

"Why shouldn't I?"

"I would prefer not to get him involved."

"He doesn't have to know why I am asking."

"He and his wife are very nosy. I am sure he would want to know more than he should."

"Okay. I will think of some other way to get the information."

"Thanks."

What David didn't tell Carmelita was that he planned to take a taxi to and from the airport. He reasoned that it would be too difficult even for both of them to manage the stroller with Elvin and handle her mother's luggage up and down the subway and bus stairs. *If she is coming to stay for a while she will have quite a bit of luggage*, he thought.

The next morning Carmelita didn't call David at 5:30. She didn't have to because he didn't ask her to and she knew that he wasn't going to work. He was up at six o'clock, showered, got dressed and fixed himself a light breakfast. By 7:15 he was ready to go. He called Carmelita. She too was ready.

"You can come down anytime you wish," she said.

"We are taking a taxi. It shouldn't take us more than thirty minutes to get there."

"David, I do not have money for cab fare."

"I do." Carmelita was silent. She didn't know what to say, so David said, "I am on my way down."

She was ready when he got to her door. He picked up the stroller with the infant in it and walked down the stairs cautiously. She locked the door and followed him. As soon as they walked out of the lobby and got to the curb, a Gypsy Cab stopped for them. "We want to go to Kennedy Airport," David said.

"Come on," said the cab driver.

"How much is it?" David asked.

"Ten."

"Is it ten dollars?" David asked to be certain.

"Yeah, man."

"Okay,"

The driver came out and opened the car trunk. At the same time Carmelita took the baby out of the stroller and David folded it and placed it in the trunk of the car. Then he joined Carmelita and the baby in the back seat.

They arrived at the airport with time to spare. Mrs. Jackman's flight had landed but she had not yet cleared customs and immigration.

"We shouldn't have to wait long. In the meantime, I will go and get a newspaper."

As soon as he returned and before he could sit down to read the paper, Carmelita spotted her mother. She was the fifth person to walk through the doorway accompanied by a porter who was carrying her luggage on a trolley. Carmelita stood up. She was tempted to race toward her mother but resisted because of the baby she had cradled in her arms.

"There she is," she told David as her mother approached the cordoned off, passenger only, restricted area in the airport's lobby. Carmelita shouted, "Mama, mama!" She immediately got her mother's attention as well as the attention of others in the vicinity.

"Mama, meet David, a very dear friend of mine," Carmelita said, and David and Mrs. Jackman shook hands in the gesture of becoming acquainted.

"How was your flight, Mama?"

"It was good."

"Were you nervous?" Carmelita asked knowing that it was the first time her mother had been on an aircraft.

"No," Mrs. Jackman replied.

She sensed that her mother was a bit uncomfortable in the new environment and perhaps reluctant to speak in David's presence, so she changed the direction of the conversation by asking, "Would you like to hold your grandson, Mama?"

"Sure," she said as she received the baby from her daughter. Then they walked out of the airport's lobby. David tipped the porter, and hailed a taxi to take them back to Herkimer Street in Brooklyn.

TEN

When they arrived at their Herkimer Street address, David stopped at Carmelita's briefly before going up to his room. Although she pleaded with him to stay a while longer he did not. He felt that Mrs. Jackman and her daughter needed that initial time together to catch up on all of the happenings, including what Carmelita was experiencing in New York City and what was occurring at home in Mayaro. He was determined also to take the opportunity to get in some greatly needed study time.

As he sat at the desk (table that is) in his room with the door open, his intention was to peruse his textbooks and glean from them information he needed. The purpose was not just to keep up with his studies but to move ahead with the assignments as outlined in the syllabi. Just when he became immersed in what was before him, he saw peripherally to his right that someone was standing at the door. He turned and there was Crystal Mendoza smiling at him.

"What are you doing?" she asked.

"I am trying to study."

"Will you ever stop studying?"

"I guess at some point in my life I will, but right now it is my sole purpose for being here."

"So, am I interrupting you?"

"Well..." David paused, hesitating to answer Crystal's question so she continued, "You can take a break, can't you?"

"I guess I can," he said as he placed a pen between the open pages. He then closed the book.

Crystal Mendoza entered the room and sat on the single bed. "Why are you home today?" she asked.

"I called in sick."

You really have no need to know that, David thought, but before he could say anything further, Crystal said, "You do not have to say why."

"Thanks, I did not intend to," said David in a detached sort of way. Then he asked, "Why are you really here, Mrs. Mendoza?"

"Call me Crystal. Why is it so difficult for you to call my name?"

"It's just the way I was brought up. You know that."

."Oh! My back is killing me." Crystal Mendoza said. She totally disregarded David's remark. Instead, she kicked off her slippers and pulled her petit frame onto his bed. David looked on in amazement. He was tempted to walk out of the room but decided against it. He didn't want to appear as being rude to his landlady again.

"Do you have another pillow?" asked Crystal. "This one is too low for me."

"That is the only pillow you gave me," said David. "I can give you a clean pillowcase if that will help."

"That is very funny, David. Oh! My back is hurting so badly," she cried out again.

"I have nothing here for pain except some aspirin."

"I cannot take aspirin. It irritates my stomach."

"Do you have anything at home that you can take for the pain?"

"No," Crystal said. She pulled up her sweater, rolled over onto her stomach and asked, "Can you rub my back right there?" She touched the spot that supposedly was hurting her. David felt uncomfortable about that but he asked, "Would you like me to use some Vicks?"

"No. Rub it just like that."

"Do you mean with my bare hands?"

"Yes, of course."

As he got up from where he sat at the desk and moved toward her, Crystal said, "You'd better close that door." Although reluctant to do so, he complied. He then massaged Crystal's lower back as she requested until she fell asleep or pretended to have fallen asleep, and he resumed his studies.

After about half an hour she got up, stretched, and said, "I must have fallen asleep."

"You must have," David said.

"Was I sleeping long?"

"You slept for half an hour at most."

"My back feels much better now. You have gifted hands, son."

What crap! He thought but he said nothing as Crystal stepped behind him and massaged his shoulders as if reciprocating for what he had done for her.

"I will see you later, sweetheart," she said. Then she walked out smiling.

"What a devious dame," he whispered to himself.

Downstairs, Mrs. Jackman told her daughter that while the flight was comfortable and the service was good, she was unable to sleep on the plane. Carmelita understood that. *There had to be some anxiety as there always is for most first time flyers*, she reasoned. She then opened the couch-bed and made it comfortable for her mother to take a nap. Lie down and get a little snooze, Mama," she said.

"Thank you."

"As you can see, the place is small but Elvin seldom cries so you should be able to sleep."

"Thanks again," Mrs. Jackman said as she lay in the bed silently thanking God for getting her to Brooklyn safely.

Carmelita took the opportunity to go through the newspaper David left there. She saw three help wanted ads that interested her but one of them in particularly, she found to be compelling. It read; *Daughter seeks companion for her eighty-seven year old mother who is in a nursing home. Call at any time.* Carmelita immediately dialed the listed number and an interview was arranged for 3:00 p.m. the next day. As if by impulse, she did not consider any of the other advertisements.

Crystal meanwhile, couldn't stop thinking of David. *There is a generation gap between us that although being real, could have been bridged had it not being for his cowardice and rigid upbringing in a culture of utter respect for one's elders,* she thought. *He has been here for three years already. That is enough time for him to realize that our age difference should be no barrier.*

She was irrational, forgetting for a moment that she already had a family, that she was still married, happily or not, and that David may have been interested in someone closer to his own age. She did not consider the fact that he had a promising future ahead of him and probably wanted to be in the company of those heading in the same direction. Instead, she sneered at the thought that David could have a friend, Mildred, who was indeed older than he was, yet he was resistant to every attempt she made at getting closer to him.

What Crystal Mendoza failed to consider was the fact that David's relationship with Mildred or even with Carmelita for that matter, could have been purely platonic. She ignored the fact also that her daughter, Dallas, shared the same birth month with David and was of the same age. Had he shown an interest in Dallas, how would she and/or her husband, Victor have reacted? No one could say. The answer to that question is still inchoate.

David had accomplished a great deal of studying that afternoon and by 3:00 p.m. he decided to stop. Although he had been absent from work, he had no intention of missing his evening classes. He packed up his books and left home earlier than usual with the intention of getting something to eat before going to class. Although Mrs. Mendoza was still leaving him dinner every evening during the week, he had not eaten her preparations since he had that experience with her putrid rice dish.

David was a focused young man, determined not to allow anything or anyone to get in the way of his progress toward attaining his goal. Some felt that his determination to persevere and subsequently achieve, even in the presence of so many distractions, bordered on obsession. Strangely enough, none of the skeptics were themselves in attendance at a college, university, or vocational school for that matter. For them, criticism was easy to engage in. To some extent that kind of bias; anti-education, anti-manners, and anti-progress among TK's peers were some of what prompted him to abandon Carmelita and their baby and leave the city.

He had not contacted them since he left and no one seemed to know with certainty where he went. Carmelita had come to terms with the possibility she may never see him again and that Elvin may never know his dad. For a while though, David, because of his caring and kindness had filled a void in their lives. Although he had given Carmelita no indication that he had any interest in her beyond the sort of friendship they developed, she felt closer to him than he probably realized. Very often the urge to tell him exactly what she was feeling seemed almost irresistible but she contained herself, fearing that what she wanted to say might change the dynamics of their relationship in a manner that might not have been for the better.

Mrs. Jackman was awake by then and resumed her conversations with her daughter. Much of it swirled around the affairs of Carmelita's childhood friend Jane Hacket. Jane's mother, Emelda Hacket and Tracy Jackman were close friends and supposedly related by descent although neither was ever ably to verify that. Nevertheless, they recognized the bloodline, imaginary or not, and their friendship endured.

Carmelita was eager for news from home and her mother did not disappoint her. It all started when she asked, "How is Aunt Emelda, Mama?" Emelda Hacket wasn't really her aunt. In Mayaro the salutation *Aunt* was often used as a form of respect for one's elders, but Carmelita continued to use it.

"She deh you know," Mrs. Jackmen said.

"How is Jane?"

"I eh see her since she had the baby but ah hear she is getting married."

"Did Aunt Emelda tell you that?"

"Yeah, guul (girl). She is so happy, although she said deh should've done that before the baby was born."

"Who is *the Mr. Right*?"

"Hedges," said Mrs. Jackman. "Everybody calls 'im Hedges. He is ah tall, lanky fella (man) from Mafeking. Me eh know 'e real name."

Carmelita's jaw dropped. "I know Hedges," she said. "His real name is Sylvester Pierce."

"Well, you young people go know them things deh."

Carmelita once dated Hedges but her mother was unaware of that. However, Jane knew. In fact, before Carmelita left Trinidad, she, Hedges, Jane, and Lucian Cove, Jane's then boyfriend spent a weekend together in Tobago.

"Is Hedges Jane's baby's father?" Carmelita asked.

"Me eh know, guul" said Mrs. Jackman. "Emelda said one of Patrick Cove's son is the father."

Without hesitation Carmelita came to the conclusion that it had to be Lucian. *Why isn't he getting married to her*? She wondered. Then it occurred to her that since she arrived in New York she had written to Jane twice but never received a reply. She also never heard from Sylvester to whom she wrote three times. *No wonder*, she thought. *They didn't have the courage to tell me about their romance*. That she found to be a convenient way perhaps to justify why she had gotten involved with Tyrone Khadevis so she told her mother, "I think now that you are here you will understand how lonely it has been for me."

"I knew you were lonely."

"The people I thought were my closest friends do not write to me, Mama."

"Me eh surprised noh."

"Mama, even after I wrote two or three letters they never responded."

"They have their reasons, child."

"Just what could their reasons be, Mama?"

"Many."

"Like what?"

"Jealousy, envy, or some sort of complex."

"What complex? Why would anyone be jealous or envious of me? As you can see, Mama, I am here struggling."

"They eh know that," said Mrs. Jackman. "They only know that you deh here in America, the land of plenty. They envy your position and some ah them think now that you are above them."

"What?" Carmelita asked and laughed at her mother's assessment of the situation. Then she said, "That is odd."

"It is not that strange really. Ah hear them old talk all the time. That is exactly how they feel, oui (yes)."

What Carmelita heard from her mother and the help and encouragement she received from David, strengthened her resolve to at least attempt what she came to the USA to do initially. *No one is going to stop me now*, she thought and told her mother, "I promise you, Mama that I shall make you proud."

"I have always been proud of you, child."

Elvin is the only child in here, Mama, Carmelita thought of saying in response to her mother's habit of calling an adult child, boy, or girl, a behavior that was common among most Trinidadians but she said instead, "I know that, Mama, and I intend to make you even more proud." Mrs. Jackman did not respond so she continued, "I plan to work and attend classes in the evening at the Municipal College of Arts and Sciences."

"How is that possible?"

"David promised to bring me an application for admission form on Monday. I plan to complete it and return it right away."

"Alright, so you return the application and you are accepted. What then?"

"I will attend."

"How is that possible? You have a young baby and you are breast-feeding him. That is like putting the cart before the horse. You should ah go to school before getting pregnant."

"Oh Mama, I was hoping you could stay a while." Carmelita did not acknowledge wrong doing or that anything was more difficult than when she first arrived in Brooklyn.

"Why?"

"So you can help me with Elvin,"

"Me didn't help you get 'im noh!" Said Mrs. Jackman. "In the first place, meh visa is for six months and meh husband expects me back by then. Secondly, I struggled to raise you and send you to secondary school by myself until I met Jeremiah, and I begged you not to make the same mistakes I did. Thirdly, I always said, Me eh raising grandchildren. Ah go help out where ah can but at the end of the day, the parents must take over."

Carmelita was silent for a while. She did not expect a rehash of the same things she heard from her mother over the years. She wanted to avoid saying anything that would have caused conflict between them, and was prepared to do whatever she felt was necessary to achieve that end. *If I have to beg and plead I will*, she thought. Then she suggested, "A month before your visa expires you can apply for an extension, Mama."

"You are still not getting it, are you?"

"What could it be that I am not getting, Mama?"

"You're forgetting that ah have ah husband in Trinidad."

"I have not forgotten. I don't think uncle J would mind."

Mr. Jeremiah Jackman was known throughout Mayaro as JJ. Since he and her mother were married, however, Carmelita always called him Uncle J out of respect.

"He eh the type who will complain but ah know what my responsibilities and obligations are."

"I understand that, Mama, but I am pleading with you to help me. I will explain my situation to Uncle J if necessary."

"There is no need for that. He already knows the situation you have gotten yourself into." Mrs. Jackman was switching her speech pattern from the Mayaro/Trinidad lilt and vernacular to Standard English as she saw fit.

"I acknowledge that I have made a terrible mistake, Mama, but I want to make amends. I feel awful asking for help but I have no other recourse. Please help me!"

"Let me write to Jeremiah and hear what he has to say about that."

"Thanks, Mama. With your help I will succeed irrespective of the obstacles in my path. Let's go to bed now, Mama. It is already ten o'clock."

ELEVEN

David did not call or attempted to visit Carmelita when he returned from classes on Wednesday night. The next morning, on his way to work, he noticed that Victor Mendoza was checking the mail boxes in the foyer although there was never any mail delivery on that block during the morning hours. *That's odd*, he thought. *It is Crystal who usually collects and distributes our mail.* He thought of her as Crystal although he was never comfortable calling her by her first name. Her given name never rolled off his tongue easily, and it was not because it was difficult to pronounce.

Victor Mendoza was also on his way to work so it was not strange that he decided to offer David a ride. After all, he didn't have to go out of his way to do that. In addition, Victor loved to talk and David was a keen listener who knew just what he should or shouldn't respond to. He was also good at lightening the tone of a conversation and leading it in the direction he preferred. The two were a perfect match. Although Victor was domineering, he couldn't overshadow David who was much more knowledgeable, but Victor never stopped trying.

"I heard that your family is very concerned about you," Victor said.

Where did you get that? David wondered. *I never mentioned it to anyone.* However, his response was, "What can I tell you, Mr. Mendoza? My family is like that, always caring and considerate."

"It is my understanding that they do not like the kind of work you are doing here."

"What's there not to like?" David asked disdainfully.

"They think that you are working too hard considering that you attended the best high school in T & T and held respectable positions there, first as a young school teacher, then as a highly ranked civil servant with the Ministry of Health."

"That confirms my suspicion."

"What suspicion?" Victor asked.

You have been reading my letters. You son of a bitch, David thought but he said, "Never mind!"

"Anyhow, I can speak with Father Sullivan on Sunday in an effort to hook you up."

"What can you hook me up with?"

"You can get a teaching position, or at least get in as a teaching assistant with the Catholic Board until you receive your degree."

"No thank you, sir. I cannot afford to work for such a measly salary when I have tuition to pay."

"How do you know what the salary is?"

"Trust me, I know, and I want no part of it, thank you," David said as Victor Mendoza pulled up to the curb to drop him off at his workplace on Fulton Street.

"Enjoy your day," Victor said before he drove off.

"Thanks."

David was upset but he tried to compose himself before walking into the building where he worked to punch in his time card. He and the other young men who boarded and lodged at the Mendoza's had long suspected them of tampering with their mail. The conversation David had with Victor only confirmed that suspicion. What puzzled him though was their motive. "Why do they read our letters? What is there to be gained from it?" He asked himself quietly but got no answers.

For a brief moment he entertained the thought of letting Crystal have her way with him if in return he could get to the root of why they tampered with other people's mail, knowing quite well that it was a Federal offence to do so. He quickly dismissed the thought that he could succumb to whatever Crystal Mendoza had planned. He respected the Mendoza's and he was grateful that they took him in as a boarder, yet he felt that he wasn't a freeloader so there was no reason for him to be subservient and succumb to their every whim.

Superficially one might think that a scrounger would have been the perfect guy for the cougar-type Crystal Mendoza who always seemed to be seeking some sort of instant gratification. More likely than not a chap like that would have been spineless and easily influenced, an easy bait so to speak. Such individuals who depend on other peoples efforts for their basic needs are generally unable or unwilling to object to anything. On the contrary, what was known about Crystal Mendoza suggests that she would have shown no interest in someone like that.

On the surface her interest in David appeared to be purely physical, but on careful scrutiny, one could see that she also admired him for his academic brilliance, his determination and drive, his kindheartedness, and his gentle but persuasive manner. She would have settled for nothing less. "I only want what I want, not what anyone else wants me to have" she once said in conversation with him.

As the day wore on and David became focused and more involved in his work, he thought less and less about Victor and Crystal Mendoza and more about Carmelita. Foremost in his mind was her expressed desire to register and attend college, which was the reason she came to the United States in the first place. He couldn't help but wonder about other capable young women he knew whose ambitious academic plans had been derailed under similar circumstances. He was aware of many of African descent who were pursued and cajoled, had fallen in love, gotten pregnant, then were abandoned because they didn't have a job or a substantial amount of money in their bank account.

Before leaving work at *Eastern Time*, a watch manufacturing firm on Fulton Street, David dialed the *Caribbean Cuisine* restaurant and ordered food for his dinner. He intended to pick it up on his way home from class. He thought of Carmelita but did not place an order for her. The classroom experience was uneventful that evening but when he arrived at the boarding house Carmelita was still awake. He could hear the sound of her television and laughter emanating from her room as he walked up the stairs. Further up on the third floor he noticed that all the lights were on in the Mendoza's apartment and wondered whether they too were awake. *No doubt Dallas is still at school or probable on her way home right about now*, he thought.

He went to his room, put down his dinner and his books and returned downstairs to the third floor. He entered the Mendoza's kitchen as he had done so many times before to get his dinner. Crystal had not stopped preparing dinner for him or for the other boarders, and he continued to pay her for it in spite of the experience he had with her fetid rice dish a week or so earlier, and the fact that he had not eaten any of the dinners she had prepared since. What happened next, although not unimaginable, was shocking. David turned around to leave. Only then did Crystal and Cedric Sebastian, another of the international students who boarded there acknowledged his presence.

They seemed surprised. With arms tightly wrapped around each other, they remained motionless, almost catatonic for several seconds before their embrace slackened. "It is not what you are thinking, David." Crystal said.

Of course not, it's just my eyes playing tricks on me, he thought but said nothing. He calmly walked out of the kitchen and up the stairs to his room. As he lay across his bed he wondered, first about the scandal that could have erupted from what he witnessed. He wondered about the repercussions, not so much for Crystal but for Cedric. "Could there be a domino effect? How would it affect me?" He questioned himself softly but got no answers. Suddenly he was afraid but couldn't understand why he was fearful. He thought of the Mendoza's mail tampering and convinced himself that Crystal was the culprit and that Victor's knowledge of what was written in those letters from home was limited to what Crystal told him.

Just when he decided to get up and get himself ready for bed, his telephone rang. He hesitated at first but then he answered hoping it would have been Carmelita but it was Crystal. "David, I need to speak with you," she said.

"I am listening."

"I need to speak with you in person."

"I am already in my PJ's," he said. He lied. "Whatever you want to talk about can certainly wait until tomorrow."

"No, David."

"Sorry, I am not coming back down there at this time."

"You will come now or else."

"Or else what, you are going to whop me?"

"You will soon find out?"

"Whatever!"

They were both adamant and stuck to their positions but they were both fearful. For the first time since her parents' objected to her getting married to Victor, Crystal Mendoza thought that her behavior could ruin her marriage. Whether her actions were entirely new or whether they were old habits, once dormant that became active again, only she knew. They were strange and scary nonetheless. David's concern was about his abode. *The worse she could do is ask me to leave*, he thought. *That might set me back a bit but I will survive.*

Immediately, he picked up his telephone and called Mildred. When she answered he said, "I am sorry to bother you this late."

"It's no bother at all, David."

"I have a predicament and may need your help."

"David, if you *may* need my help, then you do not have a predicament."

"Well, not yet but I am anticipating one. I had a tiff with my landlady earlier and my suspicion is that she might ask me to leave."

"That would be sort of drastic on her part. What did you do?"

"It is what I didn't do that is causing the problem."

"I guess you don't want to talk about it."

"It is a long story but I will tell you eventually."

"In the meantime don't worry about it. If she forces you out you can stay with me. I have an extra bedroom."

"Thanks, Mildred. You are the best."

"You are welcome anytime. I think you know that. Have a good night," Mildred said while smiling to herself.

"Good night," David said. He was elated but not for the same reason as Mildred. He thought of calling Carmelita but then decided against it, tidied himself and went to bed. He was unable to sleep though. He tossed and turned, thought of getting up to study, but he couldn't stay focused enough to do that.

It wasn't until about 3:00 a.m. that he fell asleep and he slept soundly until eight o'clock, a time when he should have been on his way to work. He felt sick. He got up but was forced to lie down again. Eventually he called his boss to inform her that he wasn't feeling well and probably wouldn't make it in to work that day. She was understanding and suggested that he take care of himself. As soon as he hung up the telephone, there was a knock at the door. He opened it and there was Crystal Mendoza smiling at him.

"I am sorry to hear that you are not feeling well," she said.

"I never told you that."

"You didn't have to. I heard you on the telephone."

"Why were you eavesdropping on my conversation?"

"I wasn't eavesdropping. I came to the door and you were on the phone so I waited."

"Okay, so why are you here?"

"Hey! David why do you always forget? I own this place."

"Yeah, yeah, I remember. We who live here have no rights."

"Why are you making it so hard on yourself?" asked Crystal. "If you just....." She paused and without completing her train of thought she moved closer to him and rested her left hand on his right shoulder. He turned his head, looked at her hand, and noticed that she wasn't wearing her wedding ring but he did not comment.

"I took it off so I could knead some flour into dough," she said when she realized how observant he was.

"I never questioned why you are not wearing your wedding ring."

"I saw that look in your eyes."

"It really doesn't matter to me whether or not you wear the ring. That is your prerogative."

"We shouldn't be quarrelling, David. I know that you are upset about what you saw last night."

"I didn't see anything, nothing at all."

Crystal laughed and said, "If one word of that gets out I am coming after you."

"If anybody could or would brag about it, it isn't me."

"Shit!" Crystal exclaimed. Suddenly she was thinking of how loquacious and boastful Cedric was.

"You should have thought of that before," David said as if he read her thoughts.

"What should I have thought of before?"

"Never mind what I said."

"What do you mean? I should just forget about it?"

"Yes."

"It is not that easy, David."

"It is not that difficult either."

"Then let's get it on." Crystal said as she held him close.

"I don't think that we are talking about the same thing, Mrs. Mendoza."

"Crystal!" she said. Then she asked, "Why is it so difficult for you to call my name?"

"I just find it to be disrespectful for me to do that."

"What? Call me by my first name or…?"

"Both," David said although Crystal never completed her statement. He had an uncanny way of knowing what she intended to say. Sometimes that amused her but at other times she was quite offended by it. On that occasion she was laughing hysterically. Her laughter emanated through the hallway and into adjourning rooms. Carmelita heard it on the second floor and wondered what was going on upstairs but she resisted the urge to investigate.

When Crystal composed herself she said, "David, this is America. People call others by their first names. It's no big deal."

"I am not accustomed to that. Where I grew up it is disrespectful to call your elders by their first name.

"No! You didn't just say that."

"You heard what I said."

"It is not what I heard that concerns me it is what is implied in the statement that gives me the willies."

"I didn't think that there was anything subtle about it. In fact, I thought I was quite explicit."

"So what you really meant was that I am too old for you?"

"I never said that."

"You didn't have to." David was confused and temporarily speechless so Crystal continued, "Everyone around here thinks that you are such a nice young man, but they have never been subjected to the venom that you exude so calmly." She seemed angry about the manner in which David spoke to her.

"Crystal, you are nuts, you know that?"

"You see! That is exactly what I mean. Wait a minute! Did you just call me Crystal?" She suddenly realized that he had called her by her first name so she smiled again. Seconds later she moved closer and hugged him. "You can come along or you can run along," she whispered in his ears, kissed him and left the room suddenly.

As she walked down the stairs, she pulled from her bosom a note she intended to give to David. She tore it up. She had written a made up story about the family's intention to sell the building and that she expected him to vacate the premises within seven days. She was going to give him the notice without her husband's knowledge and with total disregard for the law or for David's rights as a tenant. What she didn't know was that he was on to her. He anticipated her action and took some preemptive measures.

Before she reached her apartment door, he started packing the suitcase he used to travel to the USA a little more than three years earlier. The piece of luggage that once held all of his belongings was by then too small for all the things he had acquired. He placed some of his garments into a black plastic garbage bag and packed his books into two cardboard boxes before having breakfast. He was then ready for any eventuality, or so he thought. *I could cooperate with Crystal and continue to live here or I can defy her and be evicted. What's the worst that could happen*? He wondered.

TWELVE

It was mid-day on Friday and Carmelita did not hear from David. She became concerned but was reluctant to ask anyone about him. As the day wore on her concerns heightened so she called his place of employment. She was told that he was out sick. That made her extremely anxious. She dialed his home phone number and he answered feebly. "My, God! What is the matter with you?" she asked.

"Oh, It's you, Carmelita."

"Whom were you expecting?

"I wasn't expecting anyone but I thought someone from work might be trying to reach me."

"Why would they try to reach you when you called in sick this morning?"

"Welcome to the real world, my dear. It is all about trust, or rather mistrust."

"Would they actually call to check on you?"

"They have done just that in the past."

"Wow!"

"Yeah, that sums it up."

"Anyhow, I am glad to know that you are feeling better."

"Thanks, I was under the weather for a while but it was nothing physical."

"Then what was it?"

"All in my head I guess."

Carmelita didn't follow up on what David said. Instead she asked, "Are you going anywhere right now?"

"No."

"Then I will be right up."

"Okay," said David in a state of shock. "Are you sure?" he asked.

"Of course, I am sure."

Carmelita had never visited him before so the fact that she said she would be right up took him by surprise. He hurried out of bed and rushed to tidy his room. Then he darted into the bathroom, brushed his teeth and washed his face. He didn't think that he had time enough to shower. He was right. As soon as he re-entered his room there was a knock at the door.

"It's open. Come in," he said.

Carmelita was slow to enter so David thought, *My God, I hope it is not Crystal, but she never knocks.* He reasoned. *She always walks right in on the premise that she owns...* His thought was interrupted when Carmelita walked in.

"You look rather fit to me," she said.

"Looks can be deceiving."

"I know. Although sometimes it is all we have to go by."

"That's only if we are in an awful hurry."

"You may have a valid point there, David."

He pulled the chair from the desk and offered her a seat. She handed him a package she was clutching and then she sat down.

"What is it?"

"It is Elvin's Christening outfit for tomorrow. Open it."

He opened the package and was in awe. Carmelita sensed his pleasure and indulged him further by saying, "Mama bought it this morning at a little store on Broadway. She loved it so much that we never looked at anything else."

"They do have some really nice stuff over there."

"Isn't it cute?"

"Yeah, the boy is getting baptized in style."

"Thank you, David. Thanks for everything."

"You are welcome. I really wish I could have done more."

"You have done so much already. I don't know how we would have made it this far without you."

"Girl, you are a Trini. We are a resilient people. I am sure you would have survived just fine."

"I have heard it said that we can survive anything. Nevertheless, I sometimes feel so vulnerable."

"Well, I wouldn't go that far. Let's just say that we are strong, determined, and will persevere with discipline and tolerance until we achieve our ultimate goal."

"I couldn't say it better, David, you are truly an inspiration."

Just then his telephone rang. He answered. It was Mildred on the line. "I take it that you are feeling better," she said.

"I am," said David. "How did you know that I was at home?"

"I called your job and was told that you were out sick."

"Yeah, this morning I woke up feeling miserable. What was so strange though, there wasn't anything of a physical nature that I could point to as being wrong."

"You are probably worrying about the situation with your landlady."

"I don't think so."

"You may not be conscious of it but it's taking a toll on you."

"I would hope not."

Carmelita listened to David's part of the exchange with Mildred and felt she had enough. She got up, gently pushed the chair in and indicated to him that she was leaving. He held her hand and mouthed, "Please don't."

She in turn whispered, "I can't read lips." But other than that she did not object and quietly sat on the bed.

"My offer still stands," Mildred said.

"I am likely to take you up on it. I will keep you posted."

"Please do."

"Okay, bye."

"Bye, David." Mildred was smiling again."

"Was that your girlfriend?" Carmelita asked.

"No. That was a friend of mine, a classmate from…" David started to explain but his telephone rang again.

"I called you earlier with the intention of reminding you about the dance tomorrow night but before our conversation ended I forgot."

"That happens."

"That's the sort of effect you have on me."

"Do I really?"

"Yes! Anyway, I take it that you haven't changed your mind."

"No," David said. He was being terse with the hope that Mildred will end the conversation and get off the telephone. She did.

As soon as he hung up the phone, Carmelita said to him, "I have to leave now, David."

"Why?"

"Mama wants me to go shopping with her."

"I thought you already did all of your shopping," he said as he pointed to the package with Elvin's outfit for his christening.

"That we have completed," said Carmelita. "Now we are going to do some grocery shopping, but only after my appointment for that interview."

Why couldn't you do them all at once? David wondered but said, "Okay."

"If you are free I will visit with you when we get back."

"Why wouldn't I be free?"

"I don't know, David."

"Okay."

"Are you agreeing with me or are you surprised that I don't know?"

"Both I think. Anyhow, what will you do with Elvin while you are gone?"

"We are taking him with us."

"Didn't you say that you were reluctant to take him out in this cold weather?"

"Well, today is not such a bad day and in any case, he has to be out tomorrow."

"Okay." David wanted to suggest that Carmelita leave the baby with him while she went out shopping but he quickly decided against that.

"Then I will see you when I get back."

"If I am free," he said sarcastically. Carmelita smiled, said good bye and left.

He closed the door when she left, something he seldom did. However, he did not lock it. As he lay in bed looking up at the blank, white ceiling in the solitude of his lonely, little room, he couldn't stop thinking of her, and even felt somewhat pleased at the veiled jealousy she expressed when she asked, in reference to his conversation with Mildred, *Was that your girlfriend*? Obviously, neither was in a hurry to reveal to the other how they truly felt. Carmelita had been hurt before and as a result was extremely cautious. While David had never experienced anything nearly as distressing, the lyrics of the song, *Take Time to Know Her*, kept echoing in his ears.

He was dozing off when the door hinges creaked. He jumped and looked toward the door. Crystal was already inside. She closed the door behind her and sat at the edge of the bed. David moved over either to make her more comfortable or to get further away from her.

"Thank you," she said. She then patted his cheek and asked, "Are you just going to laze around all day?"

"That is the reason I called in sick today. I am feeling so lethargic."

"What have you been doing that zaps your energy and leaves you sluggish?"

"Nothing, other than eight hours of work per day and I am registered for sixteen credits. That does take its toll on ones physical and mental state after a while."

"You do not have to work so hard. You know that, don't you?"

"No! I do not know that."

"Dallas doesn't work so hard. In fact, she doesn't work at all."

"Dallas is your daughter!" David said. *You collect money from us every week in exchange for your putrid leftover food which we are never able to eat. You can afford to have your grown daughter sponge off you*, he thought

"That is true. We do help her with living expenses and her tuition is free," said Crystal. "You can also get help."

"From whom can I expect help?"

"You would be amazed if you only....."

"If I only what, sell my soul to the devil?"

"No. I can help you."

"Yeah, right!" said David as he thought, *Beelzebub's wife herself.*

"Don't be like that, David."

"Don't be like what?"

"You are so resistant." She traced his eyebrows gently then his lips with her finger tips. He held her hand at the wrist as if to indicate that's enough, stop! But at the same time he asked, "What am I resistant to, your efforts to get me killed?"

"Who would want to harm you?" asked Mrs. Mendoza. "You haven't hurt anyone." At the same time she pulled her feet onto the single bed and shared the pillow with him. He looked at her then looked at the door. "Are you nervous?" she asked.

"I have been all day. I called in sick so I that can rest and relax."

"There is nothing more relaxing than..." Crystal wasn't finished speaking when the telephone rang. *Who the hell is that at this time*? She wondered as David answered the call. It was Carmelita. She wanted to know whether he would like her to bring him dinner since she and her mother were at the restaurant and about to purchase dinner themselves. "Thanks, Carmelita, but that wouldn't be necessary. As you perhaps know, Mrs. Mendoza fixes dinner for us from Monday to Friday."

As Crystal lay smiling in his bed, David made a conscious decision to engage Carmelita in conversation; small talk, just to keep her on the line and divert attention away from Crystal

Mendoza who seemed to be craving it. He remembered an earlier incident when Crystal became impatient and left his room because she found that he was spending too much time on the telephone and consequently, paying less attention to her. He was hoping for the same kismet, and bingo! It happened. She got up and walked out without saying a word.

THIRTEEN

Mildred had a fetish for collecting men's ties and she kept a couple hundred of them in the smaller bedroom of her apartment, the room she told David he could occupy if the need ever arose. She purchased most of the ties whenever and wherever there was a sale. Was it her intention to resell them or was it just a hobby? No one knew for certain. It was strange to say the least. Nevertheless, she decided to clear the room of everything she stored there and clean it up in the event David was forced to move in with her. She moved everything; the ties, shoes, some of her clothing and pocketbooks to an empty closet in the room she occupied.

After removing her personal effects and the ties from the room, she stripped the bed of its linens and took them to a Laundromat at the corner of St. John's Place and Utica Avenue where she left them to be cleaned. She then walked over to a small discount store on Utica Avenue and purchased a wooden clothes rack to hang the many neck ties she treasured so dearly. After that she returned home, set up the clothes rack in her room and arrange the ties on it according to their width and color. That was not as easy as it sounds but she did the best she could have. When she was finished, she returned to the smaller room, dusted it, mopped the floor, and replaced the bed linen with a fresh, clean set.

She stood at the door and looked into the room proudly. It was neatly furnished. In addition to a double bed, there was an armoire with a full length mirror, a dresser, two night tables, a small desk and a chair. *He should be very comfortable here*, she thought as she reached for the telephone on the wall at the door of the kitchen adjacent to the room she had just prepared for David. She dialed his number. When he answered she said, "Your room is ready, David." There was no immediate response so she asked, "David, are you there?"

"Yes. I am sorry. You surprised me for a minute there."

"Well, it is better that you are surprised than shocked. Anyway, like I said, the room is ready. If your devilish landlady decides to throw you out you can move right in and not be homeless."

"Thanks, Mildred."

"You are welcome."

"I will always be grateful."

"Listen, we are friends. I am confident you would do the same for me if I ever had such a need."

"I would not hesitate at all."

"That is what friendship is all about."

"It is not often that I meet someone with whom I am so comfortable, Mildred."

"I feel the same way too." Mildred said. She was smiling again. Then she abruptly changed the discussion when she asked, "Did I tell you that my thesis was well received and I got an *A*?"

"No, but I would have been surprised to hear anything different."

"My professor was truly impressed."

"You write very well so I am not surprised. My question, however, is why do they call it a thesis? Isn't it a term paper at this level?"

"Technically, they are the same things. One term is a synonym for the other. However, term paper is used traditionally and more prevalently at the undergraduate level while thesis or treatise is often reserved for the final graduate paper."

"I have asked those questions a dozen times before but this is the first time that anyone has given me a thorough and thoughtful answer."

"I will always do the best I can for you, David."

"Thanks, Mildred."

"About tomorrow, what time shall we meet?"

"You tell me."

"Well, the event starts at ten. We want to be there early enough to get a good table, yet not too early to the point that we do not know what to do with ourselves."

"Why would we need to be at a table in a dance hall?"

"I take it that this is the first dance you are attending since you have been here."

"It is. I never really had the time before."

"Oh David, that is such a nice compliment. You have actually found the time to take me to a dance."

Oh, oh! David thought but he responded by saying, "I probably wouldn't do it for anyone else." He quickly realized that he was putting his foot further and further into his mouth when the normally loquacious Mildred remained silent for ten or more seconds.

"I don't know what to say, David."

"Just say where we should meet and at what time."

"Well, you already have your ticket so we can meet at the dance hall, or you can meet me here and we can take a taxi over there."

"Okay! I will meet you at home."

"You do have my address, don't you?"

"Yes."

"Do you know how to get here?"

"Of course, I do."

"Okay then. What time should I expect you?"

"I should be there around 9:30 p.m."

"Good! See you then. Bye." Mildred smiled again, a very gratifying sort of smile of which David was unaware.

"Bye, Mildred," he said.

Shortly thereafter Carmelita returned home. She had gone to her job interview earlier, and did her grocery shopping with her mother before she called David. That evening she bought dinner for him, her mother, and herself, and wanted him to join them downstairs, except that the table in her one room efficiency could only seat two. She thought it might have been possible for her to have dinner with him in his room but remembered that his small table could only seat one. He had only one chair. That in itself was not a problem. She also did not want to leave her mother at home alone that evening. Ultimately, she decided on a quick visit to David's so she could deliver his food before it got cold.

He was still lazing around as he had done all day. He anticipated picking up his dinner from the Mendoza's kitchen later that evening as he had been doing recently, but with no intention of eating whatever Crystal Mendoza had prepared. Beyond that he had no specific plans. In a strange sort of way, he was enjoying the solitude but became anxious when Carmelita knocked at his door. *My God! When will she stop being so intrusive*? He wondered about Crystal Mendoza but was pleasantly surprised when he opened the door and saw Carmelita standing there. "Come in," he said smiling.

"I brought you dinner."

"Thanks. You know that you didn't have to do this."

"I know that but couldn't you just stop after saying, thanks?"

"I should have. I am sorry."

"Sorry really doesn't cut it....." Carmelita started to complain but she stopped when David held her close. They hugged each other for quite a while before one of them eased the embrace. It was David. Had it been up to Carmelita, she would have fallen asleep in his arms. He offered her a seat and she accepted but said, "I can't stay long. Mama wouldn't eat without me there."

"I understand."

"She also needs my help in preparing a few things for tomorrow."

"There is no need to explain, my dear. I am sure we will have lots of time to spend together."

Carmelita was rather pleased. Not only did David understand her predicament, he gave the first indication that he had an interest in spending a great deal of time with her beyond being sympathetic to her situation and immediate needs. Although she wondered as to how that could be possible if they both intended to continue their education while working to support themselves, and in her case, her son too. *Perseverance is the key she decided*, and said nothing further that could limit the joy she felt at that moment.

"I know you have to leave but tell me something before you go."

I do love you, Carmelita thought of saying but she asked, "What?"

"What time does the reception end tomorrow?"

"There is no reception per se. The baptism is at 11:00 a.m. You know that, don't you?"

"Yes."

"When we get back from the church we will have lunch. There will be conversations but I do not expect anything lengthy. Mama made a black cake (a type of fruit cake) and a sponge cake (a pound cake). We also have some liquor from T & T, and I bought a bottle of wine."

"That sounds as if you are having a party and a lot of guests."

"No. I expect four people, so altogether there would be seven of us, eight if we count Elvin."

"Would the Mendoza's be there?"

"No. I invited them but Mrs. Mendoza said that they had some prior engagement."

"That's a lot of bull!"

"I thought so but I couldn't verify it. In any case, I couldn't accommodate them and the other four people so that worked out fine."

"Good! However, I still have no indication of when it would be over."

"I don't really know. I can only surmise that by four or five o'clock everyone would be gone. However, if you have something to do you can leave at any time after the baptism."

"Well, I am going to a party, a dance really, but I wouldn't leave here before 9:00 p.m."

"Then we will have some time together before you leave."

"That's possible."

"Good! Call me before you go to bed tonight."

"I will."

"Okay then, bye."

"Bye," David said as Carmelita walked out.

Shortly after she left, he went to get whatever Crystal Mendoza had prepared for dinner that evening. He entered the kitchen timorously. He was thinking of what he witnessed with Crystal and Cedric Sebastian the previous night and feared that he might once again have to pretend that he was deaf, mute, and blind. To his relief and surprise, Dallas was sitting at the kitchen table, not Crystal and, or Cedric.

"I was hoping that you would come down early tonight," she said.

"Why?"

"I hardly ever see you."

What now? He wondered but said, "You know how it is for me with work and school."

"That is why I waited up for you."

"Oh!"

"You know that I generally go to bed early."

"Yes. I have heard it said."

"Anyway, I wanted to be the first to congratulate you."

"Congratulate me, what for?"

"I heard that you have completed all requirements for graduation from MCAS"

"Do you have some inside scoop? I haven't been informed of that yet."

"That is not all," said Dallas. "I also heard that you have been accepted to one of the best universities in the nation to continue your studies toward a Master of Science degree. Congratulations!" Dallas made certain that she said everything she waited up to say to David but she never did answer his question about whether she had an inside scoop.

"Thank you," he said.

"Is that it?"

"What else did you expect?"

"I thought you would be really excited at the good news. That is why I wanted to be the bearer."

Do you really think that I should be excited that your mother continues to open my mail and pry into my affairs? David wondered but he said, "It is not as if someone handed me anything. I worked hard to achieve it."

"Even so, David, thousands of people work just as hard and fail. You should be thankful."

"I am thankful, to God that is. Failure was not an option for me, Dallas."

"Gee! What an attitude?"

"That's my attitude! What else can I tell you?"

"Okay, David. Have a good night. I will see you in the morning."

"Good night, Dallas."

David took the covered dish that had his name on it and left Dallas sitting at the kitchen table seemingly in disbelief. She was unaware of her mother's habit of opening the students' mail and assumed that David had informed her parents of his successes. After all, he was a good student and had followed the curriculum to the letter so he had some idea that he had completed the requirements for graduation in his chosen field, but while the notice of qualification was sent out some two weeks prior, he had not received it. At the time Dallas was speaking with him he had not yet received his admission letter to the Ivy League College either.

As soon as He reached his room on the fourth floor, his telephone rang and he answered. It was Carmelita. *I was supposed to be the one calling to say good night*, he thought. Carmelita was so excited that she could hardly breathe. "I got it, David. I got it."

"What did you get, dear?"

"I got the job, David. Mrs. Greenberg just called to offer me the position and I accepted it."

"That's a bit of good news. When do you start?"

"She wants me to meet with her and the staff next Tuesday."

"What staff are you talking about?"

"The staff at the nursing home where her mother is a resident."

"Are you prepared for that?"

"Yes, I am. Thank you, Jesus!"

"It is me, David you are speaking with, not Jesus."

"You are always so funny. That's one of the many reasons I love you, David,"

"Oh! What are some of the other reasons?" David asked as if he was surprised to hear what Carmelita said.

"With time you will know them all."

"Do we have that much time?"

"I am not going anywhere. Are you?"

"No."

"Neither of us is planning on going anyplace but who knows what the future holds?"

"We can only hope for the best and that time is on our side."

"Time and the good Lord I hope, David,"

"You have a great night," David said.

"You do also, sweetheart."

As soon as he got off the telephone with Carmelita, he called The Auto Rental Place on Broadway and reserved a car for Saturday, March 2nd and Sunday, March 3rd respectively. It was comparatively less to rent a vehicle for two days than to rent one for one day in 1968.

FOURTEEN

David woke up early and was the first to arrive at the barber shop on Broadway that Saturday morning. He did not want to be waiting indefinitely to get a haircut and consequently, be late for Elvin's christening. By 9:30 he left there looking well groomed. He walked over to the dry cleaners where he had taken his only suit to be cleaned a week earlier. It was the same dry cleaning plant owned and operated by Victor Mendoza. Strangely though, Victor had not yet arrived there. Beverly Camacho, the sole employee, opened the laundry that morning. She was glad to see David and quickly located his clothing. He paid her and they had a brief conversation before he left.

By 9:40 he was at *The Auto Rental Place*. The car he reserved, a brand new 1968 Chevy II Nova sedan was ready. He paid for the two days in cash and was given the keys, auto registration, and insurance documents. He questioned as to whether the vehicle was fully insured and was assured that it was. He then scrutinized the documents before driving off to Herkimer Street where he parked in front of the Mendoza's apartment building and rushed in to get ready for the christening. By 10:15 a.m. he had showered and gotten dressed, and although he always had reservations about showering and going out in cold weather shortly afterward, on that occasion, it didn't seem to matter.

He called Carmelita to say that he was ready. "We are too. I will call a taxi," she said.

"That wouldn't be necessary. Your ride is waiting."

"What do you mean?"

"I meant exactly what I said, so stay put. I will be right down."

Carmelita did not question David any further. She and her mother were already dressed, and so was the baby, so they simply waited. Within five minutes there was a knock at the door. She opened it without hesitation. David was standing there smiling.

"You are looking quite spiffy, Mr. Handsome," she said.

"Thank you. You look exceptionally well yourself," said David. "Are you ready?"

"We are."

"Then let's go."

When they got downstairs he opened the rear right door of the shiny new Chevrolet Nova and helped Mrs. Jackman into the car. When she was seated comfortably, Carmelita handed her the baby and attempted to join her in the back seat but decided against that and sat up front with David. She seemed very happy that morning. It certainly was the happiest David had ever seen her and he was very pleased. They arrived at the Saint Stephen's Roman Catholic Church on Bushwick Avenue at exactly 10:50 a.m. There wasn't a mass that morning but several people were in the church. Apparently there were three christenings earlier. What surprised David and Carmelita though, was that Victor Mendoza was among the parishioners seated in the front pew. *No wonder he wasn't at the dry cleaning plant this morning,* David thought. *Why is he here on a Saturday*? He wondered, but quickly dismissed it when Father Sullivan and two acolytes entered the church.

The cleric spoke briefly with the baby's mother and godparents. Then after a reading of scriptures from Mathew and Mark, he emphasized that the sacrament of baptism was the outward sign that signified spiritual grace. At that point, he implored everyone witnessing the baptism to accept an active role in ensuring that young Elvin Orr does not depart from the teachings of the church and the rites in which God is continuously and uniquely active. He then reminded the godparents of their responsibilities should the child's mother, for any reason, becomes incapable of carrying out hers. Through it all little Elvin remained peaceful. Not once did he cry out as so many babies do when they are anointed with oil or water that has been consecrated.

After the ceremony, Victor Mendoza met them outside of the church. He congratulated Carmelita. She was very pleased and thanked him sincerely. David, however, was skeptical. *Didn't Crystal say that they had some prior engagements and could not be at the baptism*? He wondered. *So why is he here*? *There is no mass today, so he has no responsibilities as the deacon*. The thought that Victor Mendoza's sole purpose for being in church that Saturday morning was to monitor their activities was becoming a serious annoyance to David. He excused himself and left under the guise that he had to bring the car around to the front of the church. When he returned, however, Victor was still speaking with Carmelita and Mrs. Jackman.

"That was quick," Victor said.

"I went to the parking lot, not out to California," David replied.

Victor did not respond to the comment so Carmelita asked, "Would you join us for lunch, Mr. Mendoza." It was her way of trying to deter what seemed like an impending fury. David was becoming quite impatient and angry at Mr. Mendoza who seemed oblivious to it as he went on to explain to Carmelita that although he would have liked to join them, he couldn't because he had to get back to the dry cleaning store.

"Beverly is there alone," he said.

"Beverly?" Carmelita questioned, but before Mr. Mendoza could respond she remembered who Beverly was and said, "Oh! Beverly Camacho."

"Yes, she is so dependable," said Victor. "I don't know what I would do without her."

Get one of your lazy ass, grown children in there, David thought but he said nothing, and Victor left. Carmelita looked at David but refrained from making any comment in her mother's presence.

"Shall we go?" he asked.

"Yes," said Mrs. Jackman. "We must heat up the lunch before the guests arrive." No further comment was made and they seated themselves in the car the same way they arrived, except that Carmelita held the baby with her in the front seat as they left the church yard.

"It was just wonderful," Mrs. Jackman said from the back seat.

"I am so happy! Thanks to both of you," Carmelita said as she looked at David then looked back at her mother.

"You are welcome," they both said in unison. Everyone in the vehicle except Elvin, laughed at the coincidence. In fact, the laughter startled him and he woke up crying but that was not for long.

By the time they arrived at their Herkimer Street home the baby was sleeping again. Carmelita took his warm little jumper off and lay him down in his bassinet. He was still asleep. David left to change his clothes but promised that he would return within an hour. As he walked past the Mendoza's apartment he smelled tobacco smoke coming from the kitchen. *That has to be Crystal's doing*, he thought. *She is the only who smokes in this building and she only does it when there is no one at her home.* Carmelita and her mother meanwhile, wasted no time in getting the food heated up and ready for the arrival of their guests. Then they too changed into clothes that were more casual and comfortable.

David thought of the seating arrangement at Carmelita's and decided that he would take the small table and the chair from his room to hers. First, he took the table down. Immediately it became obvious that they were identical. Carmelita placed them together side by side and covered them with a white tablecloth. "That's great," said David. "Now I will bring the chair down." He left and was back with the chair in a flash. It too was identical to the two Carmelita already had. "There has to be another one like it somewhere in this building," he said.

"You are probably right," said Carmelita. "No one buys three chairs."

"No furniture store sells an odd number of chairs. I will check with Sebastian or one of the other guys to see who has it and whether I can borrow it for the evening." David knew that each boarder had a table and one chair in his room. Although they led busy lives while working and going to school, they did at times gather in one room or another to play cards or have a drink. David, however, had never before paid much attention as to whether or not the chairs were identical. He wasn't surprised though, when Sebastian willingly allowed the use of his chair and he saw that it was the same as the other three.

Carmelita was happy with her coordinated seating arrangement but happier still that there were enough seats for everyone she expected. She always knew that the couch could seat three comfortably and possibly four in a crunch, but she was especially pleased that it didn't have to be that way. By meal time all four people she invited showed up and there had been an extra seat, so everyone was quite comfortable. The meal was served buffet style which was the only way for her to accommodate everyone without any semblance of preference of bias.

David presented Carmelita with a gift for the baby that surprised her. It was a tax free savings bond in the child's name. Although not a large amount of money, $1,200.00, it was expected to yield a tidy sum in twenty years, just about the time Elvin would have been a junior in college. Everyone else who came to celebrate her son's baptism gave her, or rather him, cash ranging in amounts of from twenty to one hundred dollars.

Carmelita was thankful but teary-eyed. They were tears of joy and everyone there realized that. No one asked about TK and she never once thought about him. After the meal, the cakes Mrs. Jackman baked were served as dessert and everyone helped themselves to the liquor that was there as they enjoyed the romantic music that was being played softly so that the other residents would not be disturbed.

Being the only male present, David was uneasy and Carmelita sensed it, yet she was unable to give him all of the attention she felt he deserved. Her guests were comfortable and enjoying the evening but she had no idea when they may have decided to leave. David understood her predicament, looked at his watch, said how pleased he was to have met everyone, apologized for having to leave and did just that.

He got up to his room aware of the fact that it would be another three and a half hours before his planned meeting with Mildred, so he kicked off his shoes, took his suit from where it hung and placed it on a hanger. He placed his shirt and his tie on a separate hanger and threw himself across the bed. Soon he fell asleep and was awaken an hour later when someone rapped at the door. *Oh my, God! Not Crystal again*, he thought. He reached for a blue cotton robe that hung over the bed head and draped it around himself before approaching the door.

He was surprised to see Carmelita standing there smiling. She handed him a plate covered with foil and said, "I noticed that you had no dessert so I brought you some."

"Thank you. Come in," he said.

"You are welcome."

She hesitated for a moment then stepped inside and closed the door behind her. She did not lock it so David did.

"Has everyone left?" he asked.

"Yes, although for a while I thought Lillian might be spending the night with us."

"What made you think so?"

"Well, she was the last person to leave and she did so exactly one hour after Cathy who preceded her."

"Well, in spite of her hostility earlier on, there must be something about you she likes otherwise she would not have stuck around."

"I am not sure about all of that."

Carmelita was still doubtful about Lillian Paul's loyalty as a friend but she bore no malice. She was that type of person, not particularly religious but an honest, caring, trusting, and loving individual.

FIFTEEN

After being with David for a little over two hours, Carmelita became concerned about her mother and baby and David was becoming anxious about meeting Mildred on time for the dance. They had agreed to meet at 9:30 p.m. He, being a stickler for time and having some knowledge of Mildred's penchant for the same, made no effort to dissuade Carmelita from leaving when she decline his invitation to join him in the shower. "I will shower downstairs," she said

"I understand."

"Thank you, and thanks for all that you have done."

"You are welcome."

"Bye."

"Good bye," said David. "Hopefully, I will see you tomorrow."

"You most certainly will unless…"

"Unless what?"

"Unless the Lord decides otherwise."

"Then I will see you tomorrow." They kissed each other and Carmelita left.

David hurried into the shower but not without trepidation. The thought that Crystal Mendoza may be at the door when he emerged, frightened him. He showered quickly and emerged relieved that there was no one there. He got dressed but his peace of mind was short lived. As he picked up the car keys and was about to leave the room, Crystal walked in.

"I didn't know that you were going out," she said.

"Well, you do now."

"Where are you going?"

"You seem to be forgetting something."

"What could that be?"

"My surname is Cassel, not Mendoza, and I am well over the age of twenty-one."

"You are so damn fresh! Nevertheless, I like that acknowledgement."

"What acknowledgement do you like?"

"I like the fact that you are legally an adult."

"What that means really is that I am not accountable to anyone, especially one whose last name is Mendoza."

"I am not asking you to be accountable to me. I just want you to..." Crystal stopped short of saying what she intended, stepped forward, hugged him and was pleasantly surprised when he reciprocated. The brief period during which they held each other close seemed like an eternity. Then he whispered, "You are going to make me late."

"You will not regret it. I can assure you of that."

Not now! Not tonight, please. David's thoughts were racing. He thought of Carmelita. He thought of the compromising situation in which he saw Crystal and Sebastian. *Is this any less compromising*? He wondered. *Could the repercussions also be dire*? There were no answers. Suddenly she eased her embrace and he felt relieved.

"Thank you," he said.

"Not so fast, sweetheart. There is more to come."

Not this evening and I hope never again, he thought but said, "I must go now."

"Enjoy your evening. I will see you tomorrow," she said and walked out of his room. She descended the stairway smiling but as she entered her apartment, the smile vanished.

David inhaled deeply and exhaled the same way in an effort to relax before running down the stairs and getting into his rented car for the trip over to Mildred's. Although he had visited her before, he had never made the journey by car. It was always by subway. On that night, therefore, he was faced with two major setbacks, his inexperience as a chauffeur because he drove infrequently since obtaining his driver's license and the task of having to read the street signs at night in order to navigate the Brooklyn thoroughfares and find his way to Mildred's before 9:30 p.m.

He overcame both impediments and arrived at her address on Union Street near Eight Avenue but there was no available parking. He circled the blocks from Union Street to Lincoln Place, down Fourth Avenue and along Carroll Street, up Eight Avenue and back to Union Street several times before a spot became available directly in front of the building where Mildred lived. He parked and entered the building through the first of two metal doors. There, in the foyer, he located and rang her doorbell. She buzzed him in without asking who it was. He pushed the second door as the lock clicked, entered the lobby, and waited for the elevator.

The lift came quickly and just as quickly he entered and pressed the fourth floor button. When he reached the floor the door opened and a woman who stood there in evening wear asked, "Going down?"

"It should," David said. He made that assumption because he was the only one on the elevator when it went up, and for the duration of the ride no one summoned it to either of the two upper floors.

He walked down the corridor to Apartment 4D where Mildred lived. The door was open but he knocked anyway. "It is open. Come in," she said. When he entered she was still not completely dressed and seemed in no hurry to do so.

"You made it here with time to spare," she said.

"Not really. It is already 9:35."

She glanced at the clock on the wall and said, "I guess I am the one running late."

"You guess?"

"I am sorry about that. For some reason I expected you to be as tardy as most other West Indians."

"Sorry to disappoint you. I am not, and never was."

"Okay, David. Give me five minutes more. In the meantime you can take a look at the room."

"The room?" he questioned.

"Yes! The room I prepared for you. It is right there, next to the kitchen."

He walked away, scrutinized the room, returned and said, "It is lovely, thank you."

"You are welcome," said Mildred. "However, you never did say what that tiff with your landlady was about. Anyway, I am ready. Let's go. We can talk about it as we travel."

"We are driving. You really wouldn't want us to ride a train or bus dressed this way."

"I never gave that a second thought," said Mildred. "I ride the trains and buses all the time."

The elevator stopped as they requested and they got on. They reached the ground floor very quickly and David placed the palm of his right hand at the small area of Mildred's lower back just at her waistline and guided her through the front doors. "Where is the car?" she asked.

"It is right here." He pointed to the Chevy II Nova parked close to the sidewalk in front of the building. They stepped forward toward the car and he opened the passenger door for her. When she was seated comfortably, he moved around to the driver's side, got in, started the vehicle and drove directly to Utica Avenue. It was a relatively short ride and the discussion about his landlady did not come up again. He was fortunate to find a parking space close to the dance hall. They walked in and were ushered to a table where four people were already seated. One of them was the very woman David saw in evening wear when he got off the elevator at Mildred's. They introduced themselves to the two men and two women, presumably couples. Then they sat down.

One of the guests at the table, a dowdily dressed woman in her early to mid forties, looked at David and Mildred in disbelief. She then whispered something to her friend whom David had seen in the building where Mildred lived. She listened to the distasteful comment but not without chagrin. Although neither Mildred nor David heard exactly what was said, the mannerisms disgusted them.

David realized how annoyed Mildred was and tried to engage her in conversation. At the same time Byron Lee, one of the three orchestras commissioned for the dance started playing one of the *Might Sparrow's* popular compositions. The band's rendition of *Jean and Dinah* was fantastic.

"That is just wonderful," Mildred said as she gyrated in her seat to the island's rhythm.

"Isn't that a Jamaican band?" One of the men asked.

"I think so," said the other man. "I could be wrong though. They may be from Trinidad.

"Maybe they are. Perhaps that's the reason they are playing calypsos," the dowdily dressed woman said with a Jamaican lilt.

"The band is from Jamaica but their specialty is calypso music," David explained.

Mildred was still gyrating in her seat so David asked, "Would you like to dance?"

She did not answer but got up, pushed her chair closer to the table, and waited. He held her hand and they moved onto the waxed, wooden area of the ballroom to dance. The eyes of the other women at their table were fixated on them but none of that mattered to David and Mildred. They enjoyed the music and the comfort of each other's arms.

When the music stopped, Mildred suggested that they get something for the table. They walked to the bar and ordered a bottle of scotch, some ginger ale, and some seltzer.

"How would you like that to be served?" the bartender asked.

"Together with a bucket of ice and six glasses," David said.

"What is your table number?"

"It is table number 16."

Mildred attempted to pay for the drinks but David objected and paid the bartender himself. She then said, "Okay. I will see what there is to eat over there." She pointed to the food court, and before David could comment, she walked over to one of the counters and ordered a basket of fried chicken wings.

The server asked, "Where are you sitting, Madam?"

Mildred wondered why she was being called madam, but paid for her order and said, "Table number 16,"

"Your meal would be delivered."

"Thank you," she said. At that very moment the band started playing another of its calypso arrangements. Mildred hurried to where David was, and although she did not observe it, the women at table number 16 were giggling. Nevertheless, she and David danced together again before they returned to their seats. As soon as they got there, the woman sitting at the table in the evening dress asked, "Did you buy the drinks and the snack?"

"Yes," Mildred answered.

"Thank you," she said.

"Meh never eat them thing deh so, chicken wings," the other woman commented.

"So, go and get yourself what you do eat," Mildred said. She didn't think that the woman responded. If she did, whatever she said was not audible because the soft, romantic music of Selwyn (Sel) Duncan's orchestra, with *Sel* himself on the tenor saxophone, suddenly resonated throughout the room.

For a moment at least, it appeared as if every couple was on the dance floor except the two men and two women David and Mildred met seated at table number 16. They were content to sit there and gossip, argue about politics, and smoke. When David complained to Mildred that he couldn't stand the smell of the cigarette they were smoking, she replied, "It is packaged like cigarettes but it's not tobacco."

"What is it then?" he asked.

"It smells more like ganja," said Mildred. "They are grazing."

"What do you mean?'

"They are smoking weed." David seemed puzzled, so she explained, "They are smoking a very strong kind of marijuana."

"Are there different kinds or is it that what they are smoking is very concentrated?"

"Oh, David, you are so bright yet so naive," said Mildred. "There are three species of cannabis: *Cannabis ruderalis*, *Cannabis sativa*, and *Cannabis indica.* All produce tetrahydrocannabinol (THC) a psychoactive drug."

"Which one of those species is the strongest?"

"I do not know. I don't think that those who smoke weed know either. They probably get their high from either one of the three species or a combination of two or more of them."

The music of Sel Duncan was followed by that of the Joey Lewis' band and the Caribbean All Stars steel orchestra. Mildred and David danced the night away together. Neither felt the need to dance with anyone else. When the function came to an end at about 3:30 a.m. David asked the other people who occupied table number 16 whether anyone needed a ride home. They all thanked him for the offer but none accepted. They had already agreed on who was taking whom home and David understood.

He and Mildred said goodbye. Everyone, except the dowdily dressed woman responded in kind. "What's the matter with her?" he asked as they walked away.

"I don't know, David, and I do not care," said Mildred. "She probably wants to take you home with her."

"Don't say things like that, Mildred."

"Why shouldn't I? She had been eying you all night long."

"You are so funny sometimes."

"I am not trying to be funny. She couldn't keep her eyes off you all night. Then she ah talk bout she doh eat them thing deh so. Why the hell didn't she get up and pay for what she preferred to eat?"

"I don't know, Mildred," David said while laughing.

"Why don't we just forget about those people and get out of here. I had a really good time at the dance. I wouldn't want to blemish the memory of that with thoughts of such low life."

"That's not nice, Mildred."

"I know but it is what it is."

By then they reached the car and David opened the passenger front door to let Mildred in. She entered smiling and quickly reclined in the seat. He walked around to the driver side, entered the vehicle, sat down, and turned the key in the ignition. They headed back to Mildred's place but soon realized the there was no available parking in the immediate vicinity.

"Go around the block," she suggested.

David drove up Eight Avenue and across Lincoln Place to Sixth Avenue and back to Union Street, but found no parking. He drove around the circle at Grand Army Plaza, down Prospect Park West and eventually found a spot on President Street near Seventh Avenue.

"This is quite some distance away from where I live."

"It is only one block away. That's not very far."

"During the day it is not," Mildred said.

"So what happens, the distance changes at night?"

"Now, you know that is not what I mean."

"I do not know. What exactly do you mean?"

"It isn't safe to walk around here this late at night, or rather, this early in the morning."

"Trust me. It is safer here than a lot of other places. There are constant police patrols here. The only area of Brooklyn that is probably safer is Borough Park."

"I wouldn't know about that. I just find it to be a bit leery here."

"Don't worry. We are together and safe."

That seemed like the clue Mildred was waiting for. She held David's left arm as they strolled back to her place on Union Street. When they reached the entrance to the apartment building where she lived she remarked, "I am concerned about your safety, David."

"Don't worry. I'll be fine."

"Why don't you come in, have a cup of tea or coffee and wait until sunrise when there is ample daylight?"

David thought of what Mildred said. He thought of Carmelita and of his own sleeping arrangement at the Mendoza's boarding house. As he pondered the situation, Mildred asked, "What are you wondering about?"

"Nothing in particular."

"Listen, if your wicked landlady, Crystal, should ever ask you to leave you would stay with me, wouldn't you?"

"I would, and I am very grateful for the offer."

"So why are you hesitating to come upstairs where you can have some coffee and be safe until daylight?"

"Okay. Let's go in," he acceded.

They entered the elevator and quickly reached Mildred's fourth floor apartment. "Sit down while I get the percolator started, or if you prefer you can try out your bed," said Mildred. David looked at her puzzled. She then said, "Go in and try it out."

"I am Okay. Really! I am," he said.

"Suit yourself, David."

SIXTEEN

It was 9:00 a.m. when David got home after delivering the car to the auto rental facility. He called Mildred as she requested to let her know that he was home safely. He then changed his clothes and tossed himself across the bed. It was not his intention to sleep in that position but he fell asleep. It was mid-day when he woke up and before he could get out of bed and tidy himself, Crystal Mendoza was at the door. "Why are you still in bed?" she asked.

"Why shouldn't I be? It is Sunday and there is not much else for me to do."

"I guess you did it all last night."

"I only did as much as I could have."

"What is that supposed to mean?"

"It can mean whatever you want to make of it."

"David, sometimes you can be so unreasonable."

"You came up here, disturbed me from my rest and claiming now that I am unreasonable. You have got some nerve!"

"I didn't come here to argue with you."

"I am not arguing. I am simply stating the facts as I see them," he said.

Crystal seemed appeased by what David said and he found that to be strange. He was hoping that she would be annoyed enough by it to leave. Instead, she stepped inside and closed the door behind her. *Why doesn't she go to Sebastian's room*? He wondered but asked, "Why wouldn't you let me sleep?"

"You could have slept all night but you chose not to."

"So?"

"So you spent the entire night with Mildred or whatever her name is, you can spend a few minutes with me?"

"Hey! You spend your nights with Victor. You have never heard me complain about it."

"You can if you want to."

"What good would that do me?"

"There is no one in the building but us."

"That does not answer my question. Nevertheless, how is that possible?"

"Victor and the children went to church and Carmelita, her mother, and the baby accompanied them."

"Where are Sebastian and the others?" As soon as he asked the question, he regretted it.

"You know that they are never here on a Sunday," said Crystal as she pulled her house dress off, eased her petit frame onto the bed, and whispered, "It's just the two of us, baby."

For a while she thought that things were going her way because David offered little or no resistance. Instead, he repositioned himself vertically on the bed to accommodate her as she snuggled up to him. Just then his telephone rang. "Don't answer it," she whispered.

"I have to. It might be important," he said as he sat up and reached for the telephone. He picked it up and said, "Hello!"

"Is this David Cassel?" the caller asked.

"Yes, it is."

"This is a collect call from Trinidad. Will you accept the call?"

"Yes," he said. Although he didn't know who was calling, he was concerned that someone was trying to reach him with news about his ailing mother.

"David, this is Baxter," the caller said. David's breathing and heart rate increased immediately as he listened to his younger brother. Crystal meanwhile, remained silent. Initially, she too was concerned. However, as she lay so close to him, she could hear both sides of the exchanges in that telephone conversation, and she soon realized that it was not a matter of grave concern as they both may have thought initially. She sat up, put her arms around David and unbuttoned his shirt. She eased the right shirt sleeve down and he lowered his right hand so she could remove that sleeve. When she did, he moved the telephone to his right ear. That allowed her to remove the left sleeve and the shirt altogether. She then stroked his back gently with her finger tips, then with her lips, and finally her tongue, to the point that David stopped responding to his brother's questions.

"David, are you there?" asked Baxter. "Let me know something."

"What did you want to know again?" he finally asked.

"I asked if you can send me one of those new stereo systems next month."

"I have no money to afford that sort of thing right now."

"How could that be when you send money home to mom every month."

"So? I do that because you who live in the house do nothing to help with the expenses."

"So things are not that bad with you. You certainly can spare a few dollars to send me the stereo. It is not that expensive."

"You don't seem to understand, Baxter, that in order for me to send anything home I have to make an enormous sacrifice, and that means doing without something I need. So since you know that the stereo is not that expensive, why can't you purchase it yourself?"

"How am I supposed to do that?"

"Just the way you expect me to."

"Come on, David. You know I can't afford that."

Then do without it, he thought but asked, "Why can't you afford it? You have a job and you do not contribute to rent nor rations in the home."

"You are in the *States* (United States), man. You can help me out when you get paid."

"No, Baxter. Obviously you do not understand the sacrifices that I am making here. Let me fill you in. First of all, I work hard for my money. No one gives me anything for nothing. I do not have one of those cushier jobs like you do in Trinidad. Every penny I earn goes toward school fees, books, boarding and lodging. There is nothing left for entertainment or recreation. I do not even have a radio. The only reason I have a telephone is that I can communicate with mom, so the next time you call, please don't call me collect. Baxter hung up the telephone abruptly but David was not bothered by it. On the contrary, he was glad.

Crystal lost her interest, focus, and concentration after listening to the conversation between David and his brother. She did not comment though, perhaps because she had much of the same information from reading the letters his mother wrote to him. Instead, she got out of the bed, got dressed, and walked toward the door. There, she hesitated before opening it, hoping perhaps, that David would try to dissuade her from leaving but he did not, so she walked out.

If David was concerned about Crystal's abrupt departure, he didn't show it. He simply went back to bed. There, he thought about moving out, but moving in with Mildred was not particularly appealing to him. He realized that she, unlike Crystal, had more than a fleeting interest in him. His primary concern, however, was Carmelita, although he never made that perfectly clear to her. *Where can I go*? He wondered. *I will get the newspaper later today and see what, if anything is available*, he thought. *All I need is one room, although a kitchenette is preferable.* With that thought he fell asleep again and slept soundly until 4:00 p.m.

He got out of bed and headed to the shower. He was careful in adjusting the water pressure so that it did not attract Crystal Mendoza's attention. Fortunately he managed to achieve that, showered, and got dressed for the evening. He was famished and thinking of going out to get something to eat. Just then there was a knock at the door. *My, God! I hope that is not Crystal again*. He thought of her by her first name as he approached the door cautiously, although he knew that she never knocked. She had always walked right in. Nevertheless, he felt that she was unpredictable and could change her behavior at any time. He was pleasantly surprised to see Carmelita standing there.

"Hey! Girl, how are you? Come on in," he said. Carmelita stepped inside but did not close the door behind her. She placed a small tray covered with a white towel on his desk and said, "I brought you something for lunch."

"Lunch?" asked David. "It is almost dinner time."

"That is true, but have you eaten anything for the day?"

"I haven't. Thanks. You are so sweet." He kissed her and she sat down without waiting to be offered a seat. That was a welcome surprise to him. *She is becoming more comfortable with me*, he thought. *I like that.* "Can you spare a few minutes?" he asked.

"Yes, I have some time. That is why I am here. I need to speak with you"

"Okay."

"Are you in a relationship with someone named Mildred?" Carmelita was direct.

"If your question suggests a romantic relationship, the answer is no."

"What other relationship could there be?"

"A relationship could be any affiliation or association, be it business, academic or otherwise."

"Let's not get hung up on the semantics," said Carmelita. "Are you having an affair with her?"

"Am I having an affair?"

"Yes, as in sexual relationship," Carmelita replied with clarity.

"No! Where did you get such a crazy notion?"

"I got it from Mrs. Mendoza."

"Did Crystal Mendoza tell you that?"

"Around eight o'clock this morning she knocked at my door just to let me know that you spent all of last night with some woman named Mildred."

David shook his head in disbelief. *What a wicked witch*, he thought. *All the good things she pretends to do are with malicious intent.* He was slow in responding to Carmelita's question, so she asked, "David, is there any truth to what Mrs. Mendoza said?"

"What she said was not without malice."

"That is not what I asked."

"I know, but that is my answer to your question."

"Oh! No. Doh gee me that crap," Carmelita said in a typical Trinidadian vernacular. David laughed, and she said, "It is not funny, David. I need to know."

"Well, allow me to explain?"

"Go ahead."

He went on to explain to Carmelita how he got the invitation to the dance he told her about and the reason he attended. He assured her that his relationship with Mildred was to that point, purely platonic. "We have been close friends since freshman year," said David. "When Mrs. Mendoza threatened to evict me she suggested that I can sublet the extra room she had in her apartment."

"Did you accept her offer?"

"I thanked her for the offer but I never accepted nor rejected it."

"That seems reasonable. You kept your options open."

"After all, I wouldn't want to be homeless in New York City."

"Again, that seems reasonable, but why did Mrs. Mendoza threaten to evict you?"

"She said they were planning to sell the place. Although I think there was more to it than that."

"I think so too since she never mentioned that to me, and as far as I know, she never mentioned it to any of the other tenants," said Carmelita. "What could it be? I do recall you alluding to something in that regard but you said at the time that it was a long story which you had no time to explain. Would you like to explain it now? Or is it that you still do not have the time for it?"

"I do not have the time or the desire to do so. Furthermore, I don't think Crystal Mendoza is worth the trouble."

"It is no trouble to me to listen."

"I know but wouldn't it be better for us to plan for the future rather than worry about Crystal's malicious intentions?"

"Did you say *us* in the same sentence with *plan for the future*?"

"Yes. I hope that didn't go over as me being too forward."

"Oh! David, you make me feel so good," Carmelita said as she got up from where she was sitting, moved over to where he sat, and sat in his lap. He hugged her, kissed her and assured her of his unconditional love.

"I promise that I will try not to be influenced by the things Crystal says," she said. Shortly thereafter they said goodbye to each other as Carmelita walked down the stairs to rejoin her mother and baby.

SEVENTEEN

On the morning of Monday, March 4th David woke up later than usual and quickly got ready for work. After he was dressed, he gathered everything he needed for class that evening and hurriedly stuffed them into a backpack which he strung over his left shoulder. As he attempted to rush down the stairs, he noticed that Victor Mendoza was leaving his apartment at the same time. He stepped back to avoid making eye contact with Victor whom he knew would offer him a ride to work which he might have felt obliged to accept, and subsequently, become engaged in a conversation he knew he wasn't going to be too enthused about.

He waited at the top of the stairs until he heard what he thought was Victor's vehicle driving off. He was right. When he walked out of the front door, Victor's car which had been parked at the curb the evening before was not there. He looked up at the thick white clouds and thought, *Thank you father*. What concerned David when speaking with Victor at that juncture, were not the conversations about his schooling, graduation, his job, his future, or leaked information from his personal correspondence with his mother. He was petrified at the thought of what Victor might have known about his wife's seductive behavior.

Although he made constant threats about what he would do, as he termed it, to anyone who messed with his family, particularly his daughter, David reasoned that if Victor ever saw Crystal in a compromising position with another man, which she always seem to be seeking, he would unleash his wrath in a most violent manner. The fact that she may have been the aggressor, and that her cougar-like behavior was due to a decline in their communication, and that their relationship had waned considerably in recent years, would have mattered little to him. As far as he was concerned, he was the father, husband, bread winner, financier and decision maker, and nothing else mattered.

Crystal Mendoza would not end her pursuit as long as I continue to live there, David thought while he worked on the assemble line at *Eastern Time,* the nationally renowned clock manufacturer on Fulton Street, Brooklyn. *What can I do to get out of this frying pan without falling into the fire*? He wondered. He thought of the generous offer Mildred made to him, and although he did not decline the offer, he wasn't ready or willing to accept it blindly unless he was forced to do so because of some malicious act on Crystal Mendoza's part.

Mildred had not suggested any terms, charges, or conditions for him to occupy the extra room in her apartment and he did not ask for any. Although their relationship to that point was purely platonic, he was concerned that if or when they occupy the same enclosed space that may change. That was not what he wanted but he wasn't certain of Mildred's stand in that regard. He realized that her interest in him had inched up a notch since she visited to borrow the textbook she needed to complete her thesis. Crystal seemed to have noticed or surmised that there was such an interest and she attempted to have it stymied by informing Carmelita of their night out together.

David was undaunted by Crystal's effort to lure him into something he was not particularly interested in, and although at times he seemed to offer only passive resistance or none at all, it was his way of keeping her appeased. He suspected that she was the vindictive type who, if rebuffed, ignored, or provoked, would spare no effort to punish him. He, therefore, couldn't bluntly refuse to accede to her seductive attempts. He was in somewhat of a quandary because he knew of Victor Mendoza's professed propensity for violence against anyone, as he did put it, who messes with his family.

David suspected that if Victor truly had such inclinations, they could be even more exaggerated if his suspicion was about his wife's infidelity. There was no telling how the violence could escalate if it became known that Crystal was cavorting around with the young men who lived under the same roof with him and whom he grew to trust. David certainly didn't want to be named the co-respondent in divorce proceedings, be physically harmed or killed, so he decided to stay the course and avoid taking the relationship with Crystal where he knew she wanted it to go. He recognized that her tenacity and malicious inclinations would make that a difficult undertaking but he was determined to try. He was fearful but he wasn't about to give up or give in.

He eventually allayed his fears by focusing on the tasks he was assigned to complete before the work day ended. When that was accomplished he gathered his belongings and left the work place for school. He arrived on campus and immediately went to the admissions office. There, he picked up two copies of the application for admission and placed the forms in a notebook to avoid getting them wrinkled. He placed the notebook securely in his backpack and headed to class. He was well focused and attentive for most of the class period except for brief lapses in concentration when he thought of Carmelita and of Crystal's effort to harm their friendship by maliciously planting doubt in Carmelita's mind about his caring and seemingly good intentions. In every instance he was able to quickly dismiss the thought and refocus his attention on the lesson that was being presented.

He rushed home after class intending to give the application to Carmelita. Upon his arrival at their Herkimer Street address he decided that it was too late to ring her door bell or knock at the door. Nevertheless, he knew that she was going to be out early because she was starting a new job. He reasoned that she might want to complete the application and drop it in the mail the next day while on her way to work, so he slipped it under her door before going upstairs. As soon as he got in the telephone rang. He answered. It was Carmelita calling to thank him for his effort and assure him that she was about to complete the application immediately so she could mail it the next day.

"That is very good," he said.

"I will make you proud, I promise."

"You have already done so simply by agreeing to go back to school."

"You have been my inspiration, David."

"Thanks. I wish I could do more."

"You have done so much already, much more than you can imagine." She was tempted to tell him how she truly felt but refrained from doing so. Instead, she said, "Good night, David."

"Good night, Carmelita," he replied. He too was tempted to express his true feeling but held back. *Those three little words are used so frequently that they seldom sound sincere*, he thought. *There would be many more opportunities for me to let her know how I truly feel.* Soon after that thought he fell asleep.

Tuesday morning he woke up a little later than usual but he felt somewhat invigorated, perhaps it was because of that brief exchange he had with Carmelita before going to bed. Whatever the reason, he moved quickly to get ready for work which was to be followed by evening classes. That had become his daily routine from Monday to Friday. He wished he could see Carmelita while on his way out but resisted the temptation to call her. At the same time, he hoped that there would be no intrusion of his privacy on Crystal's part. He knew that Victor would normally have been at the dry cleaning plant by then and Crystal could have taken that as an opportunity to pester him.

He was lucky that morning. He left home without being beleaguered by Crystal Mendoza. When he arrived at *Eastern Time* his supervisor, Charlene Brennigan greeted him so warmly he couldn't help but wonder; *what is she up to*? It soon became known when she said, "You look cheerful and relaxed this morning, David."

"Do I?"

"Yes, and that's good because I just received a rush order for two dozen time pieces."

What does that have to do with me being cheerful and relaxed this morning? He wondered.

"I know. You are wondering what that has to do with you," said Charlene. "Well, this order must be filled by Friday and I know that you work a lot better and faster when you are happy and relaxed, so I am giving you the job."

You have just ruined my day and all that was good about last night, he thought but said, "I will do the best I can."

"I know you will, David."

"Thanks," he said and began doing what he thought was necessary to fill the order by Friday. The day went exceptionally well and he left for class hoping that the rest of the week would be just as productive. Fortunately for him, it was. He completed the job by 2:00 p.m. on Thursday, March 7th.

Carmelita also enjoyed some measure of success that week. She mailed her application for admission to the Municipal College of Arts and Sciences, met with the patient she was hired to be a companion to, and was well accepted by the patient's daughter and the staff at the nursing facility. She was pleased with the duties and responsibilities that were assigned to her and felt it was the ideal setting for her to work while going to school. Although tempted to discuss all of the possibilities with her employer and the nurse in charge, she resisted and performed her duties well that first week.

By Friday, March 8th Mrs. Jackman heard from her husband, Jeremiah, and he expressed no objections or reservations about her staying with Carmelita for a year or beyond. When she told her daughter the good news, Carmelita was elated. "I knew Uncle JJ would not object," she said.

"You are lucky," said Mrs. Jackman. "You have always been so very fortunate."

"Oh! Mama I am so happy now." Mrs. Jackman was stoic but managed to smile coyly, so Carmelita continued. "We can achieve great things together, Mama," she said.

"We?" Mrs. Jackman questioned.

"Yes, of course."

"No dear. You can achieve great things. You always had the potential. My greatest achievement was supporting you through high school and seeing you graduate after I struggled so much as a single parent to raise you. Anything else you accomplish from here on would be for you and your son."

"Mama, you know that I cannot do it alone."

"What can't you do alone?"

"Realize my dream."

"Whose dream is it? Yours," Mrs. Jackman asked and answered the question. Carmelita had no comment so her mother continued by rephrasing an earlier statement, "My greatest ambition was to see you graduate from high school. You did, and for that I am proud. I am here to lend a hand so you can undertake whatever it is you are hoping to pursue. You are aware, I am sure, that my stay here is only temporary so you better be serious about what you plan to do this time around."

"I will, Mama. I promise you."

"Don't make me any promises, please, just do it."

There was a knock at the door. Carmelita responded quickly. David was there with a solemn look on his face. "What is the matter?" She asked with grave concern. He hesitated for a moment and she said, "Come in." He was reluctant to do so because he knew that her living quarters were nothing more than one room, an efficiency as it was sometimes called. There was no bedroom as such, so he was aware of the sleeping arrangements and did not want to intrude.

"I just came home and found this letter on my desk," he said after lifting his hand to reveal an airmail envelope.

"Who left it there?"

"Mrs. Mendoza, I guess."

"When did she develop the habit of delivering your mail to your room?"

"This is something new."

"It is intrusive."

"It has gone beyond that. The letter was opened before it reached me."

"Oh, my goodness!" Carmelita lamented.

"We have long suspected that they tampered with our mail."

"They tampered with your mail! Who are they?"

"Mrs. Mendoza and, or her family."

"David! That is a serious accusation."

"We believe it to be true."

"Who are *we*?"

"The others on the floor and I. Very often we never get our mail for weeks after the Post Office delivered it. On this occasion, however, after reading it, they may have considered it important enough to get it to me right away."

"Is it really that important?"

"Yes," David said but hesitated to say more.

"Is it that you prefer not to discuss it?"

"That is not it. In fact, that is the reason I am here," he whispered.

Carmelita stepped out into the hallway and pulled the door closed behind her. "Let's go up to your place, it might be easier for us to speak there," she said.

"Okay."

They headed up the stairs to David's room. There, he revealed that his mother had been taken to a hospital in Trinidad and he may be forced to rush home.

"Do you know what is wrong with her?" Carmelita asked reluctantly.

"She has been ailing for quite some time but she resisted seeking medical attention for just as long." He did not reveal what was wrong with her and Carmelita did not ask again. *Perhaps he doesn't know himself,* she thought. "Anyway, as I said earlier, I am thinking of going home soon."

"Is it really that urgent?"

"Yes."

"How soon do you plan on travelling?"

"One week from today."

"That would be March 15th. Is it not?" asked Carmelita. Then she said, "Graduation is coming up soon."

"Graduation is scheduled for May 25th."

"Wouldn't travelling to Trinidad at this time be a set-back?"

"It could be, but a greater set-back would be for me to hear that my mother passed away and I made no effort to see her while she was sick and in the hospital."

"I understand, dear. How long do you plan on staying in Trinidad?"

"That will depend on a number of factors."

"What are the factors?"

"For example, if she shows signs of improvement, I shall be back after one week. If she is not improving but not getting any worse, I may be back in a week and a half. However, if her health continues to deteriorate, I will stay there much longer."

"How much longer would you stay?"

"I really don't know."

"You are aware, I am sure, that should you stay in T & T for more than three weeks you would have an awful amount of school work to make up."

"I am aware of that. The good thing is that there are no more scheduled exams, and I believe that I can complete my writing assignments while I am there."

Carmelita's only comment was, "You know best."

"The hardest part of all is that I have to inform the Mendoza's about my plan."

"What else can you do?"

"I have no other choice."

"When would you tell them?"

David looked at his watch. "It is too late now, so I shall inform them tomorrow," he said.

"What time is it anyway?" Carmelita asked.

"It is ten o'clock."

"My goodness, David, Mama might be wondering what happened to me."

"She might already be sleeping."

"That is possible because she generally goes to bed early, all the more reason why I should leave now in the event Elvin wakes up."

"I understand," David said as he and Carmelita stood up." They hugged and kissed each other, and said good night as he watched her walk down the stairs.

He then called Mildred, told her of the news he received and of his intended plan. She reassured him that whatever happens, the room she prepared for him would still be available. They discussed his academic standing and upcoming graduation and she wished him all the best before they hung up and went to bed.

EIGHTEEN

Saturday, March 9, 1968, David woke up and immediately called home to T & T. His brother, Baxter answered the telephone. "Did you get my letter?" Baxter asked.

"I did, and I am thinking of coming home soon."

"Why? Or rather, how? I thought you had no money, so you couldn't afford to send me the stereo system."

David was shocked into silence. He didn't know what to say, so he ignored the questions and the comment that followed them. Baxter realized that David would not or could not answer the questions so he continued by saying, "Mom has improved considerably. She might be discharged this weekend so it is up to you, man. Do whatever you wish."

"My wish is to visit with her and that is what I am going to do."

"Suit yourself." They both hung up without saying anything more.

He has some gall to imply that I couldn't send him what he wanted but I can spend money to visit my mother, David thought. *I am tired of his impudence. He is a grown man and should not expect others to take care of his needs.*

After that exchange with his brother, David felt better. He decided right then that he would postpone his planned departure to April 15th. *Easter was approaching and the college would be on Spring break from April 15th to the 19th. If I travel on April 15th and return on April 27th, I would miss only one week of classes. That would be a lot easier to make up than three weeks,* he thought. *Furthermore, I can get all my writing assignments done while I am down there.*

Just then his telephone rang. He looked at the time and answered the phone. It was Carmelita."Good morning, David," she said.

"Hey! Good morning. Aren't you running late?"

"Running late for what?"

"Don't you have to go to work today?"

"David! I work Monday to Friday."

"Oh, I am so sorry. I forgot."

"That's okay. Anyway, what have you decided about your travel plans?"

"I am going later rather than sooner."

"What exactly do you mean by that?"

"Rather that traveling on March 15th, I would travel on April 15th and return on April 27th."

"That sounds reasonable. You would not miss so much class time."

"That's my thinking exactly."

"That's good."

"I am glad you think so because I need a favor from you."

"I will do anything for you, David."

"Don't say that."

"Why shouldn't I? I do mean it."

"That implies that you trust me implicitly."

"I do."

"Thanks. Anyhow, I would like you to keep my books until I return. I know that you have limited space but I don't know who else to trust and I do not want to leave them here."

"That's no problem, David. Whenever you are ready to travel just let me know and I will create some space for your books."

"Thanks, Carmelita."

"You are welcome."

"Okay, then I shall see you later."

"That's my hope."

"Okay then, bye."

"Bye, David."

Neither questioned the other as to what time they should meet. Time seemed so inconsequential on any given weekend as long as they were together. David had no reservation about spending as much time as he possibly could with Carmelita and Elvin and she looked forward to it. In a few short months they had grown extremely close, although weekends seemed like the only times they could be together.

By mid-day David was on his way out to the local Bodega to get a few essentials for lunch when he encountered Crystal Mendoza coming in. "Where are you going?" she asked.

"No place in particular," he replied while thinking, *where I am going is none of your damn business, woman.*

"Then would you mind helping me with these?" She pointed to some grocery bags in the trunk of her car. *Why doesn't she get her lazy-ass son to help her*? He wondered but said, "Certainly Mrs. Mendoza."

As he moved toward the car, she looked him in the eye and asked, "What is this Mrs. Mendoza thing about? There is no one else around."

"It is just a matter of caution, or may I say, precaution. One never knows who is listening."

"That is nonsense, David."

He did not respond. Instead, he took two of the shopping bags out of the car trunk and started to walk off. Crystal took the other two bags, closed the trunk, and followed him into the building. They walked up the stairs to the third floor and into the Mendoza's kitchen. "Please put them on the table," she requested and David complied. Before he could do or say anything else, she asked, "Can I get you something, a beer perhaps?"

"No, thank you. I am good."

"David! Why do you always refuse everything I offer you?"

"Do I? I wasn't aware of that."

"Well, you do, and it's not nice."

That's the reason right there. I do not want to be nice to you. You are too much like a stray dog; if one starts giving it food, it will never go away, he thought but said, "I shall do a lot better the next time."

"I would hold you to your word."

"My word is my honor."

"I would hope so."

Could I ever win with this woman? He wondered, but before he could say anything else Crystal asked, "How is your mother doing?"

B----! *Once again you have been reading my letters*, he thought but he said, "Mom is doing just fine."

"I thought I heard someone saying something about her being in the hospital."

You certainly didn't hear it from me, and I am sure Carmelita didn't tell you anything, so once again you are guilty of mail tampering which is a Federal offense. You can go to jail for that, he thought.

By then Crystal had put away all of the groceries they brought up in the four shopping bags. She opened a cigarette holder that was on the kitchen table and took out one of the carcinogenic white sticks. When she picked up a lighter that was also on the kitchen table, David asked, "What are you going to do?"

"What do people do with these?"

"Research has shown them to be bad for your health."

"What? The cigarette, the lighter, or both?"

"Don't try to be funny now. You know very well that cigarettes contain a host of dangerous chemicals."

"Well, I could think of something healthier to engage in but you may object to that also."

"How can you say that? You don't know what I will or will not object to."

"Oh yes, I do. You always object. If not verbally, your body language tells the story."

"Please, Crystal! Stop making up things."

She smiled as she thought, *he called me Crystal. Maybe today might be different.* She moved closer and wrapped her arms around him. He cringed. She noticed and said, "You see. That's what I mean."

"I am sorry," he said. Crystal lit her cigarette and ignored him, so he continued, "I do have something to tell you."

She blew clouds of smoke out of her mouth and nostrils and shook her left leg nervously but said nothing.

"What is the matter with you now?" David asked.

"What do you think is the matter, David? Don't you think that I have feelings? If I were a horse you wouldn't treat me this way."

"How have I treated you?"

"Forget it, David. I am just not in the mood right now."

That's a good thing, he thought.

"You probably think that's a good thing. If it is any good, it is only good for you," she said.

That is so weird. He thought but asked, "What are you talking about?"

"You know damn well what I am talking about."

"Okay, Crystal. I can tell that you are becoming very upset so I would speak with you later," he said and got up to leave. Suddenly she started crying. She was sobbing and gasping for breath as he tried to comfort her.

"I don't know, David. I really don't know," she said in a halting manner.

"What is it you don't know?"

"I know it's wrong but….."

"You don't know what it is but yet you know it's wrong?"

Crystal shook her head to indicate *yes* and for a brief moment David was bewildered. He quickly regained his composure and said, "I am planning to visit T & T soon."

"Why? Didn't you say that your mother was doing fine?"

"Yes. That's all the more reason I should visit her now when she can still converse with me."

"Yeah! Whatever, I personally don't see your point."

Crystal did not exactly question the accuracy of David's statement. She knew the facts, so she allowed him to continue. "Before I travel, I would like to pay you for boarding and lodging for two weeks in advance if I may," he said.

"You don't have to do that, David."

"I know, but it's what I want to do."

"Okay."

"Thank you," he said and got up to leave.

"Where are you rushing off to? Today is Saturday, relax!"

"That is exactly what I am going to do upstairs."

"Are you going to relax all by yourself?"

"Of course, I am."

"That's odd."

"I live alone. There is nothing odd about relaxing alone."

"Okay, David."

"I shall speak with you later."

"Bye," she said as he walked out of the kitchen.

She seemed so distraught, he thought. *I hope she does no harm to herself or anyone else.*

Crystal Mendoza never thought of harming herself or anyone else. At least she did not consider what she planned on doing as being harmful, or even wrong. It was something she had been trying to accomplish for quite some time. All she wanted was David's undivided attention. Even her little tryst with Cedric Sebastian was designed to cause him jealousy with the hope that he might be more inclined to succumb to her demands. Although that failed, she was never deterred.

As soon as David got up to his room the telephone rang. He answered. It was Carmelita calling to ask if he would like to accompany her to the open-air market at Grand Army Plaza. "What do you need from the open-air market that you couldn't get at Key Food?" he asked.

"Can you go with me or not?" Carmelita insisted.

"I will. What time do you want to go there?"

"I want to leave here soon, perhaps in half an hour."

"I can go now if you wish."

"Okay."

"I am coming down. Meet me in the foyer."

David rushed out of his room, closed the door behind him without locking it, but he walked quietly down the stairs and waited just outside of the front door so he could see when Carmelita entered the foyer. She was there in less than five minutes and they headed out. Twenty minutes later Crystal entered David's room unannounced as she always did. She expected him to be relaxed in bed but he wasn't there. She checked the kitchen on the floor although she did not expect to see him there. The young men, including David, who lived on that floor, seldom used the kitchen. Crystal pushed in the bathroom door and looked around but of course David wasn't there either.

Where could he be? She wondered. Her pleated brow showed her frustration. *I am so damn mad at him right now*, she thought as she turned and walked back down the stairs to her apartment. She was irrational and did not consider the fact that David was an adult, and as such he was under no obligation to stay in his room even when that was what he said he intended to do.

NINETEEN

David and Carmelita returned from the open-air market unnoticed. Crystal Mendoza was nowhere in sight even though neither David nor Carmelita had given much thought to the possibility of her seeing them together. Carmelita was happy that David accompanied her to the market, a good sign she thought, that he was a lot more comfortable with her than before. In addition, she had gotten everything she needed and at much better prices than she would have paid at the supermarket.

"What are you doing for the rest of the day?" she asked.

"I have some assignments to complete but beyond that there is not much else that I have to do," said David. "What are your plans?"

"Mama asked me to go to church with her this evening."

"Today is Saturday," he said in a querying tone.

"She prefers the Saturday evening mass. She always did, but I will see you when we get back."

"Okay." He kissed her on the cheek and left.

When he got upstairs he threw himself across the bed. As he lay on his back looking at the ceiling and thinking deeply, Crystal walked in.

"You finally got a chance to relax, that's good," she said. There was no response from David so she asked, "What's the matter with you now?"

"Nothing is wrong with me."

"So why are you sulking?"

"Why do you think I am sulking?"

"It is very obvious, David."

"Sometimes a man just wants to be left alone to think."

"Are you suggesting that I should leave?"

"You can interpret that however you want."

"Then I am staying. I think you need me much more than you are willing to admit."

You are just so full of yourself, he thought but said, "I got along without you before we met."

"You are so damn cheeky! I like that," said Crystal. "A cheeky man is a romantic kind of man."

You are such as ass, David thought, but before he could say anything Crystal was on the bed lying next to him. "Do you ever think of me when you are up here by yourself?" she asked in somewhat of a whisper.

"No."

"That's a lie."

"Are you a polygraph specialist?"

"No, but I can tell that you are lying."

"How did you come to that conclusion?"

"From your breathing pattern," said Crystal. "If you felt nothing by my presence your breathing and heart rate would not be so rapid."

David hissed his teeth, supposedly in disgust but that did not discourage Crystal. She kissed him and he reciprocated. Then he got up suddenly and sat on the chair at his desk.

"What the hell is wrong now?" she asked angrily.

"Everything you are hoping for is wrong."

"Who determined that?"

"I did, but I am sure Victor will also."

"How the hell will Victor know about us?"

"You may be surprised. I don't know. Perhaps you talk in your sleep."

"David, we are two consenting adults, and for your information, I do not talk in my sleep."

"We are adults alright but one of us is married to someone else who is not consenting."

"That does not change what I feel for you."

"What you think you are feeling can get one or both of us killed."

"Killed by whom?"

"Victor Mendoza."

Crystal laughed and said, "You are truly funny, David. Victor wouldn't hurt a fly."

"Perhaps you have never heard the threats he makes."

"Against whom does he make threats?"

"As he puts it, *anyone who messes with his wife or daughter.*"

"That reference could only have been about Dallas. I doubt whether he cares much about that where I am concerned."

"Why? Have you been….."

Before David could question her as he intended, Crystal interrupted. "Don't ask me that," she said as she remembered what David saw of her with Cedric Sebastian. Although that was not what came to his mind, he acceded to her request and that essentially ended any further attempt at conversation between them. Crystal was very upset and walked out of the room sulking. *Good riddance*, he thought. On the contrary, her thinking was, *believe me, I am going to get back at you for that.*

As always, whenever Crystal became upset with David he wondered about the repercussions and thought of possible ways by which he could preempt them. On that occasion he wasn't too perturbed and didn't think much about how she would react because Mildred had reassured him earlier that she was still keeping the room at her apartment vacant for him. At the same time Crystal was thinking, *I wouldn't attempt to throw him out but if he ever travels abroad he cannot come back here.*

David's thought was, *she can do whatever the hell she wants. I don't care.*

Downstairs in her second floor efficiency Carmelita had lunch ready and suggested that her mother should eat before the food got cold. "Aren't you going to eat also?" Mrs. Jackman asked.

"Yes," Carmelita replied after hesitating for a moment.

Her initial thought was to have lunch with David. However, since he wasn't aware of it, she felt it was best to have lunch with her mother who never liked eating alone anyway. Eventually, they sat down and dined while they conversed amicably. They reminisced about life in Mayaro, particularly about Carmelita's youth and especially about her high school years. Mrs. Jackman revealed some life experiences that Carmelita never knew about. She knew that it was difficult for her mother to support her through private secondary school after she failed the Common Entrance Examination which would have allowed her a free secondary education at Mayaro High, a government sponsored institution.

"I always thought that our lives were good," said Carmelita. "We were never hungry and I was well clothed, as good as anyone else I might add."

"Thank you."

"I am just so glad we were able to have this quiet chat. There is so much I may never have known about otherwise."

"Hmm," Mrs. Jackman sounded as if she wanted to hear more from her daughter but nothing else was said.

Several things were troubling to Carmelita as to why her mother had to struggle all alone to raise her. Foremost among them was her father's role or lack thereof in her upbringing, but she was hesitant to ask. Her mother never mentioned his name, his family, his relatives, his friends or his national origin. No one she knew ever made reference to her father. *Why, what's the mystery*? She wondered, but she decided not to pursue it at that time.

After lunch she called David to ask if he was free and whether she could visit him. "I am free now," said David. "You can come at anytime you wish." Carmelita did not question the remark. She assumed that he might have been studying and probably decided not to continue.

"I'll be there right away," she said.

"Okay," he replied. He did not attempt to move from the bed where he lay quietly on his back looking at the ceiling since Crystal Mendoza walked out of his room angry and disappointed. He was struggling with his thoughts and his feelings, so although Carmelita's intended visit was not expected to bring him instant relief from the doldrums, he was looking forward to it as a welcome change of pace. *She is the exact opposite to Crystal*, he thought. *She is young, smart, genteel, alluring, and unselfish.* Just then there was a knock at the door although it was open.

"Come in," he said softly and wondered, *why did she knock when the door is open?*

"Are you okay?" Carmelita asked as she entered the room.

"Yes. Why do you ask that?"

"I asked out of concern."

"What are you concerned about?"

"My concern is for your health and wellbeing."

"Thank you, I am fine though. Please sit down." She looked at the only chair in the room, the one at the desk, the table that is, but she sat on the bed next to him.

"I have created some space for your books," she said.

"You are in an awful hurry to see me go, aren't you?"

"No. I just didn't want to wait until the last minute, then to be frantic."

"What's there to be frantic about?"

"Not being able to secure your books," said Carmelita. "I know how you feel about them."

"Please don't be so uptight about that. I have already used those books."

"Are you suggesting that you can get rid of them?"

"If that becomes necessary, I can. I thought they might be useful as reference books later on but information changes so rapidly that I am uncertain about the wisdom of holding on to them."

"David! Do you know what I have been through trying to create space to store those books?"

"I can just imagine! I am so sorry, sweetheart." he said. He then wrapped his arms around her and that essentially ended any further discussions about the books and how or where to store them.

For the next hour their main focus was on each other. Nothing else mattered because they were together. It was 4:15 p.m. when Carmelita remembered that she promised to accompany her mother to the five o'clock mass.

"Oh my God, I have to leave you, David."

"Why?"

"Mama expects me to attend church with her."

"Yeah, you did mention that," said David. "Then I shall see you when you get back."

"Okay! As promised, bye," Carmelita said and left hurriedly.

TWENTY

Mildred called to ask about David's mother's health and whether she was making any progress toward recovery. He did inform her earlier about his plans to visit his ailing mother, and she assured him that the room at her place will be kept vacant until he returned. However, he neglected to follow up on it. So she was unaware of his change of travel plans. She was still of the opinion that he intended to go sooner than later.

"Is it next Friday, March 15th, that you are traveling?" she asked.

"That was my original plan but I have decided against it."

"When did you decide that?"

"Earlier this week, it was Tuesday I believe."

"Why didn't you tell me?"

"I intended to do so but we had not spoken since."

"I wonder why, David? My telephone number has not been changed."

"Well, after careful consideration and listening to many suggestions, including yours, I decided that three weeks of lectures were too many to miss and try to make up later on."

"Please don't skirt the issue, David."

"I am not avoiding the question."

"You are evasive. Why didn't you call to let me know?"

"I thought I had time enough to let you know. After all, today is March 9th. My flight plan is rescheduled for April 15th."

"I can never win with you, can I?"

David did not answer Mildred's latest question with the hope that the discussion will end there. He was right. She said simply, "I will speak with you before you travel."

"Okay," he said.

"Bye, David."

"Bye."

As soon as he hung up the telephone it rang again. "David, Crystal is here," the caller said.

"Yes," he answered. He really wanted to ask, *what the hell do you want now*?

"Could you come down here for a few minutes?"

"No."

"Why can't you?"

"I am busy."

"Today is Saturday. What could you be busy with?"

That is none of your business, woman, he thought but said, "I expect company." He hoped that was sufficient to deter her from attempting to say or do anything silly.

"I just saw Carmelita and her mother going to church."

"What does that have to do with anything?"

"Who else can you be expecting at this time on a Saturday evening?"

Dallas, maybe, David thought of saying but instead, he made a mournful sound, and Crystal asked alarmingly, "Are you okay, sugar?"

"I am fine," he said.

"I cannot accept that. I would have to check on you myself."

"I said I am fine. What more do you want to hear?"

"It is not so much what you said, but the manner in which you said it."

"How else could I have said it?" David was losing patience with Crystal.

"That no longer matters, I am coming up right now."

"Like you always said, you own the place. I cannot stop you."

"You finally got it right. I will see you in five minutes."

"Do what pleases you," said David. "But don't accuse me later on of not telling you the truth."

"What is the truth?"

"I expect company," he reiterated, but his wish was, *I hope Carmelita gets here before you do, or soon afterwards*, he thought. Then he picked up a note book from the desk with the intention of reviewing his class notes. That was a wasted effort.

Only three minutes had elapsed when Crystal, dressed only in a spotlessly white bath robe pushed the door and walked in. As usual she didn't knock before entering but David wasn't alarmed. He had gotten accustomed to the behavior although he questioned himself as to whether it was just bad manners or willful mischief.

"What are you doing?" she asked.

"What does it look like I am doing?"

"Do you ever answer a question without asking one?"

"Do you?" David asked.

Crystal's response was to grab the notebook from his hand and toss it onto the desk. David smiled, and that surprised her. She expected an outburst of anger from him but he was becoming adept at not living up to her expectations.

"Has there ever been a time when you were able to lie in bed and just relax, let your thoughts stray, on me perhaps?"

"I came to the USA to pursue higher education and that is what I intend to do. Otherwise, I might as well have stayed in T & T. I had a decent job there and a relatively good lifestyle."

"None of that answers my question. All I wanted was a simple straight forward answer."

"Then the answer you are looking for is, *no*."

"Well, we are going to change that right now."

"That is impossible."

"Why?"

"In order to just lie in bed, relax, and let my thoughts stray I would have to be alone. Right now I am not."

"That is very clever, sweetheart." Crystal said as she reached over and stroked his forehead. He held her hand. He wasn't sure why and neither was she. They looked in each other's eyes briefly but neither spoke before she got up, closed the door and locked it. She took off her robe, folded it neatly and rested it on the back of the chair at the desk. From where he lay pensively in bed David looked on but he said nothing. Crystal moved and sat next to him on the bed. She unbuttoned his shirt and he lifted his upper body to allow her to take it off. She rested the shirt over her robe on the chair. Then she pulled her petit frame onto the bed next to him. *This is going well*, she thought but she asked, "Are you okay?"

He nodded his head before saying, "Yes."

She leaned over and kissed him. He reciprocated and they remained conjoined for about one minute before being interrupted by the ringing of the telephone.

"Don't answer it," she said.

"I have to. It might be important."

As if what we are doing is not important, Crystal thought. David also thought it might be important but not for the same reason as Crystal. He was concerned about his living accommodations which for the time being at least, she controlled. Nevertheless, he took the telephone call. It was Carmelita on the line.

"David, I am running late. After church I took Mama Downtown to A & S's Department Store. We probably wouldn't get home before eight o'clock."

"Then I will see you soon."

"Okay, bye."

"Bye," David said as he hung up the telephone. He looked at Crystal and said, "That was Carmelita. She is home." He lied.

"Shit!" Crystal exclaimed. She quickly got up, put on her robe and walked out the door without saying another word.

David looked up at the ceiling and said softly, "Thank you."

Ten minutes later his telephone rang. He answered. Crystal was on the line. "What do you think is wrong with me?" she asked.

"I don't know," he said but wondered, *why is she asking me that? I am not her shrink.*

"Don't you know what is wrong with me, David?"

"I said I don't. As far as I can tell you are just fine."

"So why don't you want me, David?" He was shocked into silence or just could not answer, so Crystal continued. "You make love to me but you always find a reason to stop at the most critical time.

"Think about it, Crystal. It is you who always leave angrily whenever my telephone rings."

Crystal? He called me Crystal! She thought before saying, "You are probably right."

"Not probably, I am right."

"I am glad you recognize that."

"It is a problem you should address."

"That is something I can only do with you cooperation."

"You are relentless, woman."

"Am I relentless? Listen, you pointed out one of my weaknesses so I am suggesting that we work together to remedy the situation by addressing the problem."

"Why should we address them? If they are transgressions, they are your transgressions."

"That might be true but it takes two willing participants, consenting adults as we are to bring this thing to fruition."

David laughed and said, "You are too funny, girl."

First it was Crystal. Now it's girl. He is getting there, she thought and asked, "Do you love me, David?"

"I love you as much as I would any living creature."

"Don't be a smart ass with me now, David." said Crystal. "I need a straight forward answer."

"I could not answer that any differently until we have had a heart to heart chat."

"When will that be?"

"We can converse at any time that is convenient to both of us."

"Why not right now. Neither of us is doing anything that is more important." David did not respond so Crystal continued by asking, "Can you come down for a cup of coffee?"

"I guess so."

"How soon can you get here?"

"I can be there in five to ten minutes."

"Good, I will see you soon."

"Okay, bye."

She had coffee, with milk and sugar on the kitchen table when David arrived. "Sit down," she said, and he complied. He was very tentative, so she reassured him, "It is okay. We are just having coffee."

"Why is it you are always so persistent?" he asked.

"I am sorry if I gave you that impression but you may recall one of our earlier conversations."

"We have had many conversations. Is there one in particular that I should remember?"

"Yes, of course."

"How am I supposed to know which one it is?"

"The conversation in which you suggested Victor and I should go out together more often."

"Oh, that is the conversation you are alluding to."

"Yes. Well, it has not happened."

"Did you suggest it to him?"

"Yes."

"What did he say?"

"His response was that he couldn't do that and take care of the business all by himself."

"That is not unreasonable. He needs help so pitch in and help him."

"He has help. Beverly is always there. He often brags of how she has never missed a day of work."

"While Ms. Camacho might be a conscientious worker, her duties are in the store serving customers. I am sure Victor can use some help at home with the bookkeeping."

"He is not going to get it from me. If he spends less time at the church, he would have more time to do the things he needs to do."

"What is your aversion to church?"

"It is not that I dislike church or his attending church, but he could be reasonable and do what most people do."

"What is that?"

"Spend an hour or two at church on Sundays. Why does he have to be there most of the day?"

"I don't know, Crystal. Maybe it is his way of giving back."

"What is he giving back, and to whom?"

"I cannot answer that with certainty. I really don't know."

"Anyway, as I told you before, our relationship continues to worsen."

"I am sorry to hear that," said David. "This coffee is very good. What brand is it?" he asked out of context in an attempt to change the conversation, but Crystal Mendoza was having none of it. She wanted to give vent to her feelings and would not acquiesce.

She ignored the question about the coffee and said, "There is something I want to tell you in confidence."

Is it that you are accustomed to cheating on your husband? David wondered but he said nothing so Crystal continued, "I have what I believe is a serious medical condition."

"You did say you want to tell me in confidence but have you discussed it with your physician?"

"No."

"Who decided it was serious?"

"I did."

"Oh yes, for a moment there I forgot that you are a trained nurse."

"That is beside the point. If I had no medical training at all I would still recognize it as being serious?"

"So what exactly is it?" David asked. *I eat from you, you lay close to me in bed and we have kissed. I hope it isn't anything contagious*, he thought.

"It is nothing contagious," she said as if she knew what he was thinking.

That is somewhat of a relief, he thought as he asked again, "What is it?"

Crystal paused briefly then she said, "I suffer from repeated sexual stimulation."

David laughed and asked, "Is that the serious medical condition you believe you have?"

"Yes! It is not funny, David. I experience repeated and spontaneous orgasms."

"Then you have no need for me or anyone else for that matter," He was still laughing when he said that.

"I am suffering and for some reason you think it is a joke."

"I am sorry," he said but he was struggling to keep his emotions in check.

"This is something I have suffered from since puberty but have never before revealed to anyone."

David was becoming guilt ridden. Crystal was revealing something so personal to him and he initially took it very lightly.

"I wish I could help you," said David. "Does Victor know about this?"

"No. As I said before, I have never told anyone about it. To be honest, I have never heard anyone else complain about such feelings."

This is way beyond what I can comprehend, he thought. "I will make some inquires about it for you," he said.

"Thanks."

"You are welcome," said David. "I really enjoyed the coffee."

You will find the sex to be much better, she thought but said, "It is a Mocha."

"I must get some the next time I am at the supermarket."

"Why wait? Take some with you now." She opened a cupboard, took out a can of the exotic coffee and handed it to him.

"Thanks. You are so kind," he said.

Soon you will find me to be just as sweet, she thought but said, "Enjoy the rest of your evening, dear."

"Thanks again," he said and left smiling. Crystal was smiling too.

TWENTY-ONE

Saturday evening Carmelita returned home much later than expected. After she visited the stores downtown, she took her mother to dinner at Junior's restaurant. Mrs. Jackman enjoyed the evening. She was truly impressed with what she saw of Brooklyn and started to entertain the thought of staying longer than she had originally planned. However, she refrained from saying anything about that to Carmelita. *I wouldn't want to set her hopes too high*, she thought.

It was 10:35 p.m. when they eventually got home. Elvin was sound asleep, so too was David but Carmelita was unaware of that. She had become accustomed to him staying up late to study and was totally surprised when she called him on the telephone and got no answer. The phone rang six times before she hung up. She immediately dialed the number again. On that attempt David picked up the phone and said "Hello." He sounded groggy.

"David, this is Carmelita."

"Ah ha," he mumbled.

"I am so sorry, David. We just arrived home. I was hoping we could have been here much earlier but unfortunately that did not work out."

"It's okay."

"I brought you something for dinner though."

"Ah ha," he whispered, and within seconds she heard him snoring softly.

"Well, I guess I will have to refrigerate this food," she told her mother.

"Why?" Mrs. Jackman asked.

"David can have it tomorrow."

"Why?" her mother asked again.

"The reason is that we brought it for him."

"You cannot give that young man stale food, child. Just throw it out"

"Hmm," *I am not a child, Mama*, Carmelita thought of saying but said instead, "That would be a willful waste, Mama."

'So what will you do?"

"Eat it myself tomorrow."

"As hard as things were, when you were growing up in Mayaro, you never had to eat stale food. I cooked every day."

"That's only because you didn't have a refrigerator."

"Now that I do have a refrigerator I still cook every day."

"You are at home all day and have the time for that sort of thing."

"Don't you have time to cook a fresh meal for someone who has done so much for you?"

"That's right, Mama. You see what I have to do, and it can get really hectic when I go back to school and have to work and take care of the baby when you are not here."

"Whose fault is that?"

"I am not faulting anyone."

"Oh, that's good because the two people responsible for your predicament are you and TK."

"Thanks for reminding me, Mama. Have a good night," Carmelita said and abruptly retired to bed for the night. Her mother joined her shortly thereafter and they both slept soundly until Sunday morning.

As soon as Carmelita was awake she called David. He too was up and about, but he seemed lethargic and unenthusiastic on hearing from her. That was rather unusual and it raised some concerns, so she asked, "Are you alright, David?"

"I really don't know."

"What is the matter?"

"There is nothing in particular that I can point to as being wrong."

"Have you heard from home? Is your mother alright?" Carmelita asked in rapid succession.

"I plan to call home today. When last I spoke with Baxter he was expecting her to be discharged from the hospital this weekend."

"That means she has improved."

"Well, she was showing signs of improvement at the time of my conversation with him."

"Did he say that?"

"Yes."

"Then you should be happy."

"I agree."

"You agree, but are you happy?"

"I think so."

"Then stop brooding and start living."

"Every time I move toward achieving that goal, something or someone gets in the way," David said. He never got around to telling Carmelita about Crystal Mendoza's behavior which by then he was beginning to tolerate. In fact, each time she got cozy with him he yielded a little more than the previous time. She sensed it and resolved to be less aggressive in her pursuits. *It is only a matter of time before he succumbs*, she reasoned.

"It's not like you to allow little things to get you down, David."

"Carmelita, what's troubling me is not something I can dismiss easily. It could be ominous."

"It seems to be significant."

"Quite frankly, it is."

"Then perhaps we should get together and talk about it."

"We could meet but I would prefer not to discuss the issue right now."

"It involves Mrs. Mendoza, doesn't it?"

No! She didn't go there, he thought but asked, "Why would you even think of such a thing?"

"It's intuition, you might say."

Intuition my ass, he thought. *Crystal must have been feeding you a lot of shit.* After a brief moment of silence he said, "Crystal Mendoza is the least of my problem." He lied.

"Right now Crystal is your problem. Don't kid yourself, David."

"What gives you that impression? I really don't have a problem with her."

"Perhaps you do not see it as such but she is your problem. She is leading you on and she is tenacious, wicked, relentless, and potentially disastrous."

"You know something, Carmelita, I will cross that bridge when I come to it."

"David, you are already on that bridge. If you are not careful you wouldn't get across."

"I am a Trini., girl, and I am as resilient as they come. I will get there and I do hope that you are with me when I arrive."

Carmelita was silenced by what David said. She was unable to speak for several seconds. *What are his true feelings?* She wondered. Unlike Crystal, she didn't ask him if he loved her. His actions seem to indicate that but she had seen such actions before with Sylvester Pierce, aka Hedges, and more recently with TK, both of whom turned out to be failures. *I cannot take anything for granted*, she thought. *I believe he cares about me but does he love me? How will I know?* She wondered.

"What is the matter?" David asked when Carmelita did not respond.

"Oh, nothing, I was just thinking."

"What were you thinking about?"

"I was thinking about life in general and what it could be like with you in particular."

"Are you serious?"

"I couldn't be any more serious."

"Oh! Carmelita, I am so glad to hear that."

"Why, are you having the same thoughts?" she asked boldly

"Oh, yes. I thought you knew."

"How would I have known? You have never told me."

"Couldn't you tell from my actions?"

"No. I thought perhaps you were good at it."

"What did you think I was good at?"

"Acting," said Carmelita. Perhaps you rehearsed a lot."

"Girl, you are just too funny at times, in a nice sort of way I must add."

"Is that so?"

"Yes. I am sure you know that."

"I have heard it said. I do not know it to be true."

"It is true. That's one of the things I love about you," David said. He was reluctant to utter those three little words, *I love you,* which Carmelita wanted to hear from him so badly for so long. Yet she was hesitant to ask him directly.

"What are you doing later today?" she asked instead.

"How much later today are you talking about?"

"Let's say two o'clock or two-thirty perhaps."

"I have nothing planned."

"Can we meet?"

"We certainly can. Would you like to meet at your place or mine?"

"Have you forgotten that Mama is here? The logical place for us to meet will be at yours."

"Okay. Would two o'clock be convenient?"

"That's fine."

"I'll see you then, bye."

"Bye, David."

As soon as they hung up the telephones David had a concern, a legitimate one he thought. *Victor would be at church most of the day. Dallas and her brother are more than likely to be out as they always are on weekends. Crystal no doubt would be lonely and may be seeking his companionship. What will I do in that case?* He wondered.

As he lay on his back looking at the ceiling and thinking of a possible solution to the predicament he might find himself in, his telephone rang. He answered, "Hello!"

"David, this is Crystal. Could you come down here for a few minutes?"

"Does it have to be now, Mrs. Mendoza?"

"Crystal! Just call me Crystal. The sooner the better," she said.

David looked at the time. It was 11:35 so he said, "Okay, Crystal. I am on my way."

"Thank you."

"You are welcome," he said.

He was confident that he would be there for no more than half an hour, and decided that it would be an opportune time for him to pay her for his boarding and lodging for the period of time he would be away visiting his mother. When he got down the stairs the kitchen door was open and he smelled tobacco. He knocked at the door and entered. Crystal was sitting at the kitchen table and she smiled a seductive sort of smile that made him cringe.

"Why are you cowering?" she asked as she pushed the chair back, stretched out her legs and placed her heels slightly apart on the table top while she puffed on a cigarette.

What's up with the salacious act? He wondered before she said, "Sit down, David."

He took a seat at the opposite end of the table and that prompted her to ask, "Why are you sitting all the way over there?"

"This seat was vacant."

"So are these," said Crystal as she pointed to the seats at her right and to her left. "Or is it that you are afraid of these terrific legs?"

"They are not like anything I haven't seen before."

"I know. That is why you should be comfortable with me by now."

"Oh, before I forget, here is the money for my rent. It covers the time I would be away."

Crystal took the cash he handed her and said, "I told you that you didn't have to do that."

"I know but I may come back broke."

She counted the money, rested it on the table and said, "This is more than you need to pay me."

"I am paying for two weeks instead of one."

"Okay, suit yourself, David."

"Thank you. Anyway, why did you call me here?"

"I just felt like talking to someone."

"We could have spoken on the telephone."

"That's not the same."

"What is different?"

"We can look at each other as we speak."

"What's the difference?" he repeated.

"These," said Crystal. "I know you would enjoy them. You are just a little shy right now." David did not respond so she continued, "Seriously, David. Why are you afraid of me?"

"Why do you think that I am afraid of you?"

"Because of how you behave when we are together."

"I do not behave any differently with you from how I behave with anyone else."

"That is what you think. I have observed your interaction with Mildred and Carmelita."

"That is garbage! Mildred is a classmate of mine just as your daughter, Dallas, and that is how we interact, nothing more nothing less."

"You haven't gone dancing with Dallas."

"She has never asked me to."

"What?"

"You heard me. I am more than likely to do so if she invited me."

"That is my daughter you are talking about."

"What is so wrong? Like I said before, we are class mates and we are friends."

"Okay! What about Carmelita?"

"What about her?"

"Is she a friend also?"

"Yes, of course," David said.

"Are you trying to tell me there is no intimacy between you two?"

"I am not trying to tell you anything. You are prying, and if by intimacy you are referring to our confidence, then the answer is yes."

"Are you calling what I have been observing confidence?"

"I don't know what you think you have observed. So you can call it what you wish; relationship, understanding, closeness, whatever! It is what it is." His tone was gruff so Crystal moved closer to him at the other end of the kitchen table.

"I didn't mean to upset you," she said.

"Whether or not you meant to upset me, you managed to do just that. I will see you later," he said and left.

TWENTY-TWO

David returned to his room and looked at the time. It was 12:05, a mere half an hour had elapsed since he left to visit with Crystal. He threw himself across the bed and thought of what Carmelita said. *She was right*, he reasoned. Crystal is relentless in seeking immediate relief from whatever ails her. If I am not careful she will get in the way of what I am hoping to accomplish. *I hope she doesn't come up here within the next two hours*, he thought. *She is so driven, even when the odds are against her.* He thought of how he might be able to appease her without having to succumb to her every quirky desire. Then he fell asleep.

Two hours later there was a knock at the door that awakened him. He got up and moved cautiously toward the door thinking it might be Crystal Mendoza but hoping it would be Carmelita. *Crystal never knocks*, he remembered when he opened the door and saw Carmelita standing there smiling. He stepped aside and she walked in leaving the door ajar. She was uncertain as to whether or not it was appropriate for her to close the door. He, however, pulled it in and locked it. He had never personally locked his door before, although Crystal did at some time prior.

As he turned around, Carmelita was still standing there with her childhood memory of her mother saying, *you should always wait to be offered a seat*. David hugged her, she relaxed and reciprocated. They held each other tightly for several seconds before he said, "Sit down, girl."

"Thank you," she said as she sat on the chair at the desk.

"You are welcome, and looking fabulous as usual I should add,"

"Thanks again," Carmelita said as she smiled graciously.

"How is my godson today?"

"He was a little cranky this morning after church but he was doing a lot better when I left him."

"That's good,"

"Yeah, Mama is really good with him."

"How is she?"

"She is fine. I think she is falling in love with Brooklyn, and she is becoming very attached to Elvin."

"That could be to our, I mean your benefit," David said with a slip of the tongue and Carmelita did not miss it.

"You are right. Mama has been talking about staying longer, and taking him to Trinidad with her when she is leaving. If she does, that would give us some time to get on our feet, accrue some funds that is."

We are thinking along the same lines, David thought but he asked, "Shouldn't we make our education our number one priority?"

"It is already priority number one but to accomplish it requires resources."

"What kind of resources are you talking about?"

"Foremost is the need for financial resources."

"In our case that need has already been met."

"How have we satisfied that need?"

"Well, since I have been here I have worked and paid tuition for the first part of my education. In a few weeks I will graduate with a Bachelor of Science degree and a skill. You in turn, have made the first step in that direction by applying to college, and in your case, tuition is free. What more do we need?"

"We need each other. We need desire, drive, perseverance, and courage," Carmelita said.

"I firmly believe we have all of that."

"Then we need to make sacrifices," Carmelita said.

"We both took our first steps in that direction when we gave up our cushy jobs in Trinidad and Tobago to migrate to the USA."

"You are right but there are more sacrifices to be made if we hope to accomplish our goals."

"What more can we do, Carmelita?" asked David. "We do not squander money on overly expensive designer clothing, sneakers, shoes and, or electronic gadgets. We do not hang out at street corners, we are not into illegal drugs, or legal ones for that matter, and we are not the partying types."

"I know what we are," Carmelita said.

"What?"

"We are perfect together,"

That statement from Carmelita was exactly what David needed to hear. It provided a window of opportunity for him to interject into the conversation what he was longing to say, so without further hesitation he uttered the three little words, "*I love you*, Carmelita," he said boldly.

She was elated, sprung to her feet and tossed herself onto the bed next to him, "I love you so much, David," she said and kissed him. For the next twenty minutes or so their conversations diminished to an occasional whisper of three words or less. Then Carmelita spoke up. "I see your books are all packed," she said as she sat up and looked around the room.

"I did that a few days ago."

"You should bring them down."

"I will."

"What are you waiting for? I have already created some space for them."

"Yes, you did say that. I will bring them to you today."

"You can do that right now."

"Is it that you are ready to leave?"

"Unfortunately, yes. Elvin needs to be fed."

"I understand," David said as he too sat up.

Five minutes later they left the room together. David carried the books and Carmelita followed him down the stairs. When they reached her second floor apartment door, he waited at the left of the doorway as she rang the bell. Mrs. Jackman opened the door and smiled broad when she saw him.

"David, it is nice to see you," said Mrs. Jackman. "Come in."

Carmelita stepped back and allowed David to enter first. She then closed the door behind her and pointed to an area where she intended to store David's books. "You can put them right there," she said.

He placed the box of books where she wanted them and said, "Thank you."

"You are welcome. Please sit down," she said as she pointed to the couch in the room.

"Thank you, Carmelita but I cannot stay."

"It's okay, I understand."

He really wanted to spend more time with her and the baby but because her mother was there he felt that his presence might make her uncomfortable. To him it was really an issue of privacy, particular for Mrs. Jackman. The apartment was nothing more than a kitchenette. It was a larger space than he or any of the other young men who boarded and lodged with the Mendoza's had but it was, nevertheless, an open space.

"Bye Mrs. Jackman," David said.

"Goodbye, son," she replied as he and Carmelita walked toward the door.

"I will call you later," she said.

"Please do."

"I promise."

"Okay, bye."

"Bye, David," she said as he walked away.

As he approached his door, he heard his telephone ringing. He rushed in but he missed the call. *Who could that have been*? He wondered but quickly turned his attention to something else. He gathered all of his washable, soiled clothing and linens, and took them to the Laundromat where he dropped them off to be washed, dried, and folded. Although that was a bit more costly than if he had done them himself, he felt the time it would have taken him, could have been spent doing something else.

He returned home and completed some mathematics assignments that were due in class the next day, then he laid back and relaxed with a novel to read just for the fun of it. Reading for pleasure was a passion of his since childhood. He grew up in Belmont, Port of Spain, under strict parental supervision, in a neighborhood where there was not much outdoor activity apart from whatever he engaged in while at school. There wasn't a television in the home either.

Every Sunday after they returned home from church service David's mother took him and his four siblings to the public library. There, the boys; David, Baxter, Stanley, Ivan, and Bernard were encouraged to borrow one book each which they were expected read from cover to cover in the week ahead. *You are allowed no more than one*, their mother, Yolanda Cassel always insisted. At the end of the week on Saturday evenings, she would ask for a short review of the literature from each child. The children were never forced to read, they were only encouraged to do so, and soon it became the most desirable undertaking in the Cassel's household.

David's passion for reading had not changed over the years. He resorted to reading whenever he was distressed. He read novels, magazines, the bible, and newspapers. He was an avid reader. That kept him grounded, off the streets and out of the legal system. It has at least in part, been responsible for his resounding academic success. Although he argues that it was the maxim of *Discipline, Tolerance, and Perseverance* heard often in T & T that had been his guiding light throughout his academic pursuits. It's a dictum he insisted should be instilled in every child if we as a people hope to move out of the academic, social, and financial morasses we have been mired in.

As he lay in bed reading, it occurred to him that he didn't call Mildred to let her know that he had confirmed his travel arrangements and would be leaving for Trinidad on the morning of April 15th., a mere two weeks away. Just as he was about to do that his telephone rang. He answered. It was Crystal. "What are you doing right now?" she asked.

"I am studying," he said. He lied as he thought, *even if she walked in here right now she wouldn't know the difference. I am reading and to her probably, one book is like any other.*

His thinking was correct. Only three minutes had elapsed when Chrystal Mendoza walked into the room and asked, "Why are you always studying?" David did not answer so she asked again, "Don't you ever get tired of it?"

"I believe I told you once before that my only reason for being here is to pursue an education."

"Yeah right, you are twenty-six years old right now, what happens if you die at twenty-nine?"

"I will be buried."

"Then all of that time and money would have been wasted."

Did she tell her son that? Could that be the reason he hangs out at street corners smoking weed with friends instead of going to school? He wondered before he responded. "I may die at twenty-nine but suppose I live until I am ninety-two, what quality of life would I have without an education?" he asked. Crystal did not respond so he continued by asking, "Why do you have such an aversion to education?"

"I do not. I have never objected to Dallas going to college."

"Why then do you always have something negative to say about my educational pursuits?"

"Look, you are a man. Victor does quite well with very little education."

David was stunned to hear that from Crystal. *I wonder how many women of color tell that to their sons. Could that be the reason there are so few black men attending college?* He questioned himself but got no answers, so he said to her, "There are differences."

"What are the differences?"

"First of all, Victor is more than twice my age and it is obvious that he has had some good opportunities which he has taken full advantage of. Secondly, he lives here. This is his home. He is entitled to all of the rights and privileges as an American citizen. If it ever becomes necessary for him to draw upon them, he can. I, on the contrary, am a foreign student. I am here temporarily for the purpose of getting an education. I cannot lose sight of my goal."

"I didn't come up here to listen to your preachy shit."

"Then why are you here?"

Crystal did not or could not answer, so David continued. "I was simply trying to explain to you why I cannot behave like your husband, Victor or your son, Daniel,"

"I do not expect you to be like either of them unless..." Crystal stopped short of saying what she intended.

"Unless what?" David asked.

"You cannot be like Victor or Daniel unless you are an impressionist."

"Well, I am not an impersonator and I certainly wouldn't want to mimic your son. While your husband does have some admirable qualities, I wouldn't want to imitate him either."

"What exactly are you trying to say about my family, David?"

"All I am saying is that I like being me."

"I like you too, David, but right now you are pissing me off."

Why? I did not invite you up here, he thought but said, "I was lying here trying to get some reading done quietly. You came uninvited and find that you do not want to hear what I have to say, so why don't you leave? Oh, no! You don't have to do that. You own the damn place."

Crystal Mendoza was shocked into silence for more than a minute while David anticipated the worst. Then suddenly she smiled, got up from where she sat at the desk, moved toward the bed where David lay clutching the novel he was reading.

"You are mannish. Yeah, I always like that in a man," she said.

David shifted his tired body away from the forward edge of the single bed, not to accommodate her, but in a futile effort to distance himself from her. Crystal responded by planting her right knee firmly onto the mattress. With her left elbow on the pillow, she turned his head toward her with her right hand. Not much effort was needed because David did not resist. She kissed him and he reciprocated. What she did next was unthinkable but he was accommodating.

Shortly thereafter his telephone rang. "Don't answer it," she said.

"It might be important," he replied as the thought of his ailing mother crossed his mind. Nevertheless, he complied with Crystal's zany request.

TWENTY-THREE

David eventually got around to informing Mildred of his planned departure from New York for a short Caribbean vacation. Although she knew of his intention to visit his ailing mother in Trinidad, he never gave her an itinerary until April 6th, a little more than one week before his travel date of April 15th.

"How long do you plan on staying?" she asked

"I will be there for two weeks," said David. "My return flight is scheduled for April 27th."

"Does your landlady know that?"

"Of course she knows. I even paid her in advance for the two weeks I plan to be away."

"Did she have a problem with it?"

"I don't think so. If she did, she did not express it."

"You will be away during spring break, aren't you?"

"Yes."

"That suggests to me that you would miss one week of classes."

"That is the plan exactly," said David. "Originally, I thought of March 15th as a departure date, with the same return schedule of April 27th."

"That meant you would have missed two weeks of classes."

"You've gotten it right. I reconsidered because it is so much easier to make up one week of missed lectures than it is to make up two."

"You are right. Also, you wouldn't want anything like that to hinder you from graduating."

"That is true. I am paying for all of my courses, and there is nothing I would dislike more than having to pay for the same course or courses twice."

"That is the right approach."

"Unfortunately, too many people do not see it that way."

"That holds true only for those people who are New York City residents because the state pays their tuition. For all of the out-of-state students like me, it comes out of our pockets."

"That is too general a statement, David. I attend school as a New York City resident but I see it your way. Ultimately it's the taxpayers who pay."

"That might be true for you but many of the other recipients don't see it that way."

"Could that be the reason some of our classmates do not put any effort into their studies?"

"It just might be."

"They are squandering great opportunities."

"Unfortunately, that is not how they see it."

"How else could it be looked at?"

"I don't know, David," said Mildred. "To be quite honest, I do not care about their behaviors."

"Their failure could become a drag on society and in the end it reflects badly on all of us."

"It is not their failure that would be the encumbrance. They would."

"Is there anything we can do to help?"

"Yes, of course," said Mildred. "We can become school teachers again and exert our influence on young minds in an effort to change attitudes so they may envision a bright future through education. We can also just continue what we are doing and in the process, pull ourselves up and out of the doldrums with the hope that others may do the same."

"How many students can a teacher really steer in that direction when all around them they are bombarded with other thoughts, images, messages, and values?"

"I don't know. However, if two or three are convinced and they grow up to convince four or five, there will be a ripple effect."

"That can take several generations."

"True. If nothing is done, however, several generations later everything would be the same or worse."

"Could that be what we are witnessing on campus today?"

"Perhaps what we are seeing is the result of generations of neglect."

"You may be correct. It is the type of neglect that led so many to innovate and consequently become entwined in the legal system; either incarcerated, on probation or parole."

"I agree," said David. "Without an education, technical skill, or athletic finesse, one's choices are limited."

"What can anyone do in those situations?"

"One's only recourse is unskilled labor which may be a hard way to earn a living, but an honest way nevertheless. On the contrary though, young people with aptitude who neglected to develop proficiency and marketable skills often are resentful about doing those jobs."

"I am not so sure about that. My job can be considered menial and I do it without acrimony."

"Your approach is to use your job as a means to an end. It is not the end in or of itself."

"You may be right. If one thinks he or she is stuck in such a position with no way out of the quagmire, animosity often sets in," David said.

"I am not sure about any of that," said Mildred. "Like you, I am speculating as to why our classmates are so woefully lazy."

"Are they truly indolent, or is it that they are underprepared for college?"

"I don't know the answer to that, David."

"Neither do I. We can conjecture but that is of no help to us nor to them, is it?"

"It certainly isn't. At this juncture, I think that we are doing exactly what we need to do."

"Just what is that, Mildred?"

"We need to pursue our education as if with blinders on and not be distracted."

"That is absolutely right. We should avoid distraction until we have achieved our goal."

"Yes. When we are out of this abyss we then can concentrate on helping others."

"Do you really consider what we are doing to be abysmal?"

"Our educational pursuit is not terrible but it has placed us in a social and financial chasm."

"You are probably on to something, Mildred."

"What are you thinking now?"

"That just might be the reason so few of the brothers are on campus."

"It might be part of the reason. I believe that to be a lot more complex than you and I will ever understand."

"However multifaceted the reason may be, my question still is, why can't more of us see the benefits of attaining an education?"

"You ask the most difficult questions, David."

"Why is that so difficult? They are not on campus. They are not on Wall Street. Where the hell are they?"

"Many are in the military," Mildred said.

"If they were in college they may have gotten deferments like others have."

"True."

"Those in the military are a small percentage of the larger population of black men anyway."

"I do not know that to be a fact? Perhaps it is."

"If we were to assume that it is, the question still remains, where are the others?"

"They are incarcerated perhaps."

"How can you say that?"

"I am only repeating what is well known."

"I have never heard that said before, so where did you get that information?"

"The Justice Department's statistics show that a disproportionate percentage of black men between the ages of 20 – 29 are incarcerated."

"What is a disproportionate number anyway?"

"Statistically, 4.0 per cent of the population of black men in the United States as compared to 1.5 per cent of Hispanic men, and 1.0 per cent of white men are incarcerated."

"We need to be cautious about statistical information," David said.

"Why?" Mildred asked.

"You mentioned earlier that many young black men are in the military. You will agree, no doubt, that many have returned from the military."

"Yes."

"You are aware I am sure, that many of those who returned have come back with terrible drug habits."

"I am aware of that."

"Are you conscious of the fact also that as a consequence of their drug addiction many of these young men get in trouble with the law?"

"Yes, that may be the reason so many are currently in jail."

"Mildred, this is 1968. Many of the young black men in prison are there not because they have committed more egregious criminal acts than their white or Hispanic counterparts, but because they received more severe punishments."

"Just what are you trying to say, David?"

"What I am saying to you is that in many instances when similar breaches of the law occurred the punishment was considerably more severe for the black man."

"Are you trying to tell me that more black men are sent to prison for similar offences for which white or Hispanic men are fined or given probation?"

"In this decade and before yes, you have gotten it right at last."

"Thanks, David. That was very interesting. I hope we can continue this discussion when you return."

"You are welcome. We have been on the phone for a while now and I know that you have a lot to do, so I am saying goodbye, and I will contact you as soon as I get back."

"You can call me before you return. In fact, you should."

"Okay. I will."

"Take care, Bye."

"Bye, Mildred," David said and hung up the phone.

TWENTY-FOUR

Friday, April 12th David called in sick. He was due to start his vacation the following Monday and was scheduled to leave for Trinidad the next day, Saturday, April 13th. He was well aware of the company's policy about employees calling in sick just before they were scheduled to go on vacation or when they were due back to work after a vacation. That was something they frowned upon. He, however, saw no risk to it because that was a time of low unemployment. There were more jobs available than there were workers to fill them. *If they replace me while I am gone, I will find something else as soon as I return*, he thought.

David considered his job to be menial but in reality it was not. The company produced precision instruments. He was a trained technician who tested the finished parts used in their clocks and in helicopters built by an aircraft company that supplied the military. He was also one of their best workers on the assembly line. Whenever the need arose for him to fill in for someone who was out sick or on vacation, he performed remarkably well. He was good at what he did, although not irreplaceable.

He spent the first half of that Friday tidying his room. When that was accomplished, he took all of his dirty clothes to the Laundromat where he dropped them off to be cleaned. The attendant assured him that they would be ready in about three hours. His first thought was to use the same suitcase he arrived in the US with three years earlier. He would carefully select and fit the best of what he had in it, then throw out whatever else that couldn't fit. He quickly abandoned that thought and bought a new and larger suitcase from a discount store on Broadway. He picked up his clothes from the Laundromat when they were ready, went home, and packed all of his belongings in the new suitcase. He then leaned the old one against the door to be taken out as garbage.

Suddenly there was a knock at the door. *That's Carmelita*, he thought. *Crystal never knocks.* He moved toward the door and opened it. Crystal stepped inside and smiled. "Your place looks exceptionally clean today," she said. There was no response from David so she asked, "Are you expecting company?"

"Yes," he said. He lied with the hope that she would leave. That hope was dashed when she pulled the chair from the desk and sat down. He looked at her in a quizzing manner as if to ask, *it's Friday, don't you have anything to do at home*?

"What was that about?" she asked.

"What was what about?"

"That look you gave me. Are you wondering why I am here?"

"Yes. Why are you here, Crystal?"

"*Gee! He is comfortable with my first name now*, she thought but asked, "Are you leaving tomorrow?" She did not answer his question.

"Yes, but what that has to do with you being here right now?"

"I came to say goodbye and make a peace offering."

You said your goodbye. I do not want what you have to offer. Now leave, he thought. Crystal didn't budge. Instead, she moved from the chair to the bed, kicked off her slippers, unbuttoned her blouse, and lay back comfortably. She looked around the room and said, "You have really cleaned up the place, David."

"That's just the way I was raised," he said.

"I do not see the connection, but that is beside the point."

"Just what is the point?"

"Oh! Forget about it." David looked at her but said nothing. She smiled and said, "You don't seem happy to see me."

Am I ever? He wondered but asked, "What can I tell you, Crystal?"

You can say that you love me, Crystal thought but she did not expect him to say it nor did she express that thought. Instead, she said, "Come, sit here," and she shifted her body from the edge of the single bed to make room for him. He sat next to her and she touched him tenderly. She stroked his back, his arms, and his thighs. Suddenly he got up.

"I have some important things to do," he said.

"That can wait, David."

"It could, but why should it? I have the time now."

"David, if you leave here without…." Crystal stopped short of saying what she intended, but David responded nonetheless.

"I wouldn't be able to return?" he said in a questioning tone.

"I didn't say that. You said it."

"That's what you were thinking, that's your plan, isn't it?"

"You do not know what my thoughts are."

I am on to you, he thought but said, "Okay, Crystal, have it your way."

"I am not having it my way right now but eventually I will or..."

"Or what? I am not bothered by your veiled threats, Crystal."

She noticed that he was calling her Crystal. Not once that afternoon did he call her Mrs. Mendoza, and despite their disagreement, she continued to be hopeful that he would be tender with her. He, however, was thinking only of Carmelita. Then suddenly Crystal asked, "What is it about me you do not like, David?"

The question took him by surprise. *How can I answer that without making a bad situation even worse*? He wondered.

"You are a very nice person, Crystal. I am glad that I met you. It was a pleasure. However, we are at least a generation apart."

"I am not asking you to marry me, just…" Crystal paused then said, "I am already married."

"That is exactly the problem, or at least one of them."

"What other problem is there?"

"You are my mother's age," David said and prepared himself mentally for an outburst of anger from her.

"Why is that a problem? Older men get with young women all the time and no one complains about it," she said calmly.

"Get with?"

"Yes! You know damn well what I mean. Do you want me to be more explicit?"

I really don't care. Why can't you get it? David wondered but said, "I am not comfortable with that."

"What are you not comfortable with, David? We have had the time, the opportunity, and the convenience. What more do you want, what the hell is your problem?"

"Am I the one with the problem?"

"What do you mean by that? I confided in you and now you are throwing it back at me?"

"I am not throwing anything back at you. I am saying simply that I cannot satisfy your need."

"Do you think that I am the only one with such needs? Mildred has needs. Carmelita has needs. What do you tell them?"

"I have had just about enough of your foolishness for one day."

"You know something…," Crystal paused. She then said, "You are leaving tomorrow, just leave."

"I am all set to go."

"Then go and…." She did not complete her train of thought.

"…and don't come back," David said, completing what he thought Crystal intended to say.

"I did not say that. You said it," Crystal replied while thinking, *I will make certain you do not come back here if you continue to be difficult with me.*

"You didn't say it but it crossed your mind."

"Are you a mind reader now?"

David did not respond to Crystal's question. Instead, he thought of the many things he wanted to accomplish before night fall. Then he pointed to the trash he had collected, including the old suitcase and said, "I am going to take these out to the curb for the garbage pick-up tomorrow."

He was hoping that Crystal would leave at the same time but she did not. Instead, she made herself more comfortable. As soon as he left the room she took off her blouse, lay on her back with the palms of both hands up and under her head on the pillow. She looked up at the ceiling light, thought of turning it off but quickly decided against that. *He would like what he sees*, she thought.

David carefully placed his garbage next to a mound that was already there and walked back into the building. As he walked past Carmelita's second floor apartment he heard music playing softly and thought of knocking at the door but he did not. *If I do not get back upstairs right away, what will Crystal do next?* He wondered. Although he wasn't afraid of her, he had serious concerns about her reasoning.

As he walked into the room she smiled broadly where she lay looking like a woman's underwear model. Her skirt and blouse were hanging at the back of the only chair in the room. She beckoned him to her with a familiar motion of her right hand. He hesitated briefly at first but eventually he moved forward, sat on the bed, looked at her, but he did not speak.

"I was feeling a bit warm in here," she said.

"You didn't have to be here. Your place is air-conditioned."

"I know. It is a choice I made."

"Why me Lord?" David questioned softly as he looked up at the halo around the ceiling lamp.

"If not you who should it be?" Crystal asked.

"Are you speaking to, or for the good Lord?" asked David. "If he heard you he would probably say Victor Mendoza or Cedric Sebastian."

Crystal's response was not what he expected. He was certain that she would be very angry and probably storm out of his room, which was what he wanted. Instead, she started laughing as if she had been tickled. When the giggling stopped she hugged him, held him tightly and said, "Regardless of what you may think, I care a great deal about you."

"Yeah right!"

"I didn't think that you would believe me but it's the truth."

"None of that matters, Mrs. Mendoza. You have raised a family already. I am just coming into my own and only recently started thinking of a family."

"Is it with Mildred or Carmelita?"

"That question is rather intrusive."

"Why is it intrusive?"

"Both of those individuals are friends of mine just like Dallas is."

"Why bring Dallas into this discussion?"

"You may not appreciate hearing it, but like Mildred, she is a classmate and friend of mine."

"I am not a classmate of yours but am I your friend, David?"

David was floored by Crystal's question. After careful consideration, he responded by saying, "I am not your enemy so I guess I am your friend."

"You guess?"

"Yes."

"Yes meaning you presume, or yes meaning I am a friend of yours?"

David was in a quandary. He didn't know what to say. *Forty years from now if we are still alive, I will be sixty-five and you will be ninety-one*, he thought before he answered, "Yes, we are friends."

"Friendship implies closeness, doesn't it?"

"I believe that is one meaning of the word."

"Friendship also implies amity, doesn't it?"

"Yes."

"So we are friends, we are close, and we have good relations. Is that right?"

"You are right."

"Then why do you treat me with such disdain at times?"

"That is your view of my actions, but really, there is no derision toward you," David said. *I have been raised to respect my elders and for that reason and that reason alone, I cannot engage in a sexual encounter with you, which I believe is what you want.*, he thought.

It was as if Crystal read his thoughts when she said, "Before you leave here tomorrow morning, in fact, before I leave here this afternoon, we are going to remove that barrier, that wall of respect. I can assure you, after that you will have the highest regard for me."

"Are you giving me an ultimatum?"

"No. It is more of a challenge. I know you like to be challenged," Crystal said as she drew closer and wrapped her arms around him.

She expected him to resist and perhaps wriggle himself away from her but he did not. She smiled, kissed him, and he reciprocated. The telephone rang. He ignored it without any prompting from her. She was pleased, very pleased. Just when she was about to give up and find a way to punish him, he gave in.

TWENTY-FIVE

After wishing David a safe trip, Crystal Mendoza asked if there was anything she could do for him during the time he would be away. There was nothing he could think of and he made that known, so she kissed him, said goodbye and left. He regretted not applying for a Post Office box months earlier so that his mail could have been secured until his returned. He reasoned, however, that since those closest to him who corresponded with him by mail knew that he was coming home there was no reason for concern. *Whatever mail of mine that comes to the Mendoza's address would be of little or no significance.* He thought.

Two and a half hours had elapsed while Crystal lay in his single bed. He felt somewhat relieved after she left, but he was guilt ridden. He had originally planned to spend that afternoon with Carmelita, although she was not aware of his plan. He wondered whether the telephone call that came in during his erotic pleasures with Crystal came from her. He had no way of knowing with certainty. He thought of calling her but he was mortified. *She would be affronted if she knew that Crystal spent that much time up here*, he thought.

Once again the telephone started ringing. He reached for it quickly hoping that it would be her but it was Mildred.

"How are you, David?" she asked.

"I am fine."

"Hmm! You said that as if you weren't so sure."

"I am okay, really!"

"Well, that's good to hear," said Mildred. "I want to wish you a safe trip and I hope that all is well with your mother."

"Thank you."

"I would have liked to see you before you travel but I am sure you have a lot of last minute things to do."

"Yeah, it gets really crazy at the last minute," he said. He lied. There wasn't anything pending for him to do.

"Anyway, I hope to see you as soon as you get back."

"You most likely would."

That statement from David raised a red flag to Mildred and she asked, "Is everything okay with you and your landlady?"

"So far, yes. But I don't think that I want to come back here."

"Oh! Oh. Listen David, whatever the reason for your thinking, let me reassure you that the room here will be vacant when you get back and you would always be welcomed."

"Thanks, Mildred."

"Take care of yourself and I will see you in two weeks."

"Thanks again, bye."

"Bye, David."

He sighed but he wasn't sure what he was feeling. *Is it relief or is it a burden*? He wondered. He wasn't thinking of Crystal Mendoza's action as entrapment nor was he thinking of it as coercion. In fact, since he decided not to return to the Herkimer Street address ever again, he had put Crystal and whatever happened between them out of his mind. He had a knack for dismissing unpleasant thoughts. Mildred's kind offer came to mind but he hoped the need to accept would never arise. Finally, he decided that he should be prepared for any eventuality and would deal with them as they occur.

His telephone rang again. "Hello," he answered.

"This is Carmelita. I tried calling you earlier but I got no answer. I take it that you are still trying to get things done in the last minute."

"I am just about finished," he said.

"That's very good."

"Yes, it is quite a relief."

"Then you can join me for dinner." David did not respond so she asked, "David, are you there?"

"Yes, yes!"

"Are you free to have dinner with me?" she asked, essentially rephrasing her earlier statement into a question.

"What time would you like to have dinner?"

"It is entirely up to you, David."

"Is seven-thirty okay?"

"Seven-thirty is fine."

"I will see you then," said David. "We can ride the train downtown."

"There is no need for us to go out. I am cooking." He did not respond so Carmelita said, "I was of the impression that you always enjoyed my Mayaro, country cooking."

"I do."

"Then what is the problem?"

"There is no problem as such. I just thought…" He hesitated to say exactly what he was thinking.

"What are you thinking, David?"

"There are some things I would like to discuss with you."

"We can talk here."

"We can but I would prefer not to."

"Why not, is it because Mama is here?"

"Yes."

"Let's not make that a problem. I can bring the meal up to your place."

"I know you can. You have done that before but I would prefer to go out with you."

"Okay, David. Have it your way. I'll be ready at seven-thirty."

"See you then, bye."

"Goodbye."

He got up immediately, walked down to the Mendoza's kitchen, and picked up the dinner labeled with his initials from among those Crystal had prepared for all of her boarders. No member of the Mendoza family was present so he did not linger. He returned to his room, emptied what he thought to be putrid food into a plastic bag, took it out, and placed it in a can at the curb to be picked up as garbage.

"Please forgive me for this Lord," he whispered. "Hopefully, it wouldn't happen again."

He went back upstairs, looked at the time and saw that it was 6:45 p.m., a mere forty-five minutes before he was supposed to meet Carmelita to go out to dinner. He thought he should lie down and rest but quickly decided against that.

I wouldn't want Crystal to barge in here just when I am about to go out with Carmelita, he thought. He knew that Victor usually closed the dry cleaning plant at about that time and came directly home. He was aware also that Crystal never left her apartment when Victor was there, yet he felt some measure of trepidation. His anxiety wasn't about what Victor might think, say, or do. It was about Crystal's malicious intent, her deliberate efforts to keep him away from Carmelita, or to cause conflict between them.

At 7:00 p.m. he decided to take a walk and return on time to meet Carmelita to go out to dinner. *I am not going to stick around here and be hindered, dissuaded, or otherwise discouraged from doing what I want to do with or for Carmelita*, he thought as he left the building. On his way out he ran into Cedric Sebastian who apparently was coming home after a shopping spree.

I hope he isn't planning to give me anything to take home to his folks, David thought.

"Hey! David, how are you?"

"I am fine, and you?"

"As you can see, life is good. What else can I say?"

"Hey man, enjoy it while you can."

"Listen, David! Have you heard the rumor?"

"What rumor?"

"The Mendoza's are talking about selling the place."

"What place are they trying to sell?" David asked because he knew that Victor owned several dwellings in the neighborhood."

"This building in which we live," Cedric said.

"Why would they sell this building? It is their most profitable, Victor told me so himself."

"I don't know, man. I am only telling you what I heard."

"Thanks," David said. They shook hands and went their separate ways. Immediately, David dismissed what Cedric told him. *That's just another gossip thing*, he thought.

He walked over to the *Brothers Car Service* and reserved a car to take him to the airport for his 6:00 a.m. flight on BWIA (British West Indian Airways) the next morning. After giving the dispatcher all of the particulars, he returned home and rang Carmelita's doorbell. Somehow she knew it was him, so she came down the stairs and they met in the lobby just when he entered the building.

"You look marvelous," he said.

"Thank you," said Carmelita. "You look pretty good yourself."

They walked out of the building and hailed a gypsy cab that took them downtown. For some reason David no longer wanted to ride the train as he had originally planned. When they arrived at *Junior's*, a restaurant known internationally for its cheese cake and other delicacies, they were seated immediately and served shortly thereafter. It was just the sort of ambiance they needed to relax and converse with no fear or concern about interruptions from Crystal Mendoza or ringing telephones.

They discussed many things, including but not limited to their living conditions and what it would take to change that, their love for each other, their educational pursuits, family, politics, and the increasing decline in enrolment of black men in colleges across the USA. Two hours later when they were ready to leave, both agreed that was their first opportunity for a heart to heart talk. Each had a better understanding of the other's concerns, hopes, desires, and dreams. Their compatibility was undeniable.

They reaffirmed their love for each other but neither sought a commitment from the other. David stopped short of asking Carmelita to marry him but he felt certain that he would do so upon his return to the US. He did manage to deduce from her what her ring size was, although he didn't know how she really felt about marriage in general, or about marrying him in particular. He was aware that she hinted to TK several times before her pregnancy, during her gestation period, and before he vanished that they should have gotten married. *TK's unwillingness to get married followed by the way he abandoned them may have left her disillusioned and bitter but I hope not*, he thought.

As they left the restaurant, they held hands and walked across to the train station at Flatbush and Fulton Streets. When they arrived at their Herkimer Street address, Carmelita asked David if he needed help packing his luggage.

"I have already packed," he said.

"Is there anything at all that I can do for you?" David hesitated so Carmelita continued, "I know it is late and you probably want to get some rest before you travel. I will see you early in the morning," she said before they kissed each other goodnight. When she entered her apartment, her mother was awake but Elvin was sleeping.

"Why are you still up, Mama?" she asked.

"I couldn't go to sleep knowing that you are out there."

"I am okay. I am grown up now," said Carmelita. "Let's go to bed."

TWENTY-SIX

David was in the shower just before 3:00 a.m. when he heard a tap on the bathroom door. He turned the water off thinking perhaps, that once again Crystal was bothered by its flow. He stepped out of the tub, draped himself in a robe, moved forward and opened the bathroom door, but he was apprehensive.

"Why are you so jittery?" asked Carmelita before saying, "Good morning."

David breathed a sigh of relief and asked, "Is it that obvious?"

"Yes. You look as if you just saw a ghost."

"Sorry. I thought that witch was here again."

"Which witch?"

"Crystal Mendoza. Who else could it be?"

"David, that is not nice," Carmelita said with a scowl before asking, "Was she here earlier?"

"No!"

"Well, that was empathetic," she said sarcastically as she walked into his room and he closed the door behind them.

"Please sit down." He pointed to the bed as he sat in the chair with his damp robe still draped around him.

She looked around the room, saw his luggage and said, "I see that you are ready to go."

"Almost ready is more like it. I still have to get dressed. The taxi would be here soon."

"When are they picking you up?"

"They promised to have a cab here at four."

Perhaps I should have been here earlier, she thought but said, "That doesn't leave you much time."

"It's enough," said David. "All I have to do is get dressed." There was no comment from Carmelita.

He looked at his clothes that were laid out on the bed next to where she sat and immediately took off the robe, placed it on a hanger and hung it in the closet. "That's the only thing I am leaving here," he said.

He started to get dressed before Carmelita said, "I am sorry we can't spend more time together."

"I am sorry too, sweetheart," said David. "I wish I didn't have to be at the airport so early."

"Do you need to be there two hours before check-in?"

"That's what is suggested."

"Then I must leave you to get dressed."

"Why would you leave now? I am already dressed. You could at least wait until the taxi arrives."

He was tying his shoe laces by then and Carmelita made no attempt to leave. She was sad though. In spite of Crystal's attempts at cajoling, and sometimes badgering David into doing her bidding with the hope of keeping them apart, they remained close. They had become more than friends, and suddenly it seemed to her that she was losing him. *Every time I get close to someone, somehow, something or someone else gets in the way and eventually keeps us apart*, she thought.

"When you get into that taxi and leave here your room will be completely empty. That gives me the impression you are not planning on coming back," she said after looking around the room.

"This room might be empty except for my robe but my heart remains full."

"Full of warm blood I hope."

"Full of love for you, Carmelita."

"That is not just flattery, is it?"

"I am for real. I love you dearly. You know that."

Carmelita stood up. They kissed, and they hugged each other tightly. She started to cry but David didn't notice until the car horn blew and they eased their embrace.

"That is your cab," she said.

"Please don't cry, honey. I will only be gone for two weeks."

To Carmelita the issue was not one of time but of trust. She once placed her trust in Sylvester Pierce, aka Hedges, and was let down terribly. Years later she trusted Tyrone Khadevis otherwise known as TK, and that turned out to be a downer. She was afraid of repeating those mistakes again. *If I cannot or do not trust David, who is out there I could or should trust?* She wondered.

Although David was pursued by Crystal Mendoza for her own selfish reasons, and Mildred had an underlying fascination with him beyond that of their mutual friendship and interests as classmates, Carmelita found him to be different from either Hedges or TK. He was driven, against the odds at times in his effort to stay focused, purposeful, and undaunted in his pursuits. She liked that. She also liked the fact that he was an unselfish, caring, and giving individual. Not only did he pursue his dreams, he was encouraging her to follow hers also. *What more can I ask of him?* She wondered.

She dried her eyes, blew her nose and said, "I'll be here when you get back, sweetheart." She was unaware of rumors that the Mendoza's were trying to sell the property. They never told her, and neither did David. As far as he was concerned that was something he didn't believe, a rumor he had no intention of spreading or perpetuating.

They kissed each other again at the door to her second floor apartment, and said goodbye before he raced down the stairs, out of the building, and into the waiting taxi cab. By then it was exactly 4:00 a.m. and the driver did not hesitate to leave the scene. David was on his way and Carmelita went back to bed with mixed feelings of disappointment, hope, and optimism.

At the airport David viewed the monitors and saw that the flight to Trinidad was on time. He checked in and was directed to the appropriate gate. There, as he waited, he bought a newspaper, a chocolate bar, and a cup of coffee from one of two businesses in the area. It wasn't long before passengers in wheelchairs and those with young children were asked to come forward in preparation for boarding. After that announcement he quickly finished his coffee and placed the empty container in a trash can. Shortly thereafter a range of seat numbers including his own were called and he moved forward.

He boarded the aircraft and was ushered to his seat toward the middle of the plane. When his hand luggage was secured in the overhead compartment, he sat down and buckled his seat belt. As soon as they were airborne he leaned back, closed his eyes, thought of Carmelita and what he would like to do for her and her son. He thought of Mildred's kind offer to allow him to occupy the extra room in her apartment if that became necessary. He thought briefly of Crystal Mendoza and the possibility of her becoming a major distraction in his relentless, though guarded pursuit of an education.

During the first hour of the journey David read the newspaper. After that he fell asleep, perhaps because he had gotten very little sleep the night before. Whatever the reason, he slept soundly for almost two hours. Consequently, he missed breakfast. He requested a hot beverage and was promptly served. His choice was coffee although he could have had tea. By then more than three and a half hours had elapsed and the captain announced that it was sunny and 78^{0}F in Trinidad. He thanked the passengers for choosing BWIA as their carrier and asked the crew to prepare for the descent.

It was 10:30 p.m. when the plane touched down at Piarco International Airport outside of Port of Spain, Trinidad, Trinidad and Tobago. The passengers applauded and David wondered, *is this customary on all international flights or is it just a Caribbean custom*. Passengers were allowed to disembark at the front and rear of the aircraft. David hesitated briefly before deciding to move to the rear to exit. He felt extremely hot as he and other passengers walked across the tarmac to Trinidad and Tobago's *Customs and Immigration* at the International Arrivals Building.

Four and a half hours earlier I dressed so warmly to leave home on my way to JFK Airport. Now I am burning up here at Piarco International Airport, he thought. He did, however feel some relief as he entered the air conditioned airport building. It was an old building but it was freshly painted and welcoming. The entrance was lined with potted palms and the paintings of local artists adorned the walls.

David was not expecting anyone to meet him upon his arrival so he was prepared to take a taxi to his mother's place in Belmont, Port of Spain. He was pleasantly surprised to see that Baxter was there to pick him up. He was glad for the ride and glad also that he had taken something for his Mother and each of his siblings, including Baxter. As they drove from the airport to Port of Spain they had an amicable discussion about all the changes that had taken place since David left to study in the US. The animosity that surfaced when he refused to send Baxter the stereo system he wanted was forgotten, for the time being at least.

"How long are you here for?" Baxter asked.

"I planned a two-week stay."

"That is not enough time."

"Why isn't it enough time? My sole purpose for coming is to see Mom."

"That is my point exactly. She is fine and she has a lot planned for you, Bro."

"What can she have planned?"

"It is a long list of events that starts with a visit to the library on Sunday after church."

David started laughing before he said, "You can't be serious. No! She can't be serious."

"I am kidding about the library but the list is really long."

"Exactly what is on that list?"

"It starts with a visit to either Maracas or Mayaro Beach. There is a planned visit to the Pitch Lake, and a trip to Tobago to visit Aunt Ria."

"Is she strong enough to make those trips?"

"I asked her that very question."

"What did she say?"

"She swore that those are things she wants to do even if they are the last things she did with you."

"Huh."

"I hope you do not have other plans."

"I do not, at least not at the moment, not for my first week here anyway."

"That's good."

Port of Spain was bustling that Saturday morning as they entered the city. David was in awe as his brother maneuvered the little Asian made sedan up Charlotte Street to Queen's Park East, and across Jerningham Avenue to their home address on Belmont Circular Road.

"These cars are perfect for the narrow streets here," David said.

"That's why we drive them," Baxter responded.

"Thanks for meeting me and driving me here safely."

"You are welcome."

The brothers high-fived each other before entering their mothers living room, an indication that all was well again between them. Mrs. Cassel was sitting close to the door while waiting for them to arrive and although she wasn't as agile as David had been accustomed to seeing her move, she got up quickly enough and hugged him.

"I am so glad you are home," she said.

"I wanted to come as soon as I heard that you were ill."

"I was so sick, son. I thought I would die before I see you again."

"What made you so very sick?"

"I don't know."

Before David could question her further and before she could say anything else, Baxter interrupted. "The doctors did not suggest a diagnosis," he said.

"Are you telling me that after Mom was in the hospital for almost two weeks, they still couldn't tell what was wrong with her?"

"That's it exactly."

"That's unbelievable and unacceptable with all of the advances in medicine today."

"Those advances in medicine are taking place in the USA. This is T & T, my friend. Nothing is happening here, just look at the state of the hospital. It is like something from Joseph Lister's era."

"Is it that bad?"

"It is bad. The staff is poorly trained, conditions are unsanitary, workers are disrespectful, and most of the time they are unmannerly. It is horrible there."

"We can consider ourselves lucky that Mom is okay."

"Thank God she is better. There really isn't any thanks to them."

"They must have done something right."

"They did nothing at all. It was her will to live and the mercy of God why she survived."

Baxter was very angry as he spoke. It seemed as if he had forgotten that his mother was present. David was speechless for more than a minute or two before he said, "I am just so glad that your health has improved. I trust that you will continue to feel better." *My greatest wish is for you to see me graduate or at least know that I have,* he thought.

"I thank the Lord for his mercies," Mrs. Cassel said.

"We all must give thanks," said David. "We have been truly blessed."

Baxter said nothing further on the subject of his mother's health and no one asked what his thoughts were. *What do the others think*? David wondered. Their three younger siblings though close in age, were grown up and lived in different parts of the country; Chaguanas, San Fernando, and Mayaro respectfully. *Will I see them before I leave? Should I try to contact them now or at some later time?* He wondered but there were no answers. Baxter was not making any suggestions. In fact, he wasn't speaking at all.

"When are you going back, son?" Mrs. Cassel asked."

"I am scheduled to return on the 27th of April."

"Good. That means you are going to be here for two weeks."

"I will be in Trinidad for two weeks," said David. *Not necessarily here all of that time,"* he thought.

"That should allow us time to visit your Aunt Ria in Tobago. I am sure she would be happy to see you."

"I would love to visit Aunt Ria," David said.

"That's good. We only have to decide what we should do first."

"What else do we have to do, Mom?"

"There are a few other things I would like to do with you, but they are not pressing."

"Just what are they, Mom?"

"Well, I would like us to spend a day either at Maracas or Mayaro Bay."

"That's nice but didn't you say there were a few things you wanted us to do?"

You shouldn't indulge her, David. She would expect me to do all of the driving, Baxter thought but he did not express it.

"I would also like to visit the Pitch Lake."

"What's your interest in those places, Mom?"

"Curiosity I guess. I have never been to any of those places and people come from all over the world to visit them."

"That's fair enough."

"Please!" Baxter lamented.

"What is your problem? We are not asking you to drive us anywhere. We can take a tour just like the tourists do," said Mrs. Cassel. "You seem to think that everyone is dependent on you."

Baxter did not respond but David said, "It is okay, Mom. We will do what is necessary."

"Thank you," said Mrs. Cassel, *Why can't they understand why you are my favorite son*? She wondered. "You are always so willing, so kind and gentle, God will bless you, son."

Baxter hissed his teeth and stormed out of the house.

"What is the matter with him now?" she asked.

"He is a little upset right now, Mom."

"Why?"

"I don't know, Mom. Perhaps it is because you wished me God's blessing in his presence."

"I wish God's blessing on all of my children. He knows that."

"How are the others?"

"I honestly don't know. I have not seen or heard from Stanley, Ivan, or Bernard since you left Trinidad." She named the brothers in chronological order of their births.

David was shocked into silence for several seconds before he asked, "Where are they now?"

"I do not know for certain but I think they still live at the same places as before," said Mrs. Cassel. David knew where they lived so she felt there was no need to confirm that. Instead, she continued, "You always asked about them and extended your best wishes but I was never able to pass on that information."

It saddened him to know that his brothers were distancing themselves from their mother who struggled so much to raise them after their father's death. He was convinced that it was not because of some underlying animosity but because of the selfish nature of people in general, in a nation that was rapidly moving toward industrialization and perhaps experiencing the aftermaths of sudden wealth.

"It is good that Baxter is still here with you,"

"Not really. He is no different from the others because I see him only occasionally. Those who don't know the facts may think that because he lives here I derive some sort of benefit from his presence. No! He doesn't pay rent or buy groceries, and if I need any little thing done around the house I have to pay for it or ask the neighbor's son for a favor. God bless him. He is always so willing."

"Who took you to the hospital when you became ill?" David asked as his concerns mounted.

"The neighbor's son, Salem did. He drove me there and waited with me for several hours until the doctor decided to admit me."

"Where was Baxter?"

"I don't know. Two days after I was admitted to the hospital he showed up. He only uses these premises as his home address. Sometimes I do not see him for weeks. He comes in late at nights when I am already asleep and he leaves early on mornings before I am awake."

David was struggling with his emotions by then. *I couldn't abandon my studies to return home now that I am so close to graduation. Even if I could do that, I wouldn't want to leave Carmelita and Elvin in a lurch. I am, nevertheless, deeply concerned about Mom being here alone,* he thought.

He couldn't think of an immediate solution to what he perceived as a serious problem; his mother's day to day concerns. *Could I convince my brothers to be more compassionate, to lend a hand where and when she needs it most so she does not have to rely on a stranger as much as she currently does?*" He wondered but there were no answers.

TWENTY-SEVEN

David was happy that his mother's health had improved and happier still that he sacrificed the time to visit with her. Together they were able to accomplish everything she had planned. After they visited the North coast beach and the Pitch Lake he wondered why she chose those venues. *I hope that those were not her last wishes*, he thought. The trip to Tobago was especially gratifying to him. His Aunt Ria was overjoyed to see him and he made no secret of how he felt about meeting her again after they had been apart for twelve or thirteen years.

Three days before his return to the USA he met Stanley in San Fernando. Together, they drove to Chaguanas, picked up Ivan and headed to Mayaro to visit Bernard who lived there while working with the Petroleum Prospecting Company (PPC) in Guayaguayare. To David that was the most exciting visit. Bernard's wife, Jessica, cooked a scrumptious meal which reminded him of Carmelita's cooking. *She was right*, he thought of Carmelita. *Mayaro people can really cook.*

Bernard had quite an assortment of alcoholic drinks for them to choose from. Stanley, however, abstained from drinking because he had to drive David and Ivan back to Chaguanas and Belmont respectively. The others had no such restraint so they indulged themselves. Their preferences were rum and coconut water and there was an abundance of both, Mayaro being the coconut grove of T & T, and as such, a Caribbean paradise. Very soon what started out as a family gathering, became an unplanned party.

When some of Bernard's friends from the neighborhood joined them, Jessica started playing some calypso music, and Bernard introduced his brothers to everyone. He was genuinely happy to have them and offered some excuses, though feeble ones, to David as reasons why the brothers in Trinidad do not see each other or their mother very often.

"I understand," David said, but he wondered, *does he really think that I am buying that crap*?

As the evening wore on, Stanley suggested that the time for them to leave was fast approaching, and that prompted Bernard to ask, "Why are you rushing?"

"It is a long drive back and I still have to take Ivan to Chaguanas and David to Belmont before going home."

"Come on Stanley! It's not that far. After all, Trinidad is quite small."

Since you are so conscious of the island's size, why don't you visit Mom more often? David wondered, but he did not speak.

"Both Ivan and I have to work tomorrow," Stanley said.

"When last either of you had a day off?" Bernard asked.

"It has been a while, for me at least," Ivan said.

"Then take one tomorrow," Bernard suggested.

"Why don't you?" asked Jessica. "You will be comfortable here. There are four bedrooms and it's just the two of us."

Stanley and Ivan were tempted but David was reluctant. "I didn't bring a change of clothing," he said.

"Why can't you wear something of your brother's?" asked Jessica. "He has lots of clothes, some of which he has never worn and doesn't even remember that he has them."

David pondered the suggestion for a while then said, "I really can't. There are some things I need to take care of early tomorrow morning."

His true feeling was that he came home to visit with his mother and, therefore, he should be spending more time with her.

"That is understandable," said Jessica. "You are here for just a short while."

Just what is so understandable? David wondered but he said, "This might seem intrusive but I have to ask you, Jessica. Are you from Mayaro?"

"Yes. What's intrusive about that?"

"Well..,"

Before he could express his thoughts any further, Jessica said, "I was born here. I grew up here, although I went to secondary school in Sangre Grande."

"Did you commute?"

"Yes. I travelled every day."

"That must have been very tiring."

"No. It's amazing how much one can accomplish when one is very young and has friends who are doing the same things."

"That is so true."

David was tempted to ask Jessica if she knew Carmelita but he refrained from doing so. *They probably know each other. They are about the same age, and may have attended the same secondary school, since the nearest one is in Sangre Grande and if I am not mistaken, that is where Carmelita went to school,* he thought.

Suddenly some thick, dark clouds eclipsed the sun. There was a flash of lightning followed by the sound of thunder, a sequence that was repeated very quickly and more severely every time.

"Those are signs of an impending storm," said Jessica. "Let's get off the balcony."

The group heeded the advice and rushed inside. Jessica glanced at David and noticed a concerned look on his face.

"What's the matter, David?" she asked.

"I am concerned about the weather."

He is not the one who will be driving this evening so why is he concerned? She wondered but said, "We get those glints of lightning and rumbles of thunder all the time. Sometimes they are followed by significant rainfall. At other times they diminish and we get no rain at all."

Both statements Jessica made were relevant that evening. There was a severe downpour of rain with intermittent thunder and lightning that waxed and waned for hours. Eventually Stanley made it known that he dislikes driving in weather like that. Ivan too declared his uneasiness with driving at nights when it is raining. That left David no choice but to spend the night at his brother's.

"Will you stay the night fellas (guys)?" Jessica asked.

The other three Cassel brothers looked at David and he said, "Yes."

"Well, that's settled. I shall get your beds ready." Jessica said and left the room.

No one else attempted to leave because it was still raining heavily. Bernard's friends who had dropped in earlier without notice, made themselves comfortable and the party continued indoors until well after 11: 00 p.m.

Very early the next morning, Jessica woke up to prepare a meal for her husband and his brothers, and get herself ready for work. She had breakfast on the table and was dressed to go by 5:00 a.m. Everyone else was awake and ready to leave.

"Sit down and have some breakfast, gentlemen," she suggested.

No one, except Bernard wanted to eat that early in the morning but eventually they acceded to Jessica's request and sat down to breakfast. They ate slowly as they conversed. The men were reminiscing about their youth and growing up in Belmont with a single mother but Jessica added nothing to the conversation. It wasn't that she had nothing to add. Bernard, she reasoned already knew everything about her privileged life. She didn't want to be viewed as a showoff by rehashing the same things to his brothers so she simply listened to what they had to say. Although they had lived vastly different youthful lives, theirs, she thought were no less interesting or exciting.

"Your mother is a remarkable woman," Jessica said.

"Yes, indeed," said David. "We have learnt so much from her."

His brothers nodded their heads in agreement and quoted some of her favorite sayings, *motivational tit bits* as Ivan called them.

Jessica seized the moment to ask for an example of Mrs. Cassel's *drive talk* as she called it, and Stanley obliged.

"If you forgot or neglected to do your home work, which she always checked before you left for school each morning, her comment was, *if you keep this up you will become a beggar-man in Independence Square.*"

"We all knew the beggars in Independence Square," said Ivan. "Sometimes after church on a Sunday Mom would take us down there."

"She never told us why she was taking us there," said Stanley. "It's not as if we had anything to give them. We owned the home in which we lived but we were struggling for everything else."

"In retrospect, it was her way of emphasizing the importance of education," Ivan said.

"David got the message early and excelled in school," said Bernard. "The rest of us took a little longer to catch on but we eventually did."

David remained quiet throughout. Like Jessica, he was reluctant to join in that discussion and risk being misconstrued as a showoff. He was pleased, nevertheless, to know that his mother's sacrifice and good intentions were not wasted or lost in the spiral of life.

There was a brief moment of silence that was interrupted only when Bernard spoke, "Before David returns to the USA we all should descend on the Circular (Belmont Circular Road).

"Ascend on the Circular is more like it," said Ivan. "It is located to the North of us and uphill."

Ivan wasn't exactly correct. While the Circular was located to the North of where some of them lived, it certainly wasn't north of everyone. He did gain some attention and laughter as was intended but that was short lived. It was quiet in the room when David spoke again.

"Mom will be very happy to see us all together," he said.

"I am sure she will," said Ivan. "When are you returning to the USA?"

"I am travelling on Saturday," David replied.

"Is it this coming Saturday, the twenty-seventh?"

"Saturday, April 27th is correct."

"What time is your flight?"

Why all of these question? If you want to visit your mother, just do so. Don't use me as an excuse, David thought but he said, "The flight leaves at 11: 00 a.m."

"Then we can be there on April 26th," Ivan said as he looked to his brothers for confirmation.

"Do you realize that's tomorrow?" Stanley asked.

"That doesn't change anything," said Bernard. "We are going. In fact, I am not going to work today or tomorrow." Jessica looked at him sternly but he did not budge. "I am serious," he said.

"Well, that is settled," said Ivan. "We will be at *The Circular* on Friday."

No one asked whether I can take off from work tomorrow. Am I included? Jessica wondered. She then made it known that it was impossible for her to be absent from work on Friday because of a prior commitment. She never said what that commitment was.

"I thought it might be difficult for you," her husband, Bernard said in her defense.

"Oh! You are always so understanding, sweetheart."

"*What crock?*" Stanley wondered but suggested that they head out right away so that he and Ivan could get to work if they planned on taking off the next day.

Minutes later they left Mayaro via the Manzanilla/Mayaro Road. Stanley sped away with the intention of getting Ivan to Chaguanas before taking David to Belmont and heading home to San Fernando.

"If you drop me off at the Tunapuna Junction I can take a taxi into Port of Spain. That would save you some precious time," David said.

It certainly would, Stanley thought but said only, "Okay."

Ivan was asleep in the back seat, and he slept soundly until Stanley stopped in front of his home. By then David was in a taxi and well on his way to Port of Spain. Stanley was relieved as he entered the Uriah Butler Highway and headed to San Fernando. *If all goes well from here, I will get to work on time,* he thought. The traffic heading to San Fernando was surprisingly sparse. It appeared to be much heavier in the opposite direction and that was pleasing to Stanley. He took full advantage of it and arrived at the corporate office on High Street at exactly 9:00 a. m.

"My goodness, you are early today, Stanley," remarked a co-worker.

"We are early today," Stanley stressed.

"I get your drift," his co-worker said.

"Come on guys, make this a productive day," their supervisor said as he walked in. That essentially ended their effort at conversing with each other from their respective desks.

TWENTY-EIGHT

David arrived at his mother's home safely. Baxter wasn't there but he had no way of knowing whether he left early or he didn't come in the night before. His mother was still asleep and he found that to be rather unusual because he had always known her to be an early riser. *Is she sick again, or just tired?* He wondered. *So much has changed in the few years since I left T & T,* he thought. *If I stay away much longer I wouldn't recognize anyone or anything upon my return.* He quickly dismissed the thought and settled down to enjoy what time he had left to be in Trinidad.

He wrote a note and placed it on the kitchen table to inform his mother that he was back and apologized for not being able to contact her from Mayaro to say that he was going to spend the previous night there. He then left the house, walked down to Queen's Park Savannah, sat on one of benches at the Eastern side of the park and admired the majestic hotel perched on the side of the mountain with the lush vegetation around it and the verdant Northern Range above and beyond. After being there for about fifteen minutes, he decided to join the throng of pedestrians and walk down Frederick Street.

His intention ultimately was to visit the jewelry stores. He was thinking of Carmelita and planning to surprise her when he returned to Brooklyn on Saturday, April 27, 1968. The currency exchange at the time gave him a definite advantage. Trinidad and Tobago was a shopping paradise for tourists. Although David did not consider himself a tourist, he was spending US dollars which he earned in the USA, and that gave him an edge in terms of the quality of service and the goods he received for his money.

He walked into one of Y. De Lima's jewelry stores, the supposedly *gold standard* of jewelry outlets in the Caribbean. He was greeted warmly by a young and attractive sales representative who recognized him as being a Trinidadian but treated him differently, more like she had been accustomed to treating tourists, very special that is.

"Well, good morning, sir. What can we do for you today?" she asked with the most gracious smile he had seen in quite some time.

"I am here to purchase a diamond ring," he said.

"You are in luck. Earlier this morning we received some really nice diamonds for men."

"It is not for me," he said tersely.

"Oh oh, I am so sorry, sir."

My God, they are so polite here. She is so different from the sales reps in the department stores, he thought, but said, "It's okay."

"Are you looking for a gift?"

"You can call it a gift. I am looking for an engagement ring."

"Well, you have come to the right place. I don't have to tell you. You are from Trinidad so you know how we operate."

Then why are you telling me? David wondered. *Just show me the rings,* he thought but said, "I am looking for something elegant but not flashy."

"We have just the right thing for her," said the sales associate and she quickly asked, "What size is she?"

"She wears a size seven and a half ring."

"Come with me," she said but did not stop smiling as she walked with him to the showcase that housed the engagement rings. "These are our collection,"

He glanced at the collection and immediately saw a ring he liked. It was displayed separately in a neat ox-blood colored leather case lined with silk and set apart from the collection on the tray.

"That's a nice ring right there," he said.

"That is from the Cartier collection, a unique ring for a very special woman."

"She is indeed very special," said David. "How much is it?

"I believe it is three thousand dollars but let me check." She looked at the bottom of the case but there was no price listed there. She then asked someone she called *Miki* to get her a price list. He did not hesitate and as soon as he handed it to her she checked the list price and said, "It is better than I thought."

"How much is it?" David asked again.

"It is now selling for $2,800.00."

"Hmm! He mused and asked, "Would you consider selling it for $2,400.00?"

"If it were up to me I would give it to you at that price but I am not privileged to do so."

"Who is?"

"That would be the manager."

"Where is she?"

"He is here. The manager is male."

"Sorry!"

"That's okay," said the sales associate as she called out, "Miki, could you ask Kenrick to come out here please?"

Miki walked to the back of the store and returned with a tall and imposing character. "What is it?" the big man asked.

"This customer wants to buy something from the Cartier collection."

"So?"

Before the sales associate could respond to her manager David asked, "Would you consider $2,400.00 for that ring?" The sales associate had the ring in her hand since she checked the price.

"Twenty-five hundred would be more appropriate," the manager said.

"I will take it," David said.

The sales associate seemed stunned and remained motionless for a few seconds before she said, "Come with me."

David followed her to a cash register and asked, "Would you take a check?"

"We prefer cash but we will accept a credit card if you have proper identification."

"What would you consider appropriate identification?"

"Your passport or driver's license would be fine."

He handed her a credit card together with his driver's license. He did not have his passport with him.

"Would you like to insure this piece of jewelry, sir?" she asked.

"What is the cost of the insurance?"

"For this ring it will run you about $150.00 for the first month."

"No, thank you," David said. He didn't bother to inquire further as to what is covered or for how long.

She completed the transaction and handed David his purchase. She then extended her hand and said, "Thank you. My name is Pauline Kumar. Here is my business card."

David took the embossed business card, glanced at it, said, "Thank you," and placed it in his shirt pocket. *Shouldn't she have introduced herself to me when I first entered the store?* He wondered.

"It was a pleasure," she said.

"The pleasure was really mine."

"I think your fiancée would love the ring."

"I think so too."

"She is a lucky woman." *I wish it were me*, Pauline thought.

"I don't know about all of that," David said.

"You are very modest too, I see," said Pauline. "Anyway, enjoy the rest of your stay and give me a call on your return."

"I most certainly will, David said and smiled for the first time since he entered the store.

When he arrived at *The Circular* his mother already had lunch on the table. She was happy to hear that the others would be visiting her the next day, and she immediately started thinking of and planning the meals. David, however, was more interested in telling her about Carmelita. There was one major problem. Well, he considered it major. *How do I explain the fact that she has a young baby?* He wondered. He found it difficult to speak of her as his girlfriend but he couldn't call her his fiancée because he had not yet proposed to her. *Would she even accept my proposal?* He wondered again.

"Is something bothering you, son? Mrs. Cassel asked.

"It is so funny that you would ask me that."

"Why?"

"Something is on my mind. It is not really something that is troubling to me though."

"A mother always knows. Call it intuition if you wish."

"You are remarkable, Mom. You know that, don't you?"

"Well, I have been told so before."

"Anyway, before I leave here I must let you know that I recently met a young lady with whom I have been spending a great deal of time."

"God bless my eyesight."

"Why, Mom? You have not seen her, you are only hearing about her."

"That is all I need to know, son. Your choice is more than likely the choice I would have made for you had our custom been different and I had been given the opportunity to choose."

"Thanks, Mom."

David got up, hugged his mother, kissed her and said, "I love you, Mom." He then proceeded to tell her all about Carmelita, her baby, and the ring he had just purchased to propose to her.

Mrs. Cassel was pleased and she made it known by repeating what she said earlier, "Your choice is my choice, son, I am happy for you." She did not caution him or give any advice, and he liked that. His trip to Trinidad and Tobago was turning out to be remarkable. His mother, meanwhile, was already thinking about Baxter in a manner she had done throughout their lives; when she took care of the needs of one child, she focused her attention on the needs of another. *If only he would meet somebody nice and settle down*, she thought. *I would see all of my boys married before I leave this earth.*

TWENTY-NINE

When Baxter arrived home that Thursday evening, both his mother and his brother, David were asleep. He, therefore, was unaware that his other siblings would be visiting the next day. In his usually carefree style, he too retired to bed. By dawn Friday morning he got up, showered, dressed, and left for work. That's a routine he kept for years since he had been living there as an adult with his mother. He would not have done anything differently had he known that his brothers were coming to visit. He was like that, narcissistic. Since childhood, it was always all about him or what he needed or wanted, and nothing else mattered.

As he walked out of the house, he thought that David might think of him as being too self-absorbed because he never really stuck around to entertain him or just to converse. *There is so much we could talk about; his education, lifestyle in the USA, family, the future, or we can reminisce about our childhood*, he thought. He quickly dismissed those thoughts. *I am not here to impress anyone*, he reasoned. *Whether he sees me as selfish or selfless, I don't care.*

Soon after Baxter left, Bernard and Ivan arrived. It was no coincidence that they arrived together, but rather a result of prior planning. Bernard had driven to Chaguanas where he picked up Ivan, something they had agreed upon when the brothers gathered at Bernard's in Mayaro.

"My, God! Bernard what time did you leave Mayaro?" David asked.

"Let's just say early, very early."

"I think Mom is still asleep," said David. "She would be very surprised."

"That was the plan," Ivan said.

David wasn't sure what he was feeling. *Is it joy, sadness, or disappointment?* He wondered. Suddenly it occurred to him that he had not spoken to Carmelita since he arrived in Trinidad. He had also promised to call Mildred but neglected to do so. *If they stay here all day I may not be able to make those calls*, he thought. What he heard next reinforced that thinking.

"We plan to spend today and tonight with you and Mom," Bernard said.

"That's nice," said David although he wasn't sure. "Mom would love it."

"It does not compensate for our long absence but it's a start," Ivan said.

"It certainly is," said David. "Very often that is all that is needed; a start."

"What time is your flight tomorrow?" Bernard asked.

"My flight leaves at 11: 00 a.m."

"Then we can take you to the airport and at least see you check in."

"That would be nice, thank you."

"Hey! Look. It is the least we can do," Bernard said.

"Every little bit helps."

"Then that's settled."

Mrs. Cassel came out into the kitchen where her sons had gathered. She was shocked as she stood at the kitchen door speechless for several seconds before she spoke. "I see David got you out of your hiding places," she said to break the silence.

"We had been planning this visit for quite some time," Ivan said.

"You almost saw me at the funeral agency."

"Obviously, that was not to be, Mom," said Bernard. "We are here and you are looking good."

"Thank God for that," said Mrs. Cassel. *No thanks to you*, she thought.

"Yes! I can see that you are happy about that," Bernard said.

"What would make me really happy is for you, all of you, to go to church with me on Sunday."

"Would we go to the library after that, Mom?" Bernard asked with a big grin on his face.

David didn't think it was funny and neither did their mother when she said, "Don't make fun of me, son."

Instead of smiling Bernard became pensive. His smile essentially became a frown as his mother's words echoed in his ears. *That is exactly why I do not visit her often*, he thought. *She has no sense of humor.*

"Come on Bernard! Cheer up. Mom is not a stand-up comedian nor is she the audience of one, you know that," Ivan said.

"He knows me well enough," Mrs. Cassel said.

"I am sorry, Mom."

David was speechless. He saw nothing hilarious about the situation. *Bernard's apology was shallow and meaningless*, he thought. *He has always acted stupidly and apologized for it throughout his life.*

Mrs. Cassel wasn't upset but Bernard knew that had he asked that question at any other time she would have had a fit of anger. Her adult temper tantrums would have surfaced. That didn't happen so he felt guilty.

For a long time prior, Mrs. Cassel recognized that her sons, whom she believed she raised so well, were avoiding her. Every one of them acknowledged the sacrifices she made to feed, clothe, and educate them. However, they viewed her as a perfectionist whom they seemed unable to ever satisfy. When things were not done right, or rather, as she considered them to be right, she would yell and scream at the boys, and although she never spanked them, her hostility at times was enough to engender uneasiness and cowardice.

As soon as they completed high school, reached adulthood, and started working, one after the other, they left home and stayed away for extended periods of time. They were terrified of her. To the eyes of many Baxter was still living at home, but those closest to the family recognized that he only slept there. He was using an avoidance technique to thwart his anxiety. David, on the contrary, was in a state of constant denial. He was the first to leave home and viewed his departure only as a move toward self-actualization.

All five brothers would openly admit that their mother's influence had gotten them a first class high school education, and in David's case, an education beyond high school. Her influence had kept them off the streets, out of the legal system, and made them the progressive young men they were. With the exception of David, however, they all wished it could have been done differently, but they acknowledged that their mother did the best she knew how to do, and could have accomplished under the circumstance in which a single mother with no gainful employment had to raise five boys on a measly widow's and orphan pension fund.

The silence in the kitchen was becoming unbearable when Stanley yelled, "Hey! Guys, snap out of it. We are here to visit with Mom and David. Let's make the best of our visit."

"He is right," Ivan said.

Suddenly the mood in the kitchen changed. Mrs. Cassel, who never stopped preparing breakfast when she was so rudely interrupted by Bernard's crude attempt at a joke, had a scrumptious meal ready and on the table by the time things were back to normal. "Let's eat," she said. She did not attempt to bless the table and no one else did either. She did say, "Thank you, Lord," but she said it softly, and no one seemed to have noticed.

Since she was discharged from the hospital she had vowed to change. That, however, was the first time she had an opportunity to prove to herself that change was possible and she moved to implement it right away. *My children are all grown up now. They are doing quite well for themselves so there is no need for me to continue to be so regimented with them*, she thought.

Suddenly they were able to eat without saying *the grace*. David, the model son as far as his mother was concerned, held his table fork in his right hand, a habit he developed in the USA, and she made no comment about it.

"What a transformation!" Ivan exclaimed.

"What are you talking about?" Stanley asked

"David is eating without a knife and fork, and Mon has made no comment about it."

"Actually, he is eating with the fork in his right hand. That is a major transgression."

"Yeah, one that at other times would have triggered a reprimand but now he is getting away with it."

"Guys, would you stop, please!" David pleaded. He was becoming tired of the foolishness but his mother only smiled.

She certainly has changed, Bernard thought. He was feeling even more remorseful about his behavior earlier.

As the day wore on the young men were becoming more at ease with their mother's new demeanor and they loved it. No one spoke about it but each had his own take on it. *I love this calmer, gentler side of hers*, Ivan thought.

If only she had been like this when we were growing up, we might have been more successful, and not so afraid to take risks, Stanley thought.

Bernard's thoughts were, *we were lucky, things could have been worse*. His thinking may have been influenced by his initial indiscretion.

As far as David was concerned the Lord could not have improved on perfection. *If Carmelita could be half the woman my mother is, my life would be filled with happiness*, he thought.

Baxter was still stuck with the old view of his mother's disciplinary structure for them, as draconian. *She is never going to change*, he thought. He was unaware that she had already made great strides toward making amends. He was never at home long enough to observe them. The reasons for which he stayed away were by then disputable but he had no way of knowing that.

As the day progressed, the mood at the Cassel household mellowed, and the brothers relaxed to enjoy their brief stay with their mother and with one another. By dinner time they were chatty, cheerful, and happy together. Mrs. Cassel spared no effort in getting the best ingredients for her favorite dinner recipe. Through it all the only thing she hoped for was that Baxter would be home early enough to join them.

Her wish became a reality as soon as they sat down to dinner. It was late, around 9:30 p.m., but it was no co-incidence. It certainly was by design. Although there was no discussion about it, each brother had his own stalling tactic and used it to delay sitting down to dinner so that Baxter might arrive on time to join them. He did. They cheered; they laughed, hugged each other, hugged their mother, and although a few tear drops were shed, the warmth and joy that filled the room were just superb. The gathering wasn't planned as a family reunion but it turned out to be nothing less.

THIRTY

Saturday, April 27, 1968, Baxter left home early as usual although on Saturdays he worked for only four hours. The night before he wished his brothers goodbye, but David was awake and packing for his trip back to the USA by the time he was about ready to walk through the door. They greeted each other warmly and David promised that he would return soon after graduation.

"That's good," said Baxter. "We have something to look forward to and to celebrate."

"I hope nothing forces me to return sooner," David said. He was thinking of his mother's health.

"Don't worry. Mom is as strong as an ox," Baxter said as if he knew what David was thinking.

"It is difficult not to worry when I am so far away."

That is your choice, why are you lamenting now? Baxter wondered but said, "What will be, will be. Do not try to change the course of history."

David was beginning to lose patience with his brother's attitude. Just then Baxter said, "I will see you soon, Bro. I hope."

"I hope so too. Bye."

They hugged each other again at the door and Baxter said, "Have a safe trip."

"Thank you," David said as he stood at the door and watched his brother walk out to *The Circular*. Immediately after that, he went to the kitchen, picked up the telephone there and dialed Carmelita's number.

"Hello!" She answered.

"It's David. Good morning," he said.

"I am so happy that you called. I was worried the entire time since you have been gone."

"I am sorry that I couldn't call you sooner."

"Is everything okay?"

"Yes, yes!"

"I am glad to hear that. Now I am looking forward to seeing you later today."

"Thanks, I can't wait to see you too."

"See you then. I love you, bye."

"Bye, sweetheart."

Carmelita hung up and David dialed Mildred's number. She too was excited to hear from him and she immediately asked, "How is your mother?"

"Mom is doing great."

"I am glad to hear that."

"Thank you. I am so glad that I came."

"Well, you did the right thing," said Mildred. "How is she handling your departure again?"

"I am not sure. Up until yesterday she was fine with it but I have not seen her yet for the morning."

"With God's help she would be fine."

"Thank you."

'Hopefully, I will see you later."

"Yes," David said although he wasn't sure. In fact, he wasn't even hopeful.

"Have a safe trip back."

"Thanks again, bye."

"Bye, David," Mildred said and smiled broadly as she hung up the telephone and lay across her bed.

David rushed into the bathroom, showered quickly, and was dressed before anyone else was awake. Eventually his mother came out before any of his three brothers. She was cheerful and happy that morning simply because she had seen all of her children in one place, at home, the night before. She wasted no time in getting breakfast ready and on the table.

One after the other the brothers came out and joined David and their mother at the kitchen table. The kitchen was the focal point of family meetings when they were growing up, so it was just natural for them to gather there.

Before breakfast was served, Bernard excused himself. He was the only one in the family who smoked and he knew that he couldn't smoke in his mother's house, so he stepped outside, had a cigarette, and waited a few minutes before returning to the breakfast table. No one commented about his nicotine habit and he made no excuse for it.

"Let's eat," Mrs. Cassel said.

"Good idea," said David. "I am famished." He wasn't really. He was thinking more of his trip to the airport and the possibility that he might be delayed because of traffic congestion.

Unlike the night before, Mrs. Cassel stood up and said a short prayer before sitting down to enjoy breakfast with four of her grown children. She felt enormously proud that after her struggles and sacrifices when they were young, they had all grown up to be successful at whatever they had undertaken.

"This is undoubtedly one of the best days of my life," she said.

"Is it just one of the best?" Stanley questioned.

"It is indeed the very best," Mrs. Cassel confirmed.

David looked up at the clock on the kitchen wall. It was 7:55 a.m. and he was becoming concerned because his brothers were showing no eagerness to leave. *For years they didn't visit her. Now that they are here they do not want to leave. What's up with that?* He wondered. A feeling of hopelessness overwhelmed him. He wanted to be at the airport at least two hours before check-in time but that seemed more unlikely with every passing minute.

Out of desperation he asked, "Bernard, are you taking me to the airport or should I call a taxi?"

"Why would you want to call a taxi when we plan to be there with you?"

"Well, I thought perhaps you decided to stay a little while longer with Mom."

"Good try, David," said Bernard. "Nevertheless, we are leaving right now."

They kissed their mother goodbye and promised that they would visit with her again soon.

"Before David gets back I hope," Mrs. Cassel said.

"Certainly, Mom," said Stanley. "He couldn't get back here in a month or two."

"That would be nice."

"What are you saying, Mom? Would it be nice if they visit you in a month or two, or would it be nice if I can't get back here in a month or two?"

"Stop trying to confuse me, son. You know exactly what I mean."

They all laughed and the young men headed out to Piarco International Airport. The traffic was surprisingly sparse so thirty-five minutes after leaving Belmont Circular Road they were at the departure lounge at the airport.

David noticed that passengers were milling around the check-in counter, most with anger or with a look frustration and hopelessness on their faces. *What is wrong here*? He wondered. He didn't have to wonder for very long. A disgruntled passenger informed him that if he was going to New York he shouldn't sweat it because the flight was delayed.

He immediately looked at the monitor and saw that his flight which was originally scheduled to leave Trinidad at 11:00 a.m. was delayed. BWIA flight 1526 was rescheduled to leave at 3:00 p.m.

"What are you going to do?" Bernard asked.

"What choice do I have?" asked David. "I am not going back to Belmont and find myself hustling to get back here for three o'clock."

"Well, I am going to drop Ivan off and head back to Mayaro."

"Thank you for coming, and please give my regards to Jessica."

"I will," said Bernard. He and Ivan shook hands with David and Stanley and left. Stanley waited with David for another hour before he too said goodbye. His brothers didn't know it but David's flight which was rescheduled for 3:00 p.m. left Trinidad at 4:45 p.m. He took it in stride. BWIA flight 1526 touched down at Kennedy Airport at 10: 30 p.m. It was 11: 00 p.m. when he finally cleared Customs and Immigration.

Uncertain as to what he should do next, he called the Mendoza's home phone number. Crystal answered, "Hello!"

"Good evening, Mrs. Mendoza. This is David," he said.

To his surprise Crystal didn't ask him anything. She simply said, "We have sold the place and are in the process of packing up to move."

"Thanks, Crystal," he said.

What shall I do now? He wondered. *It is too late for me to call Mildred and I do not want to burden Carmelita with my distress*, he thought

Finally, he decided to take public transportation downtown and check-in to a hotel. While on the platform where he had gotten off the A train at Fulton Street, he observed a worker about midway on the platform washing it down. He approached the man, said good evening and asked, "Would you by any chance know of someone with a room to rent?" He waited for a response and it seemed like an eternity before the gentleman did reply.

"I most certainly do. There is one slight problem with that though, I cannot give you his number and I am going to be here until mid-night."

David looked at his watch. It was 11:30 exactly so he said, "I can wait."

"Then I will see you around 12 : 05 at the front of the station's platform, the downtown train that is."

"Thank you, sir," David said as he took a seat in the vicinity where he was supposed to meet the subway worker at mid-night.

The next thirty minutes seemed like an eternity because neither an uptown nor downtown train went by. Very few passengers were waiting at the station. It was desolate there but he was not afraid.

David had always been a mild mannered and patient individual. On that occasion it paid off. The subway worker returned and introduced himself. "My name is Heard, James Heard," he said.

"I am pleased to meet you, sir. David Cassel," he said as they shook hands.

"You have quite a predicament, I see."

"An unfortunate one it is, sir," David said. He then explained the circumstances leading up to his homelessness in New York City for the last couple of hours.

"Those are not nice people," said Mr. Heard. "You can put that behind you though because I spoke with my cousins, so they are expecting us. They live on Gates Avenue which is not very far from here and there is a nice room there for you."

By then they had exited the subway and reached Mr. Heard's car which was parked nearby. They entered the vehicle and the discussion about the Mendoza family continued until they arrived at the Gates Avenue address of Fred and Doris Linger. "We are here," said Mr. Heard. "All of the lights are on. That's a good sign that they are awake."

Mr. Heard rang the door bell to the first floor of the three story building and a tall dark-skinned man emerged. He shook David's hand. Then he shook Mr. Heard's hand and said, "Come with me, the room is on the third floor."

"No, Fred. I have to leave now," said Mr. Heard. "You are in good hands, David."

David smiled and said, "Thank you so much, sir."

"You are welcome," Mr. Heard said and left.

Mr. Linger escorted David to his room on the third floor and said, "It is late so make yourself comfortable and I will speak with you tomorrow evening. Later this evening really, it is already Sunday."

"Thank you, sir," David said but he wondered why Mr. Linger preferred to speak with him Sunday evening rather than during the morning hours. He quickly dismissed that thought and settled down.

The room was clean and tidy but small. David could tell that it once served as one bedroom of a two or three bedroom apartment. It was obvious to him that other tenants lived on the same floor, a similar situation to what he had experienced at the Mendoza's. The room was modestly furnished. It contained a twin bed, a table, and one chair. There wasn't a refrigerator, oven, or stove in the room but that was of no concern to David, not at that moment anyway.

He sat on the bed and pondered the situation. The linens were clean and freshly ironed. *That's good*, he thought. *Where is the bathroom?* He wondered. *Mr. Linger did mention that it was down the hall but where, he didn't say.* He decided to investigate and indeed, there it was at the Eastern side of the floor, a short distance from his room. He noticed that the bathroom door was kept open but there were two other doors that were closed. *Obviously there are others living on this floor,* he thought, although no sound came from either of the other two rooms.

He returned to his room and tossed himself on the bed. As he lay on his back looking at the ceiling, he silently thanked God for the intervention. He thought of Mildred and wondered whether she would accept the fact that he did not or could not call her when he found himself stranded at the airport. He thought of Carmelita and wondered, *what has become of her and Elvin. Did Crystal treat them all in the same manner, or was that her way of punishing me?* There were no answers. Finally he decided there was nothing he could do until daylight.

He slept for brief periods intermittently and was fully awake by 7:00 a.m. His first objectives were to shower, get dressed, go out to a neighborhood store, make some change, and find a pay phone from which he could call those he was concerned about and whom he felt had the same concern for him.

First he called Carmelita. She was in a quandary because Crystal had done the same thing to her. Fortunately for her, she was offered a larger place in a building on Halsey Street. The difficulty she was experiencing was in having to pack up and move her belongings herself. Her mother couldn't help much. David thought of offering to help but he did not want to have any contact with the Mendoza family, particularly with Crystal Mendoza.

He called Mildred instead and explained his situation. She was disappointed that he didn't contact her immediately when he arrived, irrespective of what time his flight came in. She had her hopes but she wasn't upset with him. She valued his friendship too much for something like that to cause a rift between them.

"I am sorry that you had such a rough time, David, but if there is anything I can do to help please don't hesitate to ask," she said.

"I think I would be okay here. There are a few quirks I may have to work around but overall, it is not bad," he said.

"Okay."

"Thanks, Mildred."

"Bye."

As soon as Mildred hung up the telephone, David called Carmelita again. "Could we meet?" he asked.

"It's funny that you would ask me that. I expected to see you here."

"I thought of it but I would rather be blinded than see those people ever again."

"I understand that you are hurting, David, we all are. What they did was wrong but we must forgive them."

"God forgives. I cannot forgive nor can I forget."

Carmelita, sensing David's anger asked, "Where and when can we meet?"

"Could you come downtown at one o'clock?"

"One p.m. is fine but where downtown shall we meet?"

"Can we meet at Junior's Restaurant for lunch?"

"If Mama will watch Elvin for me, we certainly can."

"Please ask her. I would hold on while you do."

Carmelita covered the receiver with her right palm and asked the favor of her mother. At that point David placed another dime in the pay phone to ensure that the operator did not disconnect them before Carmelita returned to resume their conversation.

"I will see you at Junior's at one o'clock," she said.

"Great! See you then. Love you, bye," David said and hurried off the telephone as if he was afraid that Carmelita might change her mind.

He was undaunted by the Mendoza family's action. *It is their building. They do have the right to sell it, but human decency suggests that they should have given each tenant adequate notice of the impending sale,* he thought. *None of that will stop me now, and I will see to it that Carmelita's progress is not impeded by their action.*

THIRTY-ONE

David arrived at the restaurant at 12:45 p.m. and was ushered to a seat for one before he could explain to the usher that he expected a young lady to join him. When he explained the situation, he was quickly seated at a much preferred table for two.

It wasn't long before a waiter came and asked, "Can I get you something to drink while you wait?"

"I will have a beer," David said.

"Is there a preferred brand I can get you?"

"Not really," he said.

He assumed that the restaurant was not likely to have the beer he liked so he was prepared to accept any brand. *If it's not brewed in Trinidad it's just a beer*, he thought. He was pleasantly surprised when the waiter returned with a bottle of the smooth, rich lager he liked, poured half of it in a glass and said, "Try this, it is really good, imported from T & T, and it's complimentary today."

"Thank you," he said.

Before he sipped the beer, he looked toward the door and saw Carmelita standing there. She was looking around hoping that he had gotten there before she did. Their eyes met and he beckoned her over. She hurried to the table and kissed him before saying, "Welcome back."

"Thank you."

She took her seat opposite to him and asked, "How was the trip?"

"Very good," said David. "I was pleasantly surprised."

"How is your mother?"

"She is much better, thank you."

He told Carmelita about the trips his mother had planned that took them to places he had not visited before leaving Trinidad. She sensed that he was very pleased and regretted that she had no similar pleasantries to report. In fact, she had some disturbing news to share with him but he seemed so very pleased about his vacation she decided to wait a while before divulging unpleasant information that did not pertain to him or to her directly. Just then the waiter returned, and David asked Carmelita whether she would like something to drink, "A glass of wine, maybe?" he asked.

"No, thank you," she said. The waiter took their orders and left.

"You look wonderful this afternoon," David said.

"Is this the only afternoon that you find me to be pleasing to your eyes?"

"Sweetheart, you are always magnificent to me."

"Thanks. You are so sweet, and I missed you so much," she said.

I missed you immensely too," said David. "I spoke so much about you while in Mayaro that I suspected my sister-in-law had gotten tired of hearing your name."

Carmelita laughed. Then she asked, "Who is your sister-in-law?"

"Jessica."

"That is a very common name in a county of one million people."

"I thought perhaps you might know her."

"David, you are the first person from Belmont that I have met and gotten to know personally."

"She is not from Belmont."

"Where does she live?"

"She said she was born in Mayaro, and that's where she and my brother live."

Carmelita was silent for a brief moment. *He did say that he visited Mayaro on his recent visit to Trinidad but he never before mentioned that one of his brothers lived there*, she thought.

"Is she Jessica Kitt?" she asked to break her own silence.

"Her name is Jessica Cassel," said David. "Her maiden name might be Kitt, I really don't know."

"I know of only one Jessica in Mayaro," said Carmelita. "Did she and your brother get married recently?"

"They have been married for two years now."

"It is possible that I know her, although I cannot say with certainty that I do."

"She seems to be about your age, and she did mention that she went to high school in Sangre Grande."

"That has to be Jessica Kitt."

"I thought you couldn't say *I do* with certainty."

"Well…," Carmelita was attempting to say something when David held her hands. That for some reason interrupted her speech.

"I believe we discussed this before but permit me to ask again," he said.

He paused, and Carmelita asked, "What is it?"

"Will you marry me?"

"Oh! David. Yes, yes!" She said with a big, radiant, happy smile.

He slipped the ring onto her finger and it fitted perfectly. She lifted her left hand, viewed the ring carefully and said, "It's beautiful. I love you, David."

"You make my life so complete," said David. "I felt lost without you in T & T."

"Now that you are back we can get lost in each other's arms."

The waiter brought their food. Only then did they realize how long it was since they placed their order. They were being served at 2:00 p. m. although Carmelita arrived there at one o'clock, a mere fifteen minutes after David. The waiter apologized for the delay.

They appreciated his apology and made that known while at the same time attributing the delay to the lunch-time rush.

"This place is always crowded," said David. "It only gets worse at lunch and dinner times."

Carmelita did not speak for a while. She was still in awe, and David grasped that a an opportunity to outline his future plans. Although they were not elaborate, she was included at every juncture. She liked that and wondered, *what have I done differently that I didn't do with either Sylvester Pierce, or Tyrone Khadevis*?

"Thanks, David. Thanks also for inviting me to lunch and in essence, an engagement party for two."

I always knew, even before TK left that one day I would ask you to marry me, and I hoped that you would say yes, he thought but said, "I feel somewhat privileged right now."

"I am the lucky one, sweetheart."

"This has nothing to do with luck, Carmelita my dear. It is because of who you are; a loving, caring, considerate, and ambitious young woman whom I love."

"Thanks for the joy you have brought into our lives. When I say *our lives*, I mean Elvin's and mine."

"You are appreciated," David said. He didn't want to say, *You are welcome. That is so cliché*, he thought.

"Before I leave there is something I must tell you," Carmelita said but stopped short of saying what she intended.

"What is it?" David asked.

"It is about Mr. Mendoza."

"What is it about Mr. Mendoza?"

"He was arrested this morning."

"What?"

"You heard me."

"I heard you alright. I still cannot conceive of it. What a hard working, devoutly religious, dedicated family man like Victor Mendoza could be arrested for?"

"The way I heard it, he apparently forgot something at home this morning, returned to get it, and saw his wife sitting in Sebastian's lap."

"You lost me somewhere. What exactly was he arrested for?"

"He drew a weapon, a gun, and pointed it at them."

"His is a licensed gun. Perhaps he got home and took it out to secure it."

"That is not what I heard."

"What exactly did you hear?"

"I was told that he threatened them with the gun."

David didn't ask Carmelita who informed her about the incident but he wanted to know how the police became involved so he asked, "Who reported it the police?"

"Sebastian called the cops."

"Oh! Oh."

David never did tell Carmelita about Crystal's behavior toward him, or of his cavorting with her, or that he once saw her in a compromising position with Sebastian. He was thankful that he was out of the Mendoza's place, forced out as it seemed by one of Crystal's devious schemes.

"I am so glad that we are no longer there," Carmelita said.

"Did they really sell the building?"

"I don't know. No one knows for certain because they are still living there."

"I feel sorry for Victor."

"Everyone seems to express the same sentiment."

"He is a genuinely nice man."

"That persona has now been tarnished."

"He will get over it once the charge or charges have been settled."

"What could he be charged with?"

"I don't know; reckless endangerment, menacing, unlawful possession of a firearm maybe."

"Didn't you say he had a licensed pistol?"

"I assumed it was licensed because he brags of being a gun collector. In addition, he owns a small business."

"I am not sure that any of that matters when human life is threatened, especially when his intended victims posed no danger to him."

"We do not know whether he saw Crystal, Sebastian, or both as possible threats, do we?"

"They may have threatened his way of life, his seemingly secure and successful family life," said Carmelita. "Beyond that he was in no danger, but eventually they would sort that out."

"Whatever! Let them squirm. We have more important things to think about."

"That is pretty harsh of you, David, considering that you have lived at their home for over three years."

"Let me correct that," said David. "I rented from them for more than three years. Where I lived on the fourth floor at that Herkimer Street address was my home, not theirs."

"Okay, David."

"Seriously though, was your home on the second floor the same as theirs?"

"I said okay. I get your drift. You win, so what more do you want?"

"There is nothing that I need or want, sweetheart," said David. "By the way, didn't we promise not to fuss with each other?"

"We did, and I kept my end of the deal. I said okay, meaning let's end it, but you chose to continue."

"That's more than enough of the Mendoza family and their problems. Eventually, we will have our own problems to contend with."

"Nothing like theirs I hope."

"I can assure you of that, it will never come close."

They stood up together to leave and instinctively hugged each other. David left a tip on the table and took the check to the cashier on their way out. As they walked out of the door and stood on the sidewalk at Fulton Street and Flatbush Avenue, he held her right hand. She rested her head on his left shoulder and said, "Thanks for the best afternoon of my life."

"You are just so delightful. I am glad you enjoyed it."

They crossed Fulton Street and were about to enter the subway when David suggested that they walk either to Hoyt-Schermerhorn or Borough Hall station instead. Carmelita didn't object, she simply complied, and they strolled up Fulton Street to Jay Street and over to the Borough Hall Station where they boarded a Downtown train.

The noisy clatter heard within the train precluded any attempt at conversation so they sat close but quietly together. Since they were forced out of their Herkimer Street address, David and Carmelita had found new abodes at Gates Avenue and Halsey Street respectively. They resided relatively close to each other, one train station away to be exact, which to them was walking distance. They were required to change trains at Broadway Junction and ride the J Train back to their designated stops. It was convenient, therefore, for David to get off at the Halsey Street stop, walk with Carmelita to her new home, then continue to his.

When they arrived at Carmelita's she suggested that he should come in and visit for a while but he declined. "That might not be convenient for your mother at this time," he said.

"I didn't think about that."

"You should have."

"You are right. Although I have a lot more space now, everything is still disorganized."

"My living quarters are about the same as before but I can relate to the disorganization."

"I was never passionate about moving for that very reason."

"That's not good," David said.

"What's not good about it?"

"Well, we have to start thinking about moving to a larger place soon."

"Why?"

"Are you forgetting that we are engaged to be married? Soon we will need at least two bedrooms."

Carmelita realized that she slipped up but she did not acknowledge it. Instead, she leaned on him and said, "You are so sweet, and you think of everything."

He kissed her. They said goodbye and reluctantly parted ways but with a promise to get together again soon.

THIRTY-TWO

Carmelita walked into her newly occupied one-bedroom apartment and looked around very excitedly as she considered the prospect of her, David, and Elvin living there together. *We do not need anything larger than this right now*, she thought. *Mama's stay here is temporary and Elvin is only two months old.* She assumed that she and David would soon be married and sharing expenses, including the rent for what would become their new residence. By then she was truly looking forward to that although she never gave it much thought before.

She greeted her mother who had just given Elvin a bath and was admiring him as he lay sleeping peacefully in his bassinet. Then she said, "Mama you would not believe this."

"What is it, child?"

"Carmelita," she said in an attempt to break her mother's habit of calling her child. Mrs. Jackman did not realize her intention so she continued. "Look at what David gave me today," she said as she lifted her left hand so her mother could view the ring.

"My goodness, child, he gave you an engagement ring! It is beautiful! Come, let me hug you." Carmelita stepped forward and they embraced each other. "Congratulations!" said Mrs. Jackman. "I always thought of him as a decent young man."

"He is, Mama."

"Consider yourself lucky. Dem (those) man and dem (they) today doh (do not) like to take on responsibility, you know," said

Mrs. Jackman with a dramatic switch from Standard English to the T & T/Mayaro vernacular.

"I am aware of that, Mama."

"Ah hope so, oui."

After that brief exchange with her mother, Carmelita sprang into action. Immediately, she started to unpack whatever she still had in cardboard boxes in an effort to tidy the living room. She moved the box containing David's books and placed it closer to the door. *He might be coming to get this soon*, she thought.

At about the same time David had arrived at his new home on Gates Avenue. He looked around and thought, *it's a little more spacious than what I had on Herkimer Street but with the same inconvenience; the bathroom is communal and is located down the hallway.* He tossed himself on the bed but quickly jumped to his feet. *I can't lay here idly*, he thought, *I must go out, find a pay phone, and give Mildred a call.* He gathered some coins from the table and left. From a telephone kiosk at Gates and Bedford avenues, he dialed Mildred's number.

"Hello!" She answered.

"Mildred, this is David."

"Oh! My goodness, I am so glad you called. How are you?"

"I am okay."

"Are you calling from Trinidad?"

"No, I am in Brooklyn," said David. Mildred did not respond immediately so he explained the events that unfolded the night before when he returned to New York and called the Mendoza's residence. "I was desperate," he said.

"You should have called me."

"It was very late."

"That would not have mattered. You could have called me at any time," Mildred said. She sounded disappointed and sad.

"I am comfortable. Also, the landlord and his wife appear to be nice people," he assured her.

"I was looking forward to having you as a roommate,"

David felt guilty and confused. He was apologetic but that did nothing to appease Mildred and ease her disappointment. In an effort to comfort her and salvage their friendship, he promised to visit with her that evening. She perked up immediately.

"What time will that be?" she asked.

He looked at his watch and saw that it was exactly 5:00 p.m. "Within the next hour," he said.

"I will see you then."

"Okay, bye."

"Bye, David," she said and hung up the telephone. She was smiling again.

Instead of returning home as he had originally planned, David took the subway train to Mildred's. She was delighted when he arrived and she quickly put together a snack for them to munch on as they conversed. As usual, their conversational topics were varied. They discussed numerous things that were of interest to both of them. They were relaxed in each other's company, but David knew he had to find an opportune time to inform her that he had proposed to Carmelita. He expected a dreadful response from her, so he broke the news as gently as he could. He was pleasantly surprised at how graciously she accepted it.

"I know you, David. I have not met the young lady but I am confident you made the right choice."

"Thank you."

"You are welcome," said Mildred. *What else can I say*? She wondered. *I am disappointed that I am not the chosen one but in all fairness to you, we were never more than good friends*, she thought.

"We have had a long and enduring friendship which I hope will continue," David said.

"I hope so too, but that is no longer entirely up to us."

"I don't think Carmelita would be too concerned."

"If you base your relationship and eventual marriage on understanding and trust, there would be no need for concern," said Mildred. "I do want to wish you the very best though. I have enjoyed being your friend. You have been wonderful and I hope that our friendship would continue, but if for any reason it doesn't, I would understand and hopefully, be able to accept that."

David was silent, puzzled and confused it seemed. *How could any human be so reasonable*?" He wondered, and he struggled briefly with doubt as to whether or not he made the right choice. Finally he concluded, given our ages and cultural differences, I probably did the right thing but only time will tell. He remained silent in his amazement, so it was Mildred who spoke again.

"Life offers no guarantees," she said.

"While that is true, it is not a good enough reason why we should abandon our hopes and dreams."

"You are correct. We must persevere in spite of the odds. You may not have known it but you have been an inspiration to me, David."

"You have been instrumental also in my educational pursuits and my drive to succeed."

"There is no doubt in my mind that you have been equally responsible for many of my initiatives. I always had one or another plan but when I lacked the desire and determination to implement them, you were there as my inspiration."

"I take that as a compliment."

"It is."

"Thank you."

"In your quest to begin a new phase of your life which carries with it new and different responsibilities, try not to lose your momentum and drive to succeed."

"I wouldn't. I have been emulating you for a while. You are one of the best at it."

"Yes, I will admit that I have been driven, sometimes on my own but by you at times."

"You have been driven against the odds, and so have I."

"That's how it is, David."

"I know. Success never came easy for us but here we are, one month away from graduation."

"Thank you, Jesus," Mildred said.

"Do you plant on attending the graduation?"

"Yes, of course. What about you, will you attend?"

"Yes."

"Are you sure? Graduation is scheduled for Saturday, May 25, and that might be in conflict with your wedding plans."

David laughed, and Mildred did too. That was exactly what she intended, to lighten things up a bit.

"We are not getting married in such a hurry. If we were, it would be in June rather than May."

"Well, I don't know that."

"I do. Seriously though, should we decide to get married soon, will you attend the wedding?"

"If I am invited I would attend of course, short notice or not. I am like a boy scout, always prepared."

David was pleased to hear that. *She is taking it well*, he thought. "We have no concrete plans. It is only earlier today that I made the suggestion," he said. He was reluctant to use the word *proposal.*

"Whether you suggested about getting married or proposed to get married, it's the same thing, what's the difference?" Mildred asked.

"The difference is subtle but there is a difference."

"Okay, David. Let's not get hung up on the semantics. I will be straight with you," said Mildred. "I had my hopes and desires but obviously, those were not your wishes. I understand that, and the manner in which you approached it has heightened my regard for you."

"You are truly amazing, Mildred."

"I would prefer adjectives like marvelous, wonderful, or loving to describe me or what I am about but I will take *amazing.*"

Both David and Mildred were choosing their words carefully. Neither one wanted to say anything that may have caused the other emotional distress. Their conversations which have been many since they first met have always been of a cautious nature. No wonder they remained close friends for so long and neither expressed a romantic interest in the other.

THIRTY-THREE

David arrived at his new home at 11:45 p.m., a full hour after he left Mildred's. He felt pleased with his accomplishments. He had informed her of his engagement to Carmelita and of his new abode at Gates Avenue and she accepted both graciously. He had hoped to call Carmelita but by the time he arrived in the area of his home, he found it was too late to sit or stand at a public telephone booth to make the call. *I must find time during the day tomorrow while I am at work to call her and also to call and ask the telephone company to transfer my phone service to my new address*, he thought.

He was unaware of any mail delivery for him while he was away. Carmelita didn't mention anything about the mail situation at their former address at Herkimer Street, and when he called the Mendoza's upon his return from Trinidad and Tobago, Crystal made no mention of his mail. Since she was in the habit of pilfering, tampering with, and sometimes hording other people's mail, the fact that she made no mention of mail delivery was not an indication that nothing was mailed to him during his absence.

His last thought before he fell asleep was, *I will go to work tomorrow as scheduled. If I am reprimanded for calling in sick before my scheduled vacation, then that's it.* The next day he arrived at *Eastern Time* half an hour earlier than the 9:00 a.m. scheduled start time and greeted some of his co-workers who were already there. They had coffee together and were soon joined by their supervisor. She was enthralled to see David and greeted him warmly with a hug. "How was your trip?" she asked.

"It was wonderful, truly wonderful," he said.

He had never mentioned his mother's illness to his supervisor or co-workers so the question of her health didn't come up. As with most industrial plants, the conversation quickly changed from personal greetings and small talk to the business of the day. "Come with me," Charlene, the plant supervisor said. David followed her into her office. "Have a seat," she said.

He sat down nervously as she rustled through some papers on her desk. David was uneasy. *Will I be reprimanded or terminated*? He wondered. He was still bothered by the fact that he called in sick just before his scheduled vacation.

"Oh, here it is," said Charlene. "I knew it had to be right here on my desk."

The suspense was becoming unnerving but David maintained his composure until Charlene looked up at him and smiled. "This work order came in last Wednesday but we want to have the units assembled by Friday." she said.

Why did you hold the order until now? David wondered but asked, "How big is the order?"

"The order is for two dozen clocks."

Although he felt relieved that no immediate action was taken against him for company rules violation, he wondered about the volume of work he was being assigned. Normally, no one individual was ever required to assemble more than a dozen time pieces in a five day period. That policy was in place to ensure precision and excellent quality, things for which the company was renowned.

Am I being set up for a fall? David wondered but he felt confident that he could get the job done in the scheduled time and maintain the quality that was expected of *Eastern Time*.

"Can you handle this volume of work?" Charlene asked.

"It is a bit excessive but I will try."

"That's not good enough, David," said Charlene. "I'll tell you what. I am going to add six of these to Pablo's workload."

"Wouldn't that be an over tally for him?"

"Not really. Right now he is working on an order of twelve for another store. If I give him six more, you both would have eighteen pieces each."

That seems fair, David thought but all he said was, "Okay."

By Friday, May 3rd both David and Pablo completed their assignments to the supervisor's satisfaction. The orders were sent out on time and Charlene was delighted. David had returned to classes at the Municipal College of Arts and Sciences, and things were looking up. Graduation was quickly approaching. He still had a job, was engaged to be married so the future seemed bright.

Why should Carmelita and I wait to be married? He wondered. *We would save a great deal on rent and other household expenses if we pool our resources now*, he thought. *I will discuss that with her this evening.*

Earlier in the week David had turned in all of his outstanding assignments to his professors. He felt comfortable about not attending classes that Friday evening, so he called Carmelita to inform her of his intention to visit her after work. She had no objection. On the contrary, she was delighted. He then called the telephone company to request that his telephone service be transferred to his new address, even though he questioned the wisdom of his decision in light of his marriage proposal to Carmelita. *If she agrees to what I am about to suggest this evening, there would be no need for me to install a telephone at my new quarters at Gates Avenue*, he thought.

At 5:00 p.m. he rushed out of *Eastern Time* and headed to the Halsey Street address where Carmelita had moved to with her mother and baby. He was visiting her there for the first time since they both relocated and he was excited about it. A day earlier he had walked her home but he did not enter the premises. On that occasion, however, he intended to sit with her and discuss their future plans. He wasn't concerned about her mother being present. Mrs. Jackman, he had observed never got into many discussions with them.

When he arrived and rang the door bell, Carmelita was surprised that he came as early as he did, although she was hoping that he would. She was glad to see him and they greeted each other warmly with a hug. Mrs. Jackman was happy to see him also but she stopped short of hugging him. After they exchanged some brief pleasantries, she retreated to the bedroom with Elvin, leaving Carmelita and David to themselves in the living room.

David wasted no time in outlining his thoughts. He couldn't call it a plan at the onset but it soon emerged to be just that. Carmelita understood his reasoning and agreed that they shouldn't wait indefinitely to get married. "We can have a small ceremony here and a year or so later for our first anniversary we can celebrate with family and friends in Tobago, or Trinidad if you prefer," she said.

"Tobago is fine," said David. "From what I have seen during my recent visit, it is ideal."

"Then that aspect is settled," said Carmelita. "We must now decide on a date."

"Are we deciding on a date for the ceremony or for the celebration?"

"The ceremony comes before the celebration, isn't that how it works?" she asked and chuckled.

"Amuse yourself." David said as he looked around to see if she had a calendar on the wall.

"It's in the kitchen," she said.

"What's in the kitchen?"

"The calendar you are scanning the walls for."

David smiled as she got up, walked back to the kitchen, retrieved the calendar, returned, and handed it to him.

"Graduation is May 25th," he said as he circled the date with a pencil. Then he asked, "How does two weeks after that sound?"

"It sounds good to me."

He handed the calendar back to Carmelita and said, "Pick a date."

"June 8th", she suggested without hesitation.

"That's the date," he said. It was the very date he had in mind but he refrained from telling Carmelita that.

She was elated, and although she tried not to let it show it was very obvious to David. She was happy and that made him very happy. I may not see you before weekend because I leave the campus very late at nights during the week.

"I realize that," said Carmelita. "I wouldn't want you walking around here that late anyway."

"Thanks."

As David got up to leave he saw his books at the left of the doorway and said, "You could put those out of sight. I will not be taking them with me tonight or anytime soon."

"You are not taking them anyplace anytime, ever!" Carmelita emphasized.

"You've got it."

Before leaving he asked her, "When will you break the news to your mother."

"In a few minutes if her mood is right."

"What happens if it's not?"

"Then I shall wait until tomorrow, but certainly no later than that."

"You are marvelous."

"Thanks. You are no less than fabulous. I love you, David."

"I love you immensely, sweetheart."

They laughed, hugged, and kissed each other before saying goodnight. Both made a deliberate effort not to say goodbye."

"I will see you on Saturday," David said as he walked away.

"See you then, bye."

"Bye, gorgeous."

As he walked away from Carmelita that Sunday evening, he remembered the promise he made to his brother Baxter before returning from his vacation in T & T. *I told him that I would return soon after graduation but I didn't say with a family*, he thought. *It is only fair that I bring him and the others up to date. This will come as no surprise to Mom because I hinted as much to her while I was there.* When he arrived home he sat down and wrote a lengthy letter to Baxter which detailed the events that unfolded since his return. He would have preferred to call him on the telephone but since he didn't have a phone in his room, he reasoned that a letter would suffice. He knew that Baxter was somewhat detached from the rest of the family so he wrote three similar letters to each of his other brothers. After that, he felt very pleased with himself and went to bed.

The week of May 6th to May 10th seemed uneventful. His daily routine was very similar; he went to work every day and attended classes every evening. He did speak with Carmelita often, twice a day on occasions. He called Mildred once, but apart from that, all that he had done was pretty mundane, to say the least. On Saturday, May 11th he had a 9:30 a.m. appointment to have a telephone installed at his new digs. It was essentially a transfer of service from Herkimer Street because he was assigned the same telephone number. The New York Telephone technician was on time and finished the job within an hour.

His first telephone call was to Carmelita. She was happy to hear from him but wondered about the wisdom of him installing a telephone when, according to their wedding plans he would soon be relocating again. *Well, it probably is necessary in the event of an emergency*, she reasoned. As their conversation progressed, David asked, "Did you discuss our plans with your mother?"

"Yes."

"What did she say?"

"She was okay with it."

"Did she say that she was okay with it? If so, what does that mean?"

"Her exact words were, 'You know best, my dear.' Then I informed her that there should be no inconvenience to her because we would be out all day for most days in any given week. I assured her also that after our wedding she would continue to occupy the bedroom and we would sleep in the couch-convertible."

"How did she take that?"

"She didn't mind at all."

David felt relieved and he suggested that they visit the Brooklyn Botanic Garden the next day, Sunday, May 12th.

"That's a good idea," said Carmelita. "I have never been there."

"Does that mean you are accepting my invitation to visit the garden?"

"Yes!"

"The weather is forecasted to be fair, clear, and warm; a good time to take Elvin and your mother out."

Carmelita was silent. Previously she thought that she alone was invited so she was surprised when David mentioned Elvin and her mother. *That's such an unselfish act*, she thought. *It's a far cry from the drinking and partying I experienced with Hedges, or TK's marijuana smoking binges.*

She was beginning to understand what set David apart from either Sylvester Pierce or Tyrone Khadevis and she loved him even more for it. By noon they were still conversing on the telephone and Carmelita suggested that they meet for lunch.

"Where shall we meet?" David asked.

"We can meet downtown," said Carmelita. "There is a diner at the top of Court Street. The food is said to be very good there."

"I take it that you have not eaten there yourself."

"That's true but I think it is worth a try."

"Can you be there by two o'clock?"

"Yes."

"I shall see you then."

Carmelita nursed the baby and informed her mother that she was meeting David downtown for lunch. She arrived there at 2:05 p.m. and joined him at the table where he was already seated. They were served quickly and enjoyed their lunch as they conversed. After lunch Carmelita suggested that they take a walk up Montague Street because she wanted something new to wear to his graduation. Their walk had not progressed far up Montague Street when she spotted a dress she liked in the window of a little boutique a short distance away from Court Street. They entered the store. She tried on the dress which fitted perfectly, so she purchased it.

While still in the store, it occurred to her that she might find something there for her wedding. She continued to look around. David suggested that they visit the bridal departments at Martin's and A&S's department stores but she declined saying, "Ours will be a simple ceremony. We should save the elaborate attire for our planned celebration in T&T.

"That's fine with me," David said just when Carmelita found something she liked.

"Do you really like it?" she asked in response to what she thought was his approval.

"Yes," he said.

"I will take it." she said to the sales associate who assisted her.

As they left the boutique she said, "I am pretty much set for your graduation and our wedding."

"You still need shoes," David said.

"I have enough shoes I can choose from for both occasions. What about you."

"I have shoes and I plan on wearing the only suit I have."

"You can't do that."

"Why can't I?"

"It's your wedding, for Christ sake!"

"It is a new suit. I have worn it only twice before."

"That doesn't matter. You can wear it to your graduation but you are getting something new for our wedding."

"Okay," he said while thinking, *boss woman,* but he admired her take-charge attitude nonetheless.

They walked down Fulton Street and entered Bond's Men's Shop at Fulton and Jay Streets. There, David purchased a new suit for his wedding. They were both satisfied with their accomplishments that Saturday afternoon. They enjoyed their lunch together and as far as Carmelita was concerned, they got some badly needed shopping done.

We have spent more than half of our combined weekly income, David thought. *This, however, is a unique situation and does not indicate our future spending habits.* Both of them seemed satisfied with the role the other played. *If this is any indication of what lies ahead for us, we are on the right track,* Carmelita thought. *I am now looking forward to a happy and successful marriage with David Cassel.*